THE WRECKED, BLESSED BODY OF SHELTON LAFLEUR

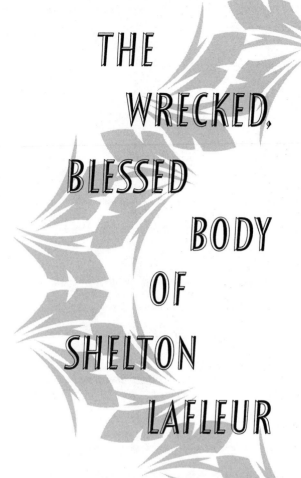

THE
WRECKED,
BLESSED
BODY
OF
SHELTON
LAFLEUR

JOHN GREGORY BROWN

Houghton Mifflin Company

BOSTON   NEW YORK

1996

Copyright © 1996 by John Gregory Brown

For information about permission to reproduce selec-
tions from this book, write to Permissions, Houghton
Mifflin Company, 215 Park Avenue South, New York,
New York 10003.

For information about this and other Houghton Mifflin
trade and reference books and multimedia products,
visit The Bookstore at Houghton Mifflin on the World
Wide Web at http://www.hmco.com/trade/.

Library of Congress Cataloging-in-Publication Data
Brown, John Gregory.
The wrecked, blessed body of Shelton
Lafleur / John Gregory Brown.
p. cm.
ISBN 0-395-72988-2
I. Title.
PS3552.R687W74 1996
813'.54 — dc20   95-38114   CIP

Book design by Anne Chalmers
Text type: Janson Text (Adobe),
Festival (Monotype), Whirligig (Emigré)

Printed in the United States of America

QUM 10 9 8 7 6 5 4 3 2 1

The epigraph is taken from the eighth of "The Duino
Elegies," from *The Selected Poetry of Rainer Maria Rilke*,
by Rainer Maria Rilke, translated by Stephen Mitchell.
Copyright © 1982 by Stephen Mitchell. Reprinted by
permission of Random House, Inc.

FOR CARRIE

and in memory of

G. GERNON BROWN, JR.

and

ARTHUR M. McCULLY

CONTENTS

Who has twisted us around like this, so that

no matter what we do, we are in the posture

of someone going away? Just as, upon

the farthest hill, which shows him his whole valley

one last time, he turns, stops, lingers —,

so we live here, forever taking leave.

— Rainer Maria Rilke

THE

WRECKED,

BLESSED

BODY

OF

SHELTON

LAFLEUR

1 MOTHER AND CHILD

WATCH NOW. It's my hands that speak, not my voice. Just picture a child who, lacking words for his thoughts, flits and flutters his moth-soft fingers before your eyes and asks you to see. *This is what happened to me*, the child's hands say. *I'll show you.*

Of course I'm not a child but an old man, and a frightful-looking one at that, more skeleton than skin, face like a weatherworn stone, my body casting the shadow of some half-starved animal on the verge of collapse. You'd guess, just looking at me, I was eighty-five or ninety. You'd guess I was about to slip, in a single shallow breath, straight from this world to the next. Maybe you'd even swear you'd seen the likes of me on the porch outside some falling-down old folks' home, my body bound to a creaking cane rocker, spit clinging to the corners of my mouth.

No, that's not me, though it might as well be. The fact is, I'm only seventy. I just look older. I feel older.

Even so, inside this body there's a child's story stirring, wanting to break free. Watch, my hands say, and I'll show you the story of that child, a child made strange and silent by circumstance, a beautiful dark star of a child who sixty-two years ago dropped to the ground as though he'd fallen from the sky.

In truth, the fall was from the great swaying branches and thick rustling leaves of a single tar-patched and withered Audubon Park oak. As he fell, the child's body crashed from branch to branch, and for those quick few moments he didn't know up from down and could hardly tell which limbs were his own and which the tree's, feeling only the sharp kick and swish and wallop of tumbling, a tumbling that would leave his body bruised and broken and wrecked.

Sixty-two years later and the ruin of that child's body, now an old man's, remains. With the passing of one slow year to another, one creeping day to the next, that body grows more burdensome and debilitating and frail, as though the fall from the oak occurred not just once but again and again, each fall worse than the one before it — swifter, more painful, more difficult to endure.

Even my dreams, though they've got a lifetime from which to take their stories, have now become dreams of falling. Mornings I wake, as often as not, with the sensation that I've just landed there in that bed after plummeting through the air, my body pressed so deep into the mattress that it seems buried in the earth. I feel chilled and nearly take myself for dead. I run my hands across my arms for warmth and wonder how it is I've sprouted these two frail twigs, so coarse and insubstantial. They hang down from my shoulders as if some farmer has stuck them there to scare the dimwitted crows from his corn.

How, I ask myself, do this sunken chest and bent back manage to contain a beating heart, the same one that pumped inside a young man, a child, an infant? Such a change seems so improbable, so devastating.

Sometimes it feels as though my body has set about becoming the tree that, sixty-two years ago, it found itself falling from. Skin of bark and hair of moss — I practically scare myself.

But my hands. Watch as I raise them up, as I place them in view of my swimming and searching eyes. See the fingers swollen out to their knotty, arthritic joints. See how the nails have gone cloudy and cracked. See how the crescent-shaped blisters bubble out at the base of each thumb and jagged creases cut through the palms as though my fingers have just peeled open, after years and years, from the clenched fists they first formed.

You'd never guess that these hands have provided, through my long life, a measure of strength that my body has otherwise lacked. They've put food on my table, earned me a livelihood as real and true as any man has a right to expect. They've offered themselves in forgiveness and friendship and longing.

They've done more, though. They have. Keep looking and you'll see how they've waved grace over from its hiding place, waved and waved until something has finally swooped down as if from heaven or shot up from the ground like a pale new shoot. You'll see how each time I waved, there grace was, found where and when it was least expected.

Look: There's Minou Parrain, come to save the child.

Look: There's Edward Soniat, there's his frail daughter Margaret.

There's Genevieve Simmons, small and scared and terrifying.

There's proud Isabel and shy Adrienne.

There's Olivia and Elise, just children.

They've all got a gift for the child, don't they? They've all got a place in shaping the child's life, waving and waving to grace for the child's sake, for their own.

Who's going to save the child's life? Who's going to save his own? Who'll take the broken wings the child's limbs have become and show him the when and where and what-for of setting them in motion?

Well, it's been grace, nothing more or less, that has made its great good appearance before my eyes, taking on the most surprising of shapes. And I've made of it only a single request — that

3

I be allowed, when my voice can't or won't, to speak. Time and again, grace has answered. Time and again, it's said yes.

Go on, it says now. *Tell your story while there's time.*

I will, I answer. *I will.*

And so my hands start their trembling, start their shaking, and speak.

❧ ❧ ❧

Sixty-two years ago, then, a child fell as if he'd fallen from the sky, and when he landed, he landed not just in the dirt and oak leaves and roots and not just beyond the hearing of family ears and the sight of family eyes but in a place beyond everything he'd ever seen or heard or known, and for the first time in his eight-year-old life the child realized, in the midst of his pitiful wailing, that he was utterly alone.

In fact this child had wailed like this before, still streaked with the blood of his birth, while two dark hands held him with the greatest of care, raising him high like Abraham raising Isaac in the forest's moonlit clearing, his mind full of heavenly fire. And then the child was set down, those two hands clutching him tight, thumbs crossed against the child's chest, fingers joined tip to tip on the child's back, those two hands barely able to let go but letting go nonetheless, letting go forever.

At the time the child didn't know, couldn't have known, but only a few hours old, he'd been left like another of the Lord's early children, like Moses among the rushes, though not at the windswept banks of a gurgling stream, not wrapped in fine cloth or resting on silky corn-thread leaves, not destined to be found by a maiden who'd make him a slave-freeing king.

No, he'd been left in a wood-and-wire banana crate, sticky paper peeling off its ends, at a certain Garden District doorstep in the city of New Orleans in the dripping summer's heat of 1926, a year when — for the lucky and rich, I mean — high times still swirled like a straw in a cold tall glass, a year when the turmoil and crisis and ruin that lay ahead had yet to step forward and

4

show their faces. One war was done, and who knew there was another to come? Who knew the rich would soon turn poor and the poor turn desperate? Who was looking and listening not for the here and now but for what lay ahead?

And here was this child, left alone on the very day and hour of his birth, come from a world those swirling high times hadn't touched, hadn't thought to pay any mind. Here was this child. Here was this single, inexplicable abandoning.

No, it's worse, my hands tell me. Not just *abandoning*.

This *transaction*.

This *purchase*.

Well, whatever its name, it was there, beyond that doorstep, past the white marble halls and floral wallpaper walls, through a patio garden of wisteria and oleander and persimmon, on back to the leaning white clapboard structure that had served once as rank and rotten slave quarters, now as the neatly appointed rooms of an unfortunate, privileged daughter — it was there that the child would be looked after, cared for, loved.

His mother was to be — and what difference could this screaming newborn infant discern? — not the dark, desperate, secret woman who'd given birth to him but a crippled white girl of seventeen, a girl who wanted what she otherwise would never have: a child of her very own.

And look who has stepped up to give his daughter just what she's asked for. It's the widower Edward Soniat, adoring father and devout Roman Catholic, importer of fine European furnishings, sole proprietor of Edward P. Soniat International. He's got one office on Canal Street in New Orleans. He's got another in Paris and one more in Florence. He's got fingertips so fine they know in an instant what's oak or ebony or pine, what's the crinoline inside a woman's skirt, what's the cotton picked in a white-hot sun. Yes, his hands, just by the touch of his fingertips, know all that, for he's got arms and legs that stretch, like a Roman god drawn across the sky, from one continent to the next.

Don't be fooled, though. Edward Soniat knows the very in-

5

sides of pain as if it's an animal he's hunted down and split open. He's watched his wife die from a sickness that spread like fire from her womb; he's watched the child that womb produced grow into a girl who for twelve years was happy and healthy and whole but who in the thirteenth year was not and would never be again, the doctors, one after the other, explained. Over time, they said, every muscle in that sweet girl's body would cease the give-and-take that allows a leg to bend, an arm to reach, a mouth to swallow, an eye to blink. Over time, those muscles would grow brittle and coarse, would stretch tighter and tighter, as if they'd been twisted, would bend the child's bones the way a string bends a bow, curling her limbs until they became useless for walking or reaching, for pulling the blankets over her body, for turning the pages of a book.

Over time? the girl's father, Edward Soniat, asks. *How long does that mean?*

But the doctors say their guesses are only as good as his own.

How long? he asks again.

Ten years, they say, and one adds, *If you're lucky, Mr. Soniat, it might be fifteen.*

But the father shakes his head, quiets his sobbing by closing his eyes, covering his face with his hands.

If you're lucky. If you're lucky.

But luck, he knows, has made its home in a foreign land, in some distant place where, though he'd go anywhere, he'll never go again.

So Edward Soniat, as age overtakes him — swift as an arrow, sharp as that arrow's sharp point — finds himself transformed as surely as his daughter. He's become, through the years of her suffering and his own, a man as much of progressive temperament as of considerable means, believing as he does in nobility and decency, in women's suffrage, in mankind's equality, in Christian determination and forbearance and responsibility. Edward Soniat presides, doesn't he, over a not-so-secret society that gathers in his grand New Orleans home, drinking the drinks that sailed back from across the globe in his sole possession, pondering questions of immense and impressive difficulty. They've promised, every one of these men, to entertain, then undertake, certain affirmative measures; promised to improve the earthly lot of one and all, black as well as white.

And so Edward Soniat is busy, this summer of 1926, devising his life's single greatest act, an act of devotion and love and grand charity.

Watch.

Soon enough, with all care and good speed, he has provided precisely what his daughter has asked for, the only thing she truly wants, she has said. Yes, he's provided it. Provided him. Provided this Negro child. Shelton Gerard Lafleur.

I'm an old man now, yes I am, but there's still time to consider, is there not, the manner in which such charity as Edward Soniat's might have taken root and grown, fueled by a daughter's sad, sweet longing, by a father's Christian commitment, by one mighty, daring scheme.

Did this man, good as his gold, devise his plan among the books and green-glass reading lamps of his nut-wood and tapestried library? Or did he simply hunt, street by street and door by door, through the city's ramshackle Negro neighborhoods in search of a woman expecting a child she didn't want and couldn't feed, a woman in need of a few folded dollar bills more than this helpless body, this hungry mouth?

It's no matter, really. What's done is done.

Watch. Here it is. A child.

And here is Edward Soniat, good Christian soldier, ready to call this new child from the ragged blankets and clinging dirt of a bloody bed, ready to give that child a clean and shining home, providing not just the clothes for that child's body and not just the food for that child's mouth but much more, much worse: his very name. Shelton Gerard Lafleur.

The child, that dark flower, was named out of nowhere, was he not? It was the very same nowhere from which he had appeared, only to land on that Garden District doorstep. Let's be clear: There were no Lafleurs in the Soniat lineage, no Sheltons or Gerards. And there was not, one can be certain, a note pinned to the crate granting the child a Christian name. *Tasty and delicious,* the peeling paper might well have declared. *Try some today!*

Look. There he is. Just a wailing child.

Well, here's two guesses in answer to a lifetime's question. Maybe the child was named by the young girl herself when she first took him into her arms, looked down into his dark but squeezed-shut eyes, held his thrashing body tight against her empty breasts, the girl crying with joy, shedding no end of tears, the name appearing on her lips as if it had come to her in a blinding white moment of divine intervention.

That's his name, Daddy. I just know it, she says, looking up at her father through her tears.

Or maybe her father, Edward Pfister Soniat, is the one to speak. Isn't it his voice, after all, more than his daughter's, more sometimes than my very own, that still rings in my ears this many years later, one fine rich voice in a lifetime's mighty chorus? So maybe it's Edward Soniat who provides the name, just as he has provided this child.

Yes, *he* would have named the child, wouldn't he? I don't have to listen long or hard to hear his voice rising above the mighty chorus: *I've given my daughter a child.*

Watch, and you'll see what I see: There's Edward Soniat lowering his head as if in prayer, his oiled hair flopping down like a wave against his forehead, the wave's crest pricking at his eyes like a thorn. He pushes his hair back, runs the comb of his fingers over his head, runs it down to his neck, sweeps the palm of his hand across his brow. He frets, sweats, and worries, then resolves that sure enough, he has done the right thing, has done a good thing, proper and just.

8

Keep looking and maybe you'll see Edward Soniat that same evening, alone now, staring at the green-glass library light, the great question he has put to himself hanging in the air, surrounding him, like it's been woven into the lingering cloud of his sweet tobacco smoke. Doesn't he hear, past the patio and garden, from his daughter's bed, the child's cry, the quiet that follows? *It's her wish but mine also*, he declares. *I am a man, God knows* — and he frets, sweats, and worries — *whose aim is goodness and grace and charity.*

Again Edward Soniat runs his hands through his hair, lets his fingers come to rest at his neck. *And mine*, he goes on, *is a charity that flowers with twin blossoms, taking from one who can bear but cannot provide, giving to one who can provide but cannot bear.*

Even so, this many years later, the question stands: Where'd the name come from? A tribute to some dead friend? To some secret, treasured association, some deep affinity or affiliation, some personal affair? Maybe he chose the name at random, guided by a certain unacknowledged disquiet and hesitation, by a reluctance to wholly confirm the trick he'd performed, the transaction he'd undertaken and now, having handed the child over to his daughter, completed.

This *purchase*, say these hands.

Years later, when that child had become a young man, his wrecked, blessed hands painted a self-portrait with fierce, angry strokes, finished it with green lines running up and down the dark throat, swipes of white and red and yellow cut into the dark eyes, cut throughout the dark face, then named the work, the pen's point scraping on the coarse, painted paper the way Edward Soniat's must have scraped on his own years before: *The Final Flowering of Shelton Lafleur.*

I didn't know anything then, did I, for I'd go on to paint other self-portraits, a dozen of them, and each seemed to me a final flowering, with my right hand raised between the self I was and the picture I'd set about creating, my fingers pinched so low on the brush I could feel, or imagined I could, each bristle stick, bend, and then give as it spilled color onto the canvas. And each time I was done, when the work was finished, I'd lower my hand and discover not what I'd made of myself but all I still didn't know, all I couldn't even guess at or, having guessed, comprehend.

And is it too much to suggest that I felt this not-knowing most fully when I raised my hand again to sign there the name I'd been given, the name that still sounded in my ears like a small, nagging question? *Where'd I put that shiny nickel? Shelton Gerard Lafleur?*

There I am at eighteen, at twenty, at twenty-seven, at thirty-five, gone north to make a name for myself, that name remaining the question it would always be.

There I am at forty and forty-one, forty-six and forty-nine, folks marveling at the gentle touch of my hands, swearing how it must be a miracle for one such as me, a poor, crippled Negro from New Orleans, to paint works that swing so wide of the primitive, far beyond what those works ought to be.

And there I am at fifty and fifty-three, at sixty-one and sixty-nine, back in the city of my strange, unfortunate birth, my terrible fall from the sky.

There, each and every time, the oil paint cracked, run through with lines, thick and swirling or thin and fine — there's that question, my question: *Shelton Gerard Lafleur?*

Call that name and it's me who answers. Say, *Hey, take a look, straight over there. The crippled one, the one leaning on those two canes, the one in that baggy coat and too-long tie, the one whose eyes trail off into nowhere, the one who looks, sure enough, about ready to die. That's that painter, that's that artist. Shelton Gerard Lafleur.*

Well, that's me. It is. Still, there's that question; there's that child.

※ ※ ※

Seventy years old now, my body bruised and broken, but like a never-satisfied, ever-inquiring child, I'm still full of questions, one after the other in a steady line. So here's one more question for good measure: Doesn't truth, whether grim or glorious, always manage to provide a witness, one who sees and knows and understands, one who'll bear the news to all others?

Not always, maybe, but this one time it did, for there was, on that sweltering summer morning in 1926, another body there in that room, though it was pressed into the corner like a frightened mouse, like the smallest of the earth's creatures, eyes alight. It was the nursemaid, Genevieve, quiet and small but unable to disguise, had anyone looked to see, her trembling at this transaction, at the handing over of this child, the giving to this child a name.

Genevieve, ashen and ancient, would have been old enough, wouldn't she, for such a moment as this to spark some dim recollection or at least call to mind some frightful story she'd once heard.

A child pulled off his mother's breast and sold.

A man and woman divided.

A family torn apart.

How could she not have wept at such a sight?

So she did weep, invisible and silent though that weeping might have been, with remembered sorrow, with hidden rage. Yes, she wept and she thought and she prayed and finally, who knows how much later, she dreamed and imagined and plotted, holding the child's life in her hands as surely as the others, who passed him around from crate to doorstep, from charitable Christian father to grateful crippled daughter to that pair of untouched breasts.

So everyone in that white, bright, sunlit room — father and daughter and child and nursemaid — was, each to his own ends, weeping. Somewhere else another voice was joining theirs, though no one heard it, though no one could. That voice, don't you think, was weeping too.

Well, it takes a lifetime for such a picture as this to show itself, to take its true shape in memory. The worst of secrets are left to unravel inch by inch from the cloth into which they've been woven. And then, so many years later, who's left to weave those secrets into something new?

You are, my hands say.

I'm too old, I say back. *And anyway, I've already tried. Look at my pictures. Look how I've tried.*

And besides, this is only a child's story, and isn't every such story, every child's, just a sad, pleasing fable, a tale of wonder and surprise, of mystery and miracles and coincidence, of people and places and incidents that appear before the child as if they've fallen, like the child himself would fall, straight down from the open sky?

So here he is, here's the child Shelton, a child who couldn't see, wasn't told, and so didn't know that he was born in some other house, to some other mother, that somewhere beyond the rough and tumble and tears and joy of early childhood was another woman weeping.

But I did try. My hands tried, I mean, though they had to imagine it and could imagine so little that my painting showed only the crown of the child's head cradled in his mother's arm, the child's head a large, mottled orb, the mother's arm sinewy and splotched, the perspective so magnified and close that my hands were able to depict, running through both the child's head and the mother's arm, the flow of blood, the purple, branchlike veins, and nothing more.

Mother and Child, the width and height of my two hands, framed in old, chipped, gilt plaster but kept hidden in some dust-filled attic or drawer. The work of a sentimental, unskilled apprentice, the work cherished.

2 ORPHANS

EIGHT YEARS OLD, and true memory begins, takes over from what can only be recovered in the smallest bits and pieces. The child's first seven years were as fine and light as porcelain chips flicked off the rim of an old china cup, the child's world no larger than the size of a room filled with flowers and books and hand puppets and wooden blocks, with the scent of strange lotions and medicines and syrups, with a mother's lilting voice and clenched screams, a voice that becomes the child's school and religion and comfort, screams that become the child's dreams.

Then the child turns eight and, itching for escape and adventure, wanders off one morning. He rises up from his bed when it is barely light and dresses quickly, glances again and again at his crippled mother, still sleeping, then wanders off, even though wandering off has been forbidden, even though he does not have anywhere he knows to go.

Does he open the door with hesitation, with even the slightest notion of what he is doing, of what he is about to do? Is it this that makes the child turn, as he begins to shut the door, to look again at his mother, twisted and curled in her bed, asleep in that impossibly contorted position from which she now can hardly unfold herself?

Her body becomes each day, it seems to Shelton, smaller and smaller as his own body grows. Her voice becomes softer, just a whisper, just a rush of air. Her screams of pain become so familiar that they're just one instrument in the orchestra of the city Shelton doesn't see but hears: a train's whistle, an automobile's choking roar, the clop and mud and thumping and clacking of horse-drawn carts, the cry of children's voices, mothers calling those children home, a thrashing that might be the child's own breathing or his mother's but sounds sometimes like a flock of pigeons taking flight.

But what eight-year-old Shelton sees and understands this morning is this and nothing more — that right now his mother is peaceful and sleeping. So he closes the door and doesn't wake her. He steps outside, looks up at the line of windows in his mother's father's house, and sees no light nor movement nor presence — Mr. Edward has sailed off, hasn't he, to London or Paris or Florence, to some impossibly distant and magical land — and so the child swings open the patio gate and kicks it closed with his heel as though he has done this a thousand times, as though he's the one now who's got a boat to catch, a sea to sail across, a fortune to acquire. Doesn't the child hear, through some thrown-open window, a strange, sweet melody, a woman singing, her voice pitched so high and clear it could be a bird strumming the first rays of the sun, the world become only voice and music, confirming how far the child has gone already, the new place to which he's already come.

Then he races down the alley, the echo of his steps rebounding from the walls of one house, the next, and the next, and skips across the streetcar tracks of St. Charles Avenue to the green fields of Audubon Park. He has gone off in search of nothing, really, but sets his sights soon enough on the dusty touch of a clump of Spanish moss there in that one great withered oak, chosen at random, chosen simply because its thick limbs swoop down like a snake's arched back before shooting up to the sky, the coarse bark marked by patches scraped smooth as polished wood by the years of other children's climbing.

The oak is surrounded, Shelton notices once he has climbed enough, by a circle of smaller trees with leathery, olive-colored leaves. He has seen these trees before. He has touched those oily leaves and learned to name them from an illustrated drawing in one of the hundreds and hundreds of books he and his mother, through the eight years of his life, have paged through. His mother would sit propped up with pillows in her bed, with Shelton situated next to her, clumsily turning pages, his mother's curled finger pointing: sparrows and bluejays and finches, the names and configurations of the constellations, the United States and its capitals, the shapes of lakes and mountain ranges and shorelines, myths and fairy tales and fables, insects and flowers and —

That circle of small, dark trees, that's what? His mother's voice.

That's magnolia. His own.

Magnolia, whose sugary scent he detects now in the rustling breeze as he climbs and climbs the oak. He'll learn, years later, to paint the magnolia's blossoms, carrying them inside, setting them down in a vase. He'll learn to show, with the dark wash beneath, the slight change of texture as the blossoms dry, capturing the touch of brown like a rust stain on linen.

Still Life with Magnolia, and I still hear, don't I, the voice of my mother naming them, and the voice of Lawrence Parrain, known to all as Minou, the one who would teach the child to draw, the patter of his speech behind the child, the whispering in his ear: *It's not enough to look. You've got to see, Shelton. You've got to see.*

But for now, the child just looks and looks and climbs. And

then, just like that, for no reason at all beyond a child's uncertain step or grasp or balance, he falls. And before his body has even reached the ground, his hands bear, from their clawing and scraping against the branches, a remarkable resemblance to what they will look like sixty-two years later, what they look like now.

And as his body approaches the ground, it seems for an instant that the child might land as though he meant this fall all along, his body straight now, upright, his legs stretching down, as though his feet will gently touch the ground and he will be left standing, will merely brush himself off, raise his head, walk, take a look around.

But the child's forty pounds have become, after twenty feet of falling, four hundred. So his ankles and knees buckle; his muscles stretch, rip, and tear. His legs pop, like two tight corks, out of joint at his hips, the ends of his thighbones pressing out just below the skin like the oak roots just below the ground beneath him.

His spine does not give, though, and his head does not crack. But when the child ceases his pitiful wailing and tries to stand, he can't. He rolls over and over in the earth as though he is on fire. He screams; his legs burn and keep burning. He puts his face in the earth and oak roots and leaves and keeps it there, dirt on his bleeding lips and tongue, dirt in his bruised eyes and nose. He waits and waits and, if the truth be known, is waiting still, though minutes later he is found by a gentleman out for a June morning's stroll, a gentleman who pokes with his cane first at the child's legs and then at his shoulders and asks, "You alive, boy?" as if he is merely curious, as if he doesn't care one way or another whether he has stumbled upon an accident or the aftermath of some act of bright white vengeance — a black child left for dead beneath the swaying branches.

But Shelton moves, groans, spits the dirt and blood off his lips, and the gentleman, his voice shaking with fear or maybe simply with age, says, "Well, I'll get you some help, I guess."

Minutes pass, and still Shelton doesn't move, can't. He sees his mother miraculously rise from her bed, call his name, run after him. He sees Mr. Edward standing by her empty bed, dropping to his knees at the wonder, offering heavenly thanks for this cure. He sees the nursemaid Genevieve standing there too, daring to raise a hand to the man's bowed head, saying, "They're gone, Mr. Edward. They're gone, yes they are." Smiling her secret, hidden smile. He sees his mother holding him by the hand while the two of them run. Yes, they're running together.

Then Shelton groans again, at another touch. Two police officers are standing over him. "What did you do, boy?" they ask, and Shelton tries but can't answer. The officers step back and look around as if they're hoping to find one of the boy's black buddies or shiftless parents lurking nearby so they can scold and threaten and be done with this child. Failing that, they try to lift the child to place him in the back of their white and black and red-light-flashing cruiser, but the child screams so on being jostled or even touched that they think better of it and one tells the other to fetch the boy an ambulance.

"You got some folks nearby?" the one still leaning over him asks, but Shelton groans and screams once more and then is silent.

"Can't you talk at all, son?" the officer says. "Can you hear what I've just said?" But Shelton doesn't groan or scream or speak or even move his head.

"Oh, good goddamn," the officer says, but when he puts two fingers to Shelton's neck and sees the rise and fall of Shelton's chest, he gets up and walks over to the car, sits down inside, and takes a long drink from whatever he's got in there.

Shelton waits, hears the sounds of his breathing, feels the push of his lungs inside his chest, and thinks again of his mother and wants to call out to her. He tries to call, tries to say *Mama*, tries to say *Please*, but there is only blood and dirt and spit.

Then Shelton sees his mother again, though this time she

hasn't risen up from her bed but is still lying there, sweat streaking her face, pressing her long hair flat against her head, her whole body writhing and shaking, and he is running off in search of Genevieve or Mr. Edward, running from room to room in the big house, running up and down the stairs, the names he calls echoing back to him as if it's someone else calling, someone who follows him from one room to the next but stays hidden.

Then he turns to head through the library door but runs right into Mr. Edward, who in one quick motion lifts him high, pulls him close, laughs and laughs until Shelton can say, though he doesn't want to say it, doesn't want Mr. Edward to put him down, "It's Mama."

So Shelton's mind leaves him there, suspended in Mr. Edward's arms, until in due time, who knows how long, the ambulance arrives and two men slide a white board under his body, the board like a knife slicing through his skin, and then deliver him to the charity hospital. On the great iron doors they carry him through is carved a story the child can't comprehend: muscular men raising axes and shovels, women bent at the waist, their hands touching the ground, a sun and moon and bolts of lightning all scattered above their heads, the face of some great horned beast split in half as the doors divide, opening for him, for the splayed, broken body of this child.

There, inside, they clean that body with a yellow sponge and warm gray water and, while Shelton bites and bites his tongue to keep from screaming, put his hips back into joint by pulling first on one leg and then the other, two masked men and two masked women holding Shelton down as they tug at his legs, their fingers pressing down through his skin to the muscle and bone beneath until the child is sure they mean to tear the legs straight off him.

And when they are done, Shelton decides he can breathe again and so does, though he knows something is still wrong with his legs but can't tell them.

He needs to speak, this child. He needs to tell them to go back, to keep pulling on his legs, to keep turning and twisting. He needs to tell them to cut him open, cut him nearly in half, fix whatever it is inside him that's still bent or twisted or broken.

But when they have wiped their own brows dry and torn off their masks and shaken hands all around, they turn to Shelton and ask how he feels, how he's doing.

Now. Tell them now. That's just my own voice, my own hands, calling back to the child.

But the child can't hear me, can he, so he nods, then shakes his head from side to side, as if what he's hearing in his ears is only the whistling of air, only the rustling of oak leaves, only the flailing of his arms as they swing out for the sunlight, as they catch on a shadow, his own shadow, as they cut through the breeze. Yes, all my shouts and screaming and instruction are no use. The child still can't make his mouth speak, can't answer any of the questions put to him, as if his fall has left him this one further injury.

So after a moment's wonder about this silent child, who maybe isn't bright enough to understand the language they're speaking, the doctors and nurses turn away, shake their own heads, let the poor colored child sleep.

He does sleep, and in his sleep he steps out of bed and back to his mother's side, to lie down beside and against her. She tells him stories, ones she's told him before — of her father's poor childhood, of his determination and daring, of the romance that blossomed, her mother a princess, her father a prince, of her mother and father dancing at their wedding beneath the sparkling glass of a grand chandelier, a hundred specks of light above them like a sky filled with lucky stars. And Shelton falls asleep to the swirling music of his mother's voice, to the flickering light of a hundred million stars, to the gentle swaying that must be just like Mr. Edward feels on the boats that take him from here to there, so far away.

In the morning, though maybe after days and days of drifting in and out of such dreams, Shelton wakes to the sight of two black-robed women, two Catholic nuns, standing over him. They've brought in a bowl of thick, cold soup and some bread, and while he eats, soup running down his face, crumbs gathering on the sheets, they ask the very same questions asked but unanswered beneath the bright lights of the operating room.

What is your name?

Shelton doesn't answer.

Where do you live?

He doesn't know.

By the park where you were climbing? By the park where you fell?

Yes.

What is your father's name?

He doesn't have one.

Passed away?

Shelton stops, thinks for a moment. Yes.

What is your mother's name?

Mama.

Her name?

Miss Margaret.

Miss Margaret who?

Shelton doesn't answer, isn't sure, doesn't know, though he's got a catalogue of names in his head: Austen and Duplantier and Gallier and King, Merrick and Milton and Soniat and Zacharie, names he knows from books and newspapers, from illustrations and visitors' calling cards, visitors from whom he often hid, whose comings and goings he spied through a window's curtain folds or through a closed door's keyhole, once even, while playing some solitary game, through a warped panel of Mr. Edward's dressing closet, a cedar-floored pine armoire whose musty formality, with the rough scraping of Mr. Edward's wool suit coats against his bare arms and legs, left him feeling suffocated.

He'd seen a woman that time, hadn't he? He'd seen the delicate fingers pinch open one button, then another, until a man's hands, Mr. Edward's, brushed them away as though they were an already answered question. He'd seen the dress slip from the woman's body, seen the woman's white cream shoulders, the arc of her back, Mr. Edward's thick arms become a ring around it. He'd seen them step, dance, fall away from the dressing room, laugh. He'd seen them disappear into the darkness.

"My mama," he says now to the Catholic nuns, then stops. How to describe that familiar face, that curled, crippled body? "My mama," he says, looking at the two women, at their dark eyes, at the blank, empty sympathy registered there but aimed somewhere above the bed where he lay — at the crucifix hanging on the wall, Shelton guesses, or at the crack in the plaster where the nail holds the cross, twelve crooked lines running out from beneath Christ's head. Shelton had counted the lines again and again when he'd woken to the empty room, wondering if, were he to reach up with one finger, the faint green paint would flake from the wall, as gentle and remarkable as snow.

"My mama's white," he thinks to say, he doesn't know why, seeing the snow he imagined, knowing only that it's true and it's something he once wondered about the way he'd wondered about all the rest — why he didn't have a father, why his mother lay day in and day out in that bed, why one minute she could be singing and laughing, the next be screaming and kicking to get her covers off, all of it both too important and too ordinary ever to speak aloud or ask about or even consider in the form of a question.

But now the two women look at him, shake their heads, almost laugh but don't.

"Dark as you are, child," one says.

"Careful," says the other.

"She is," Shelton says, and the two women's fingers dance through the folds in their robes and they twirl around but twirl back and tell Shelton to sleep, they'll come visit him again, they will.

Later that day, or maybe a few days later, the two Catholic nuns — the same ones, Shelton thinks, but isn't sure — appear again in his room. They bring him clothes and stand by and watch him get dressed, Shelton clinging to the hospital bed the whole while because his legs aren't working right, something is broken or ripped or torn. His legs feel turned the wrong way and hurt.

"Time," says one.

"You'll see," says the other. "Though it helps to pray, of course."

Then Shelton is done getting himself dressed, and they lead him out through the iron door, its carved story reversed, to a big black car that pours out smoke and says CRESCENT CITY TAXI. The women open the car's doors, robes flowing this way and that until swept up into their tiny fists, feet squeezed, Shelton sees, into dusty, black-laced leather boots, and a man takes Shelton and the two women for what they have told him is just a drive, though Shelton knows somehow it isn't.

The man drives and drives and Shelton sees more of the city in these twenty minutes than he has seen his whole life: brick streets sliced in half by streetcar tracks, a thousand different faces, white and black, those faces turned, Shelton imagines, to this car as it drives past, faces that interrupt their conversations to ask, *Who and what is that?*

A child out for a taxi ride with two Catholic nuns?

On his way to heaven, no doubt about that.

"Maybe I could find it," Shelton says, frightened now.

"Find what?" the two women ask.

"My house," Shelton says. "The tree where I fell."

"Dear Lord," one says.

"Hmm," says the other, looking out the window, silent, shaking her head.

Shelton searches the faces out on the street, wishes and wishes for one that will, miracle of miracles, take on the shape of Mr.

Edward's. By now isn't he out hunting Shelton down? Hasn't the news of Shelton's fall reached Mr. Edward's home or his Canal Street office or Paris or London or Florence, wherever else he might be found? Wouldn't he sail across the ocean as soon as he learned of Shelton's absence?

So Shelton looks and looks, but then the man up front turns the car onto a wide street by the name of Elysian Fields, then turns into a long drive just past a sign that Shelton can read, a green sign whose white letters spell out MILNE COLORED BOYS' HOME.

The women sigh together, one long loud breath, and Shelton feels that breath against his face, warm and sour and strong, feels it send him off a thousand miles in the distance like it's the huff and puff of a fat-cheeked cloud and he's a paper boat set adrift in a giant sea. Here, he barely hears the women tell him as they step out of the black car, robes gathered again in their fists — here, at the orphans' home, is where he'll live, be taken care of, looked after.

They wait; Shelton is silent, a thousand miles away, body rocking this way and that, a paper boat taking on all that water, threatening to collapse.

But only, they say, until someone shows up to claim him or until — Shelton turns to see their fingers dance again in the dark folds of their robes — until he learns to tell them something they can use to find his family, something that is true and not some made-up, mixed-up, child-fallen-from-the-sky story.

"A white woman," one says.

"Lord forgive us," says the other.

"By his name, I've seen none darker."

"Nor me."

Orphans' home? Shelton thinks. "I'm not an orphan," he says, and that stops the two women's talking, stops their slow steps beside him. They pat their hands on Shelton's shoulders, shake their cloth-covered heads.

"Of course not," one says.

"You're just lost," says the other, and they lead him inside, to a thin, gray-haired white man who nods and nods until the two women have said their goodbye to Shelton, turned away, closed the door behind them.

"I'm not," Shelton says again, but the women are gone, and the gray-haired man can't hear him or pretends not to or doesn't care. He puffs out his cheeks, looks right and left, then asks Shelton a few questions, different ones from those he's been asked already. Can he read? Can he write? Has he been baptized in the Holy Roman Apostolic Church? Has he suffered head lice, influenza, fevers? How'd he wind up crippled? Polio? A mule kick? Mistreatment?

Shelton nods and shakes his head, can't speak.

"Well, we're a family here," the thin, gray-haired man says. "We work hard. We provide for one another. We keep our home clean. We've got a group of good boys here, and the ones who aren't just need a little coaxing, a little shaping. You understand?"

Shelton nods again and lets the gray-haired man lead him to his bed, to his dark wood clothes chest, his soapdish and toothbrush, his pencil and paper on his rusted metal desk.

"Can you tell me your name, son?" the man asks.

Shelton looks up. "It's Shelton," he says, and he waits, expecting the man to ask him more, to ask about his mother, to ask about the tree where he fell.

But the gray-haired man has no more questions for Shelton. "Every boy," he says, "no matter his individual faults or talents, is equal in our eyes. You are all, though you're colored, though you've no parents of your own, the Lord's children."

The man pats Shelton on the head and leads him out to the other boys, gathered in a circle on the green lawn, every one of them dressed in white shirt and brown pants. "There," the man says and puts his hand on Shelton's back. "There's your new family, Shelton."

The man's hand moves from Shelton's back to his shoulder and stays there, squeezing his collarbone, painful and kind.

And years later Shelton's hands, my own hands, would paint that same circle of boys, though I found them this time on a blacktop Catholic school playground, the shirts still white but the pants now navy blue, a worn leather basketball rising up in the air at the center of the circle, rising higher and higher and then falling, each of the boys hollering and cursing, shouts and curses they mean more than they know, the ball like a dull brown sun rising and falling again and again on their upturned faces.

Orphans, I named that work, knowing what I know of such children, understanding all I understand, seeing in my mind's eye, though I didn't dare paint it, the one time that ball forgets to fall, rising and rising instead, the circle of upturned faces struck now with wonder, with the miracle of what they've just witnessed, a miracle that makes them laugh and smile into the bright sunshine until finally, one by one, they've got to lower their heads and look down at their hands to find them empty.

3 THE GREAT SEA

WELL, SHELTON WAS NOT like the others and told them so. He was not an orphan. No, no, no. Yes, he was as black as the rest of them, even blacker, but not an orphan, not that. He had a mother, he told every boy who'd listen. "I'm not an orphan," he told them, one and all.

And before long, after time and again patiently placing their hands on their hips or crossing their arms against their chests, they did the only thing they knew to do — they tackled Shelton or punched his arm or walked away cursing. And in time, though not nearly soon enough for Shelton to kneel down and ask their forgiveness, he learned that each one of them, some time or another, had had his own mother too — somewhere in New Orleans or up in Mississippi or in Chicago or Memphis or Washington, D.C. Or their mothers were buried beneath the ground in some distant, never-seen cemetery.

Or maybe their mothers weren't dead at all, the boys conjectured. Maybe they were alive somewhere and one day would prove it by strolling into the Milne Home and carrying away their dear lost children, shorn lambs saved at the last minute

26

from slaughter, slaves swiped from the stinking bowels of a ship, treasures dug up, unearthed, beneath the green grass or sandy beach at some invisible X.

But Shelton was different, and he told them so, told them he had a mother, one who wasn't hiding or in prison or buried or gone up north — a white mother, he said once, and the eyes of the boys caught fire, set ablaze by Shelton didn't know what.

White! one and then another screamed.

White as fine white sugar! they said, and laughed.

"White," Shelton said, looking from one face to the next. "My mother's white."

Look out now! one boy said.

Here's the Holy Ghost! said another.

White! they all said together, stunned, amazed, incredulous.

"White," Shelton said, Shelton whispered, Shelton pleaded.

And she was, wasn't she? She was as white as the Milne Home's white brick walls and white porch and grand white pillars, which Shelton soon learned he and the other boys would paint, over and over, all summer long.

Their dark hands and dark arms would be, by each day's end, colored white with the white paint, which they washed away at sunset, standing in line to dip their arms in the dark metal drum of turpentine out back behind the kitchen, where everything but the turpentine itself smelled of burned fat and shrimp heads and boiled cabbage and rotten oranges.

One by one, the boys stepped forward and reached down until their elbows touched the drum's sharp cold lip and their fingers found the drum's bottom, muddy with the congealed white paint that had settled there. To Shelton it felt like the cold silt and ooze beneath the sun-warmed surface of the City Park lagoon where the boys were taken once each summer for a swim. They were promised a penny for each old golf ball their toes or fingers found and rescued from the slippery bottom, and the boys descended again and again, like divers in search of shiny pearls.

When it was time to clean up after painting, Shelton saw that if he pulled his arms out of the drum quickly, lightning fast, the congealed white paint would drip from his fingertips like melted butter and leave white rings on the turpentine's calm surface. He watched as each white ring grew wider and wider, less and less distinct, separating by some trick of light into two rainbow-colored arcs the moment before the paint disappeared.

At night, lying in bed, Shelton could still smell the sweet, fiery sheen on his hands, could feel it burning beneath his fingernails and in the lines of his palms and at the roots of the downy hair on his arms.

Those nights when he felt the burning, Shelton thrashed in his bed and whimpered until the thrashing and whimpering woke him, and he'd see the boys, woken from their own sleep, gathered around him as though they were conducting a late-night vigil, their faces lit by the moon through the dormitory's latched but curtainless windows and struck with fright and wonder, as if they were watching not the fretful dreams of a boy like themselves but the final gasps and shaking of some dangerous injured animal.

"Shelton Lafleur!" they'd finally scream together, and Shelton's arms would shoot up and his hands would reach out, and the boys would laugh and laugh, hysterical, wild.

After the first few days of painting each summer, Shelton and the other boys scratched and scratched at their hands and arms all night long. By morning the dormitory's green tile floor would be covered with white flecks that would cling to the boys' bare feet when they got up and dressed and trudged off to breakfast before being sent out to paint again.

There was no mistaking the other boys' footprints for Shelton's, which left behind only the smudged imprint of his toes and the balls of his feet, never his heels. Anyone could see from those imprints, even if they'd never seen Shelton walk, the way his feet turned in at an awkward angle and slid across the floor in a movement more like the sweep of a broom than a step.

That Shelton did not walk like the other boys simply confirmed for them that this pitch-black child who lied like a dead dog, like a criminal, about his mother's color was strange and dangerous and had to be watched, had to be fought, had to be beaten. Most of all, though, he had to be tamed, brought low, made small, shown what was truth and what was not. So they named him, and when one name did not prove enough, named him again and again: *Shelton the Shuffler. Stutter Step. Bird Bones. Pigeon. Creampuff Sissy. Eightball. Dogwood. Baby Boy.*

Shelton didn't care. He was not like them and told them so. He wasn't an orphan but the son of a sugar-white mother. Though he was asked again and again, he couldn't and so did not try to explain how he'd been taken away from her, why she had not come, as he swore she would, to rescue him.

And how was it that a white woman was mother to this black black child? He didn't know. The boys laughed and laughed, teased and tormented him.

And this, as his years in the Milne Home passed, as he learned more and more from the other, older boys about the workings of the world, about men and women lying down together — this became Shelton's own conclusion: If he was actually flesh of her flesh, if he had emerged from between her young girl's white-twig useless legs like a bloody midnight storm, then surely his mother was a woman who, when she could still walk, if she'd ever walked at all, had gone somewhere she shouldn't and ended up in the hands and arms and loins of a black man — a man like Shelton and then some, a man hideously, impenetrably black.

Or, worse, she'd simply lain in the bed where she'd always lain but had been seduced one night by the devil, for only the devil, Shelton was told, could put inside a white woman's body a child the color of coal, a deformed, crippled, lightning-smart child, a child who all the white folks at the Milne Home — the teachers and the gray-haired man and the priests who arrived once a month to hear the boys' confessions — concluded was just making a show of his meekness and goodness and kindness, a child who was hiding his actual stripes deep down within him, waiting and waiting with the patience of a saint for the one moment when he'd let his true nature loose on an unsuspecting world.

And Shelton finally felt what he was meant to feel. He felt ashamed.

But what the child told himself was that he didn't care. He'd go on being nice as nice could be. He'd go on behaving as his mother had told him he needed to behave if he was to avoid the fate that would otherwise befall him, a fate that would, before anything else, take into account his color, would place civility and decency aside if given half the chance, would deny him opportunity, would pass judgment blindly, without forethought or hesitation or mercy.

"None darker," one of the nuns had said, and Shelton had felt the frightened amazement, the half-hidden wonder.

The child was too young, of course, to understand his mother's words, which she was too young to have formulated on her own and thus had taken, like the array of medicinal syrups she took each morning, from her right-thinking, charity-minded father.

What the child Shelton did understand from these speeches was only a single admonition: Behave. So he did, and he continued to do so no matter his circumstances, waiting and waiting for his mother to send someone to get him, to lead him home so she could touch her feverish hand to his head, pull him close, curl his body against her curled own.

The image of his mother and of Mr. Edward, of his Garden District home and of the tree where he fell — they all slipped away from Shelton from time to time like the white paint washed off his hands and arms. His memories would become just a story he'd once heard and repeated, a story that now, except for one thing or another, he'd about forgotten.

Then a new boy would wind up at the Milne Home, and all the other boys would gather around him, eager for the words this new child was set to speak, for the story this boy would tell.

He'd been beaten, had he?

He'd gone hungry for weeks and weeks on end?

He'd lived with an aunt who'd passed away asleep in her bed?

He'd been handed from one house to the next until he'd run away, swearing and swearing he'd never go back?

Well, that's nothing, is it, Shelton? Come here, Bird Bones. Come over here, Pigeon. Tell this boy your story. Tell him everything. What's that about your mother? What color you say she is?

※ ※ ※

When one year and the next and the next had passed, Shelton telling his story a hundred times, still no one had arrived to speak his name. And when Shelton had finally had enough of answering the boys' taunts and teasing with politeness and good humor, he admitted to himself what he now understood, that he was not just an orphan but an orphan twice, and it was that admission as much as anything, as much as the taunts and teasing and torment, that led him to do what he did: He stopped speaking.

He didn't have any other choice, did he? If he didn't speak, if he didn't address them, wouldn't they eventually ignore him, just leave him alone?

They did not, though, and his silence became, he knew, a weapon, the only weapon close at hand. Beaten now, and not just by the boys but by the once-friendly teachers and by the thin, gray-haired man, Shelton still wouldn't speak. He wouldn't say anything. He wore his silence, they said, like a crown, and they beat him again and named him anew: *Button-lips. The Idiot. The Dumb Child. Silent, Stupid Shelton.*

When the days of the child's silence had passed to weeks and the weeks had passed to months, there was talk that behind that silence lay some grand notion Shelton had gotten into his head. The coal-black child who thought he was white was training, one boy and then all the others said, to be a holy man, a monk or priest or even Jesus Christ Almighty. So the boys beat him worse, now with a bamboo switch which they passed around from bed to bed, tucking the switch under their blankets for sweet dreams of what they'd do to Shelton. Even the youngest of the boys, who stared wide-eyed at the wonder of a crippled child, were coaxed and cajoled and threatened until they agreed to strike out at Shelton too.

He didn't scream, though, or cry out, or so much as breathe a single breath when the switch hit his legs or tore into his back or slapped the palms of his open hands. Silence coursed through his body, mixed with the blood in his veins, and strengthened him when he was beaten again.

Years later, his hands, these hands, my own — they found such treatment easy to depict. It was there all along, contained in their misunderstanding, in what they thought was on the child's mind but wasn't. My hands painted Jesus Christ in the grip of the Romans and bent beneath their spears and helmets and suffering in his last moments with the blind consent of the heavens above him. My hands painted the fourteen stations of the cross, and when a fire consumed them, painted all fourteen again. I put the child's wounds on Christ's body, and why not?

The child had first seen carved pictures of that story when the boys were all taken to a special Catholic mass at St. Louis Cathedral. For just that one day, the church was filled with colored families dressed in their Sunday best, the fathers and sons in dark suits and neckties, the mothers and daughters wearing lace and netted hats pinned with bright flowers, so many of them that Shelton squinted his eyes and imagined the congregation was a great expanse of earth giving rise to a glorious, flowering garden. Here was an image that would stay with the child, and some twenty years later the man he'd become would see it again, the worshipers gathered now not at St. Louis Cathedral but just outside a tiny church in St. Francisville, Louisiana.

I thought to paint the two scenes, past and present, as though they had been joined together, removing the men and women

32

and children one by one from the cathedral until they were no longer bathed in the sunlight washing through a row of stained glass windows but were standing in a bare, flat field, every face flushed with the leaping flames of a burning clapboard church.

I tried to remember and recreate in the painting what the child had seen in the cathedral but I did not see in that field in 1958: the orchids and gardenias and magnolias and azaleas that had adorned the women's hats, the bloom of life cast now, by the joining of these two scenes, near the raging, spitting threat of an awful fire.

If it was grace that led me to this burning church so I could set about painting what I witnessed, it was a grace that took more than it gave. I'd spent that Sunday afternoon driving my car down the winding River Road from New Orleans to St. Francisville, passing oil refineries and immaculately restored plantations, painted with the same kind of blinding white paint as the Milne Home's. I arrived just in time for the evening service, where a priest named Father Jerome Gautreaux was to consecrate my own stations of the cross, the fourteen paintings that the parishioners had worked to purchase with money they'd raised from two years' worth of bake sales and bingo games and raffles.

The church, though, was already in flames when I drove up, and I stepped out to hear the priest lift his voice above all the sobbing and weeping. "There's a great sea crashing over this nation," the priest called out, wiping away his own tears, the only one in that field turned not toward the fire but away from it, as though he'd already seen the flames and understood their meaning, as though he had emerged from the fire itself to tell its story. "There's a great sea washing everything clean," he shouted. "It's a sea, my brothers and sisters, whose waves won't subside at the empty threat of one small fire. It's a sea whose waves won't subside at a hundred burning churches or a thousand burning crosses or a hundred thousand more."

And while the rubble the church had become still smoldered,

the priest went ahead with the mass in that field, and even I, Shelton Gerard Lafleur, who could not make myself believe, nearly believed for those few moments, as if the burning church had indeed summoned some kind of holy presence, which reached out with the flames' fingers to touch every face, to heal both old wounds and new, to promise change.

After the mass was completed, I stepped forward and looked out over the faces, the gray ash from the fire settling like a gentle snow. I said that I'd go ahead and paint the stations again, that I'd paint them in the memory of this terrible misfortune.

Which I did. I'll admit here, though, that the whole time I painted I kept in my mind the image of that congregation, huddled and frightened in the bare, flat field, and of that earlier congregation in the cathedral.

There's Christ praying again in the garden. There's Christ dragged away and falling and getting crucified. There he is, rising a second time, as if that first time weren't enough to do all that needed doing.

And ten months after the fire, just as soon as I was done with the fourteen stations, I set about painting what I'd kept in my mind, what I remembered. When I was done, I gave to this painting the name the priest had provided me: *The Great Sea.*

In others' eyes and, I'll admit, my own, that painting was to be my greatest, so grand and magnificent that even with it hanging in one of the great white-ceilinged, white-walled rooms of the New Orleans Museum, you couldn't stand far enough back to take in the whole work at a single glance but would have to look, the way the child had looked in that cathedral, from one face to the next.

The work was admired and praised and celebrated for the artist's remarkable eye, for my ability to see in those faces the whole of the Negro's struggle and longing and aspiration, so I just kept to myself this secret — that the eyes that had seen and studied and held on to this sea of people weren't those of a fully grown man, the surehanded crippled Negro artist from New Orleans by the name of Shelton Lafleur. They weren't eyes seeing the pain and longing of an entire race. They were simply the eyes of one lost Milne Colored Boys' Home child.

Yes, when I turned to memory to see and feel and paint that congregation, what I found there was the child who'd searched each and every one of those faces that Sunday morning in hopes that just one would turn toward him, would meet his eyes and show some glimmer of recognition, that one person in the mighty crowd would think *I know that boy's mama* and push through to him and lead him home.

Which, of course, no one did, and so the boy had to grow into a man and paint all those pictures and live long enough to manage to tell his story, with paint first, with stroke after stroke of his hand, until that hand shook and ached and trembled.

҂   ҂   ҂

There was only one place in the Milne Home where the child felt welcome, where he felt he'd stepped beyond the boys' taunting and teasing, and that was in the infants' ward of the Milne Home. He'd been assigned as punishment for his silence to the one job no other boy wanted. Before going on to breakfast, he had to make his way over to the infants' ward to sweep and then mop the forever sticky floor and wipe off the countertops and haul the stinking diaper bags over to the laundry. The other boys who'd done this job had raged over the constant crying and the smell of the soiled diapers. They couldn't stand being every moment in sight of the colored women who volunteered to look after the babies, the dark-eyed, God-fearing women who held those babies tight and gave them bottles and rocked them to sleep with their singing all day and night until those babies were old enough to be passed on to the care of the Milne Home proper.

Shelton, though, didn't complain or throw curses this way

and that or threaten to smack a crying baby if he didn't shut up. So the women in the infants' ward came to like him, despite his strange silence, or maybe because of it. Some of them seemed to see his sealed lips as a sign of contemplation and devotion.

The women in the infants' ward all wore white dresses with gold crosses pinned to their chests and white scarves tied over their heads and white shoes with thin brown lines running through them where the leather had creased and cracked from the women's pacing back and forth with babies in their arms. These women would, like the boys, tease Shelton, though they teased him with kindness and endless banter and mysterious blessings, their hands raised high in the air, their eyes welling up with grateful tears. They told Shelton that inside his meager, crooked body was a good strong man who'd blossom one day like one of those night-blooming flowers, which could change from a scrawny weed to a heavenly blossom in the midnight blink of a watchful eye.

Each morning when Shelton finished his chores, they offered him a moment's parting wisdom. He should eat his greens smothered in butter and garlic for good luck. He should find himself a tarred rope, make nine knots in it, then tie it around and around his waist. He should make his prayers to Mother Catherine or Father James Joseph or to the One Holy Church of the Innocent Blood, where they promised to light a long row of sweet white candles on his behalf.

One of the women, stranger than the rest, with hands that shook and eyes that shone and a voice that seemed like a croaking toad's, told Shelton he should spread a pinch or two of St. Joseph's powder in his shoes or gather up some goofer dust and rub it on his soles. "That'll make those feet dance," she said. "Just watch them."

Shelton had never heard of goofer dust or St. Joseph's powder, and he just stared at the strange woman and lowered his head. "Don't you worry," she said. "I'll get you some." But she never did.

Though Shelton paid these women little mind and didn't care to hold the babies when they were offered to him, he did like to listen to the women when they were singing. He liked how one of them would start on a song, little more than a whisper, with a baby in her arms, and then the rest would gradually, one by one, join in, every inch of the infants' ward bathed in music, the morning light breaking in through the windows.

Though he was only a child, that child could hear in these women's voices, in their songs, a lovely, enveloping sadness. They sang "It's Getting Late in the Evening" and "Motherless Children." They sang "Way Bye and Bye" and "Precious Lord, Take My Hand." Some days the women's voices seemed to take root in Shelton and linger there all day long, even until he lay down to sleep, when he'd think sometimes he was still hearing them, hearing their voices, and they were singing to him.

"Find your strength in the good Lord, Shelton," the women beseeched him. "Lift your voice up to heaven." Though he didn't, though he couldn't, their voices stayed with him. And though the child couldn't know that he would, he'd keep on hearing those voices the rest of his life. From time to time, and he never knows when, they lie with him as he lies down to sleep; they rise with him when he drags his body from its bed. Though it's been half a century and more, those voices still linger. Someday, first with his hands, then with the child's voice that is now a man's, he'll sing with them.

In my own way, my own sad manner, I'm singing now, am I not? *One morning soon*, my hands sing. *One morning soon.*

One Morning Soon, and the day came when I made of those voices, out of oilpaints on a block of oak wood, a song of my own, a song that showed the memory of how the sweet red lips parted to sing, how the white dresses and scarves shone, how the white shoes split and cracked, how the gold crosses gleamed and the sunlight poured in, how the wrapped black orphan children, Shelton just one of them, found sleep through their tears and managed to dream.

※ ※ ※

From time to time, Shelton and the other boys were herded onto a bus to do this or that: to go to that special mass at the cathedral or to take their summer swim in the City Park lagoon or to pick a few peaches for some friendly farmer in St. Bernard Parish or to sing Christmas carols for retarded white children in a special school, a school that looked and smelled different from the Milne Home but also, Shelton thought, Shelton understood, the same.

They'd also gone, one cool and windy Saturday, to watch an exhibition Negro League game at Pelican Stadium. The boys were crowded shoulder to shoulder in the sagging, splintery left-field bleachers, each of them given a shiny silver nickel to buy cotton candy or Roman taffy or Coca-Cola, which they'd all done except for Shelton, who'd slipped the nickel into his shoe when the other boys stood to watch a ball crash off the bat and fly clear over their heads.

Shelton figured one day he'd find some use for the nickel, and when they returned to the Milne Home he hid it beneath his desk drawer and then under the mattress at the corner of his bed. Then, as time passed, he moved it from one hiding place to the next until he forgot where he'd last put it. He searched and searched but couldn't find it.

One other time the boys were all taken for a short drive to the edge of Lake Pontchartrain. Already dressed in their swimming trunks, which had appeared one day at the home in a giant crate — a gift, the boys were told, from some rich Negro benefactor living up in New York who'd himself once been a Milne Home orphan — they'd peeled off their shirts and poured from the bus, heading straight down the gravelly, trash-strewn beach and on into the water, wide and blue and clear.

The day had been such a glorious one that Shelton, who had sworn himself to silence, had to bite his lip to resist whooping and hollering like the other boys, fifty or so of them scattered through the water, bobbing up and down like fifty fishing corks, splashing like fifty just-hooked catfish.

Shelton had never seen Lake Pontchartrain before this trip, though his young-girl mother had pointed it out to him on a map of New Orleans. It looked like a robin's egg turned on its side, with a thin line stretching out of its top to show the canal that connected the lake with the wide Mississippi. Though he'd seen the lake on the map and pictured it in his head, Shelton had never imagined there could be so much blue water in just one spot, more than the whole world could swallow, he figured, even if every person on the earth came there with cup in hand to take a drink.

Only one boy hadn't rushed into the water. Emanuel Jackson, a year older than Shelton, had been delivered to the Milne Home only a month before the swimming trip. His mother and father and two younger sisters were dead, the other boys said, from a fire that had burned down nearly an entire block of shotgun houses somewhere uptown. The boy had escaped through an open window, the windowsill burning his hands as he climbed over it.

Emanuel Jackson, his hands still bandaged, sat on the seawall steps instead of swimming, and Shelton looked back at him from time to time from the water, feeling sorry for this boy in a way he didn't feel sorry for the others, figuring that Emanuel Jackson had lost in the flames what he'd lost when he'd fallen that morning from the Audubon Park oak. From the water, Shelton watched the boy lift a bandaged hand to shield his eyes from the sun, which must have felt to his body, to his still-warm skin, like the flames from that terrible fire.

At the end of the day, when they filed back onto the bus, Shelton made sure to take the seat next to this boy, which in

39

any case no one else wanted. But when Shelton sat down, the boy slid to the end of the seat, pulling his shoulder in as if he wanted to be certain Shelton's body didn't touch him. Then he looked over at Shelton and said, "You're smelling like a rotten fish. You know why?"

Shelton kept his silence but looked down at his lap and then over at the boy's bandaged hands, which were coated with some kind of yellow cream that seeped out at the edges of the dirty white gauze.

"I'll tell you anyway," the boy said. "Because you can get mighty sick from swimming in that lake."

Shelton looked up at the boy's face now, and the boy smiled. "It's the truth," he said. "That water can make your skin rot. It can make it so it peels off like a dried-up onion." The boy lifted his bandaged hands. "Like this," he said, and he laughed.

There was something strange, Shelton thought, about this boy's face — it looked more like a girl's face than a boy's, the high forehead and cheeks as smooth and shiny as a pecan shell, the eyebrows two thin black lines drawn, it seemed to Shelton, by a fine pencil.

"I'm Emanuel Jackson," the boy said now, his laughter turning into a smile. "I know who you are. You're the one who don't talk."

Shelton nodded.

"I hear you can talk but don't. That true?"

Shelton looked at the boy, met his eyes. He smiled too.

"Well, my problem's the opposite," the boy said. "Or at least that's what my mama said. She said I talk too much. She said I go on and on like a twilight cricket."

The boy turned to look out the window, and Shelton wondered if this mention of his mother had brought back to mind for him all that had happened, if he were seeing again in his head all those flames, if he were seeing again, if he'd seen it before, his mother's and father's and two sisters' burned bodies, the way Shelton saw again and again, as if he were standing at a distance and watching, his own body slip and twist and fall.

But then the boy turned back to Shelton and said, "You ever been to Carville, Louisiana?"

Shelton shook his head.

"I have," the boy said, "and they've got a place there just like the Milne Home, only you know who it's for?"

Shelton shook his head again.

"Lepers," the boy said. "Lepers. But I bet you don't even know what that is."

Shelton did know, though. His mother had liked reading all the miracle stories in the Gospels, of the lame made to walk, the blind made to see, the demons cast into the swine who went and drowned themselves, the lepers wrapped in sackcloth who managed to get cured with a single magic touch of Christ's hand or even just the ragged hem of his robe.

Shelton drew in his breath, leaned close to the boy, and spoke, his voice hoarse, less a sound than a rush of air. "I do know," he said.

"Hey," the boy shouted, jumping up in his seat. "It's a miracle! The dumb child speaks!"

The other boys on the bus stopped their shoving and screaming to listen, but Shelton wouldn't say another word. They slapped his head and punched his arm, but he kept quiet, looking at them one by one, blinking his eyes as if he'd forgotten again what speaking was.

The boys all turned now to Emanuel Jackson, shoved the back of his head, flicked fingers at his ears, called him a no-'count liar and, knowing what they knew, called him a mama's boy, a mama's boy — the worst of the worst names you could call someone.

"Give me a quarter. Give me a quarter, and I'll make him speak," Emanuel Jackson told them, raising his bandaged hands, which the boys didn't dare touch, to hide his eyes, to protect his face.

When the boys finally turned to whistle and yelp at two girls standing on a corner, Emanuel Jackson leaned toward Shelton. "Okay," he said. "I've got your game. I'm sorry." Then he leaned his mouth closer to Shelton's ear. "Of course, if I was you, I'd get myself a pocketknife and put that in their face when they go to slap you again. Like this" — he jabbed with his bandaged hand at Shelton's side, and Shelton felt him wince — "but that's just me, I guess."

Now he leaned away from Shelton. "Anyway, I was talking about all those lepers in Carville, so I'll tell you. Their skin peels off, so you know what they do?" He looked at Shelton. "I'll tell you what. They go swimming in the lake. The Pontchartrain Lake, only clear across on the other side. They go swimming because the doctors say all that salt in the water is good for them. The doctors told me the same thing, too, like I was a fool. Well, I'm not."

The bus bounced as it turned into the Milne Home, and the boy put his elbow into Shelton's side, a friendly nudge. "I'd take a bath if I was you," he said. "If that leper skin washes across the water and comes to touch your own, you'll wind up in Carville before you know it."

As they stepped off the bus, the boy pushed Shelton again and said, "You didn't see any white folks swimming in that water, now did you?"

Shelton stopped walking, and the boy stopped with him. "You tell me why that is," the boy said. "You tell me one good reason and I'll eat my words alongside a whole damn plate of that leprosy skin."

Shelton shook his head.

"I will. I will," the boy said, laughing.

Then Shelton simply watched as Emanuel Jackson left him behind, as he ran ahead to catch up with the others, squeezing between two boys' shoulders, separating them, starting in on some other wild story.

Shelton tried to picture what these lepers looked like. He squinted his eyes and saw the backs of the boys in front of him, saw their shirts tear away, the skin peel off and blow out behind them. And that night, as he lay in his bed, he couldn't help but imagine his own skin peeling off his whole body the way the white paint would peel off his hands and arms after painting. But then he drew in his breath and told himself that Emanuel Jackson had just made that story up. Maybe there really was a place for lepers in Carville, Louisiana, wherever that was, but there wasn't any way that the lepers' rotten skin could wash across all that water. Emanuel Jackson had just made up that story out of his head or had heard it from someone else who'd made it up. So what if the only white folks he'd seen had been sailing by on fancy boats or sitting way down the shore by the seawall steps with blankets and a picnic lunch? That didn't prove anything, did it?

So lying in his bed, Shelton made up his own story, mixing up the Bible stories and ghost tales and children's books his mother had read to him time and again. All that water, he told himself, carried the power to make him better, not sick. It was a power that could put the strength back into his legs, let him climb again any oak tree he wanted.

Here's my work named *Pontchartrain:* fifty black boys bobbing in the water, hands raised high above their heads, water pouring from their fingers like each one of them's a fountain, legs kicking up just above the surface like the tails of diving fish, the boys' backsides, red and green in their swimming trunks, bright as the flowers atop the women's heads in that other work. One of those bodies of course belongs to Shelton, swimming as free and strong beneath the surface now as a shark, shouting and shouting as his mouth fills up with the water, which he drinks and drinks until his body is, like the water, clear and shining and blue.

※ ※ ※

And finally, after five years of taunting and teasing at the Milne Home, the boys all gave up and let the child be. Even the teachers and the gray-haired man now steered a clear path around Shelton wherever he might be, as though they were on the verge of believing the truth of the boys' taunting — that there was indeed a strange and frightening strength in this crippled child, a strength you wouldn't believe unless you'd seen his silence go on, as they had seen it, for so long.

Then the gray-haired man decided to call in a doctor, a special doctor, he said, with a quiet, defeated grin — a sallow-skinned man who flashed a bright light into Shelton's eyes and ears and mouth, who knocked at the child's knees and heels and arms.

"What's the matter, boy?" the doctor asked when he was done, and this time Shelton let himself speak.

"Let me be," he said, spitting his words out, mangling them, and the doctor did let him be, storming out the door and saying he had better things to do than waste his precious time on some stutter-mouthed, smart-ass nigger.

The next morning, just before dawn, just as he'd done five years before when his mother lay sleeping beside him, Shelton Gerard Lafleur stepped out of bed and pulled on his clothes and, for the first time since he'd fallen, tried to run.

He did run, though it might not be what others would call running, but to Shelton it was, his legs swinging out and around in wide, scraping circles across the dormitory floor and out past the great white house and the great green Milne Colored Boys' Home lawn and out to the street named Elysian Fields, almost tripping himself with each swing of his legs. But he ran anyway and kept on running.

Shelton Gerard Lafleur, this strange and silent child, this dark flower, was now thirteen years old.

Almost a man, he decided. Almost grown.

And for the first time in those thirteen years he felt something he'd never felt before, a feeling he'd never known.

Well, there was that one moment when he'd wailed and wailed on that Garden District doorstep before being swept inside.

And there was that one moment just before he fell from the sky, that one moment when he'd looked out through the green leaves and swaying branches and thought he saw something swinging way up high. There'd been something there, fluttering above the horizon, almost still but not. Then the form or shape, whatever it was, had swept down toward him with a message, with words he didn't know and couldn't imagine but longed to hear, words he'd one day learn weren't words at all but pictures.

Yes, there were those two moments. And now, now. Here was another one. He was free.

4 ONCE UPON A TIME

S o he ran, such as his running was, and stopped only when he couldn't drag his legs another step. Then the child, dog-tired and soaked with sweat, collapsed more than sat to catch his breath on a bus-stop bench at the corner where Elysian Fields met a boulevard named Robert E. Lee.

That name, which young Shelton recognized, was etched in pale blue letters on ten white tiles embedded in the pavement, and he wondered if this corner was the very spot where the general had been laid to rest, buried in that gray, gold-buttoned vest and wide-brim hat he was wearing in every picture of him Shelton had ever seen.

His chest rose and fell with his short, quick breaths, and Shelton looked down Elysian Fields, past the long line of green-shuttered houses with their red-brick steps, past the row of leaning palm trees in the neutral ground. He could see all the way back to the Milne Home, which, no matter his exhaustion, wasn't more than a hundred yards away, if that.

The child knew just what he wanted to do. He wanted to see

the water of Lake Pontchartrain again. He wanted to watch the sun rippling off the calm surface as if someone had lit a fire there and let the flames keep spreading. He wanted to lift his sore feet out of his shoes and let them slide into the water, to dip his whole body in bit by bit, his shins and thighs and hips and chest and shoulders disappearing beneath him, only his head up above the calm blue surface, his eyes trained on the sun's bright reflection. After taking that swim and drying himself in the sun and slipping his old shoes back on, that's when he'd decide what to do next, what might be done with this newfound freedom.

No, he already knew what he'd do — he'd go find his mother. He'd wander up and down every one of this city's streets. He'd look and look until he found her and he'd say, *Here I am*, letting her reach for him the way the boys' hands had reached up in the water, reached for the sun and clouds and sky. He'd say, *Here, Mama, now I've got a story for you*, and he'd let her close her eyes and listen as if he were the one now reading out of a book, reading a children's story that began *Once upon a time*.

Once upon a time, he'd say, *there was a child, a beautiful dark star of a child, a child who fell from a tree as though he'd fallen from the sky.*

And his mother, her eyes closed, would smile and smile, knowing the story's happy ending — how that child would finally make his way back home, how he would wind up in his mother's arms.

Once Upon a Time. Which one of my works is that? There's a pitch-black sky containing a million stars. There's a great oak tree with branches that form a canopy stretching like fingers above what rests beneath: a child who's found a quiet spot to spend this night. And at the place where the dark earth should meet the darker sky is a line of blue, squeezed so by the dark colors above and below that you're not sure that blue line is truly there at all.

So Shelton sat on the bench and thought about the lake. He closed his eyes and saw the clear blue water. He let his head fall down near his aching knees while his chest still heaved and his shoulders shook. He was tired. He was sleepy tired, as if he could, if he wanted to, just keep his eyes closed and fall asleep right here at this very spot.

Maybe he did fall asleep. Maybe he did. But in any case, when he opened his eyes, he saw the sweat running from his forehead down to his pants, which were speckled with drips of white paint and with dark, oily stains of turpentine. Though he'd worn these same pants every other day for going on a year, the other pair exactly like them, they were still too large, the waist gathered in fan-folds by the brown leather belt above his hips, the bottoms of the legs rolled three times and pinched closed with diaper pins he had secretly slipped over the edge of a countertop in the infants' ward of the Milne Home, quick as spit, the one and only time he'd stolen in his whole life.

The other boys stole all the time, Shelton knew, taking whatever they could find — pencils and paper from the teachers' desk drawers, tins of food and loaves of bread from the kitchen pantry, paintbrushes and twine and hammers from the storage shed, magazines and picture books from the Milne Home's dark and dusty library. The boys were reckless with their stealing, with what they'd stolen, passing the objects around at night from bed to bed and saying, "Look what I've got. Look."

Although Shelton had felt the thrill of stealing when he'd slipped the diaper pins into his pocket, though he'd wanted to pull them out and say, "Look what I've got. Look," he knew the boys would just have laughed and laughed, teased and tormented him, named him anew.

Shelton guessed it was there in the infants' ward where he'd first be missed. He wondered what the women would do when he didn't show up for his chores. Would they call over another boy and send him off to the dormitory, instructing this boy to roust Shelton with an angry bit of shaking? Or maybe they'd figure the good, quiet child deserved a morning's sleep every now and again and so would make do without him. Shelton didn't know.

There had been other boys, of course, who'd run from the Milne Home, even some who hadn't, after a day or two, come back. What the child Shelton didn't know or understand was that the freedom he'd run off to gain had been his all along, for there wasn't any interest among those who operated the home to find such children. They had enough others already and always more to come, children whose mothers had died or landed in some asylum, those left on doorsteps, like Shelton, doorsteps where they weren't wanted and wouldn't be fed or looked after or loved. There was a great depression holding in its grip, though the child Shelton didn't know this, not just the city of New Orleans but the whole entire country, and white families as well as black couldn't feed or clothe or shelter their children. What was one more Negro child lost on the streets going to matter? The folks at the Milne Home did what they could.

Usually it was the boys who'd be sent off in a year or two anyway who ran, boys who were fifteen or sixteen, not so young as Shelton. Maybe they found jobs sweeping up at the wharfs along the Mississippi River or found a merchant boat to take them on a cotton or sugar cane or coffee run. Maybe they had an uncle or aunt who hadn't been willing or able to look after them as children but who would now let them work in a corner grocery store or newspaper stand, let them ride along hauling fruit through white folks' neighborhoods on a creaking ramshackle horsecart, the boys' voices deep and strong enough now to carry their shouts from busy street to open window to bustling kitchen.

Shelton had heard those shouts as a child, hadn't he? He'd heard them carry around Mr. Edward's house and back to the patio garden, where he was engaged in some imagined enterprise, gathering leaves and berries to make some strange concoction, leaping off the mountain that one of the iron chairs had become. He would run inside when he heard the cart man's shouts and ask his mother if he could please buy an orange or apple. She'd say yes, always yes, and reach for the tiny cloth bag she kept in the drawer of the table next to her bed, taking so long to pull it toward her and open it and find a nickel that the child was shaking, jumping up and down, for fear that he'd be too late, that once he was out there the cart would be gone.

Then, with the nickel gripped in his hand, he'd race out to the patio and then through the front house and then out the front door to catch the cart man by surprise just as he was pulling off. Shelton would hand the nickel over and point to what he wanted, and the cart man wouldn't speak a single word, would just shake his head as though he'd been struck dumb by the sight of a small black child running out of such a house, no one shouting after him, no one saying he should get his little black behind inside right this very moment, right now.

Now Shelton thought he'd laugh to see one of the Milne Home boys become a cart man. That would be a fine job, wouldn't it, handing out fruit and vegetables, driving a horse from one neighborhood to the next. Some of the boys who ran off, though, Shelton had been told, wouldn't find a job, and they'd get caught stealing or lying drunk in the French Quarter or putting a knife to some white man's side and would wind up, after only a week or two of freedom, in the other colored home, by the name of St. John Bercham's, a home for colored juvenile delinquents, which was uptown and surrounded by a ten-foot wall of brick that had ivy growing over it to cover the razor-sharp shards of glass pressed into the mortar at the top.

That was the last place, Shelton had been told, where you wanted to end up. They had chains to keep you sleeping in your bed. They had whips that would make the Milne Home boys' bamboo switch seem like a soft blade of grass.

And this was the fear that accompanied Shelton's new freedom — that he'd be found and then dragged kicking and screaming to St. John Bercham's. So it startled him and made his heart stop cold when he heard, his head still down to his knees on the bench, his head heavy with the sleep he had or hadn't given in to, a voice in his ears.

"There's a poor pitiful piece of work indeed," the voice said. Shelton didn't dare look up. He told himself that he'd just imagined the voice, that he was simply playing in his head some remembered taunt. There was always, wasn't there, one voice or another sounding out in his head, if not the women singing, then one of the boys or a whole handful of them calling him some name or another, daring him to do this or that, threatening him with the bamboo switch. Through his months of silence, of keeping his mouth buttoned up, he'd learned to talk back to the voices, to say inside himself the things he wouldn't say out loud, answering in kind whatever those voices demanded.

But here now was the same voice again, louder, laughing, crashing headlong into Shelton's ears: "A poor pitiful piece of work indeed!"

Shelton did raise his head now to look and saw first the morning's low, blinding white sun. He shut his eyes and felt there the salty sting of his sweat, then opened them again to see a man standing over him, a black man with skin nearly as dark as his own.

"Let me be," Shelton said, but he couldn't hear his own words. "Let me be," he said again and coughed.

"Let you be?" the man said, laughing louder now, taking a seat next to Shelton. "I just might do that, though I suspect there are folks who wouldn't."

Shelton felt the man's leg pressing against his own. He felt the man's arm stretch along the back of the bench right over his shoulder. "Some folks," the man said, leaning near Shelton's ear, "use their eyes to see. I'm one of them. Should I tell you what those eyes have just witnessed?"

"I don't care," Shelton said, shouted, though it came out as a whisper.

"Speak up, son."

"I said I don't care."

"You don't care?" the man said, and he brushed his hand across the top of Shelton's head. "You don't care that these eyes have just seen a boy head out from that asylum down the road?"

Shelton tried to jump up, but the man caught him by the arm

and pulled him back down on the bench. "Hold on," the man said. "Here's what else I've just seen. I've seen the most awful pair of legs ever to carry a child carry him down right here to this very bench, the one where you happen to be sitting. Those legs seem to have about worn themselves out. Am I right or not?"

Shelton didn't answer, and the man took his arm off the back of the bench and reached over as if he meant to lay his hand on Shelton's leg but then pulled his hand back. "You born that way?" he asked.

Shelton shook his head.

"Someone do that to you?"

Shelton shook his head again. He turned to look at the man, who was leaning his head back as though he were just warming himself in the morning sun, as though Shelton were the one who'd sat down next to him and the man either hadn't noticed or didn't care to acknowledge his presence.

Shelton studied the man's face, watched the lids of his eyes close, his cheeks pinch up. His jaw was lined with small red cuts. Though he didn't seem old, he had gray streaks running through his hair, and he wore glasses, which Shelton didn't think he'd ever seen on a colored man. Or had he? Maybe he had seen this man before, raking leaves or cutting branches on the grounds of the Milne Home or delivering boxes to the kitchen or infants' ward. Or maybe when he'd seen him was years ago, performing this task or that for Mr. Edward, hauling into the house some heavy piece of furniture just arrived by boat from London or Paris or Florence.

"I've got ears as well as eyes," the man said. "Speak up."

"You going to take me back there?" Shelton said, and the man's eyes opened, though he didn't turn to look at Shelton.

"Take you back?" the man said. "Now what makes you think I'd go to such trouble?"

"Then how come you were watching me?" Shelton said, and the man did turn now to look at Shelton.

"I already told you," he said. "I'm one who keeps his eyes open, even when they're not."

The man shut his eyes again, turned his head up, and waited. Then he reached into his shirt pocket and pulled out a package of cigarette tobacco and paper. Eyes still closed, he rolled the tobacco in the paper, raised it to his lips, licked the edge, and sealed it. He pulled a box of matches from his pocket, slipped one match out, and lit the cigarette. His eyes were still closed.

"You see?" the man said, and he opened his eyes to look at Shelton and smiled.

And Shelton, for the first time in as long as he could remember, smiled too, and then laughed.

"How'd you do that?" Shelton asked.

"That's nothing," the man said. "Just watch." He closed his eyes again. When a small brown bird shot past them overhead, the man said, "That's a sparrow."

Shelton laughed again. "And that" — the man raised his hand and fluttered his fingers — "is a single falling leaf."

Shelton looked down and saw the green leaf lying on the pavement near his feet.

The man opened his eyes now and turned to Shelton. "These eyes are something special," he said. "What's more, they were already on the lookout for you. Yes, they were. Here I was thinking I'd have to devise some complicated plan, the thought of which had just begun to trouble me. Then I see I've got nothing at all to do, because look who's strolling out in that pitiful manner, no one but the child himself, just like he heard me calling his name. You heard me, now didn't you?"

Shelton shook his head.

"You sure now? My voice is something special too."

"I didn't," Shelton said.

The man lifted his cigarette to his mouth, inhaled, and blew out a cloud of smoke. "Well, you should have heard. That's if you're who I think you are."

Shelton watched the man's mouth turn up into a smile.

"Well, are you?" he asked.

"What?" Shelton said.

"Who I think you are."

Before Shelton could answer, the man grabbed hold of his arm and stood up, pulling Shelton with him. Although there hadn't been another person in sight except for those riding inside the few cars driving past, a white woman with a small child in her arms was now crossing the street, heading toward them.

"Good morning, ma'am," the man said, and he looked over at Shelton and nodded.

"Good morning," Shelton said.

The woman didn't answer. She looked at them a moment, then took a seat on the bench and held the child in her lap.

"Over here, son," the man said to Shelton, leading him away from the bench and near the steps that led up through a white gate to a red brick house.

"Let's get this figured out right now," the man said. "What's your name?"

"Shelton," Shelton answered.

"That's not much to go on," the man said. "You wouldn't think there'd be more than one child with such a pitiful name as that in the entire city of New Orleans, but you never know. What's your whole name?"

Shelton hesitated. He didn't know what to tell the man and what not to. He wondered if as soon as he said his name the man would drag him back to the Milne Home and collect whatever money they paid for returning boys who'd run away. He told himself he should have kept his mouth shut. He should have done what he'd done at the Milne Home. But he hadn't, and now he couldn't. "Shelton Gerard Lafleur," he said, and he thought, *Could I run again? Would he try to catch me?*

"Well, I guess that's it, then," the man said. "I guess you're the one."

"What?" Shelton said.

"The one I was looking for, unless there's another boy with such a name in that asylum."

"There isn't," Shelton said.

"And now there's not even one, is there?" the man said, and he laughed and slapped Shelton's back.

Shelton laughed too. He laughed and laughed. He let himself laugh along with this man who could see even with his eyes closed and he said, "You're right. There's not even one," and he laughed some more.

And Shelton was still laughing, eyes closed, eyes shut against the sun, when all of a sudden the man took him by the arm again and said, "Shelton Gerard Lafleur, there's somewhere for us to get to."

And just then a public bus pulled up at the corner. Shelton thought again about running, about shaking himself free of this man and setting off toward the lake and that blue water, setting off to find his mother, but he couldn't make his body follow his thoughts. He saw himself, as though he were looking at some strange child, quietly closing the door to his mother's room, kicking the gate shut, running down the echoing alley, crossing St. Charles Avenue, climbing the oak.

And the moment before he had slipped and fallen, what had he seen in the distance, drawing near, flying through the sky, swinging way up high?

Then the white woman stepped onto the bus with her child, and Shelton and the man followed close behind, the man's hand still gripping Shelton's arm, helping him up the steps. The man let go and reached into his pocket, pulled out two coins, and tossed them into a wire basket near the driver.

"Could you wait a minute to get going, sir?" the man said. "This child's a cripple." The driver, a white man with a pockmarked face, didn't turn his head but nodded.

But as the man was leading Shelton back along the aisle, the bus lurched forward and Shelton stumbled. He tried to catch himself by placing a hand on the back of a seat, but his hand slipped, and he knew now he was falling, his legs buckling like the legs of a broken chair.

Then he felt two hands catch him at the shoulders, felt the squeezing of fingers there, gathered in his shirt, tight against his shoulder blades, a grip that both did and didn't hurt.

"I've got you, son," Shelton heard the man say behind him. "Just keep yourself going."

5 MONKEY HILL

YOU WOULD UNDERSTAND, wouldn't you, that in
the first moments of the bus's lurching its way back up Elysian
Fields, back in the direction from which the child had just run, it
seemed to Shelton that his every gangling, tortured step had
been nothing more than wasted effort. He was being taken back,
wasn't he? There again, just outside the window, close enough to
touch, was the great green lawn of the Milne Home. There again
were the white bricks and white porch and white pillars of the
home itself. There again, though small as a line of ants, were
the boys shuffling off to breakfast, slapping one another's backs,
heads turning this way and that, ears filled for a moment with the
churning engine of this very bus.

The boys turned to look, didn't they? Didn't their voices
ring out?

Look, goddamn, there's the cripple Shelton.

Falling all over his two pigeon feet.

Gone for a ride like he's got somewhere to get to.

Shelton still felt the man's arm on his shoulder and found, at his instruction, a seat two rows from the back of the bus. He swung his legs and body around with his hands clasped, to keep from falling again, to the metal bar of the seat directly ahead. Now Shelton couldn't help but look out at the Milne Home, couldn't help but hear the boys' voices ringing out.

Gone with the nickel pulled from out his shoe.

Couldn't be. We stole it, didn't we?

Yes, we did. Yes, we did.

So Shelton looked and listened to the boys but thought again of his mother, thought of stepping up to her and telling her the story not of his fall from the tree but of his escape from the Milne Home. And what would he tell her? He'd tell her how he was afraid.

He thought of all the stories his mother had read to him, all those children's stories with their illustrated drawings that she'd held before his eyes — there was always, wasn't there, some injury, some not-so-secret threat: a harpoon buried in a beast's bulging gray belly, lost children stumbling upon a candy cottage glowing with the fiery, blood-red rays of the evening's sunset, an arrow slicing through the apple atop a man's head, another arrow still to come and then another. It was always fear that drove those stories forward, a fear that knotted itself in the child's throat, that curled his fingers into fists and squeezed at his chest until he wanted to shout, *Look out now! Look out!*

His mother had seen and understood how the child was swept up in those stories. "This is a good one?" she'd ask, teasing, pausing just when the child couldn't stand it, just when they were a page or two away from some miraculous escape or divine intervention.

And all those stories ended fine, didn't they, the harpoon catching on the bones of a buried shipwreck and dropping off as if it were nothing more than a splinter, the children returning home salted and seasoned but uncooked, the man rescued just as the final arrow sailed from the bow directly toward his head. And

Shelton would drift off to sleep at his mother's side, her arm cradling his head, mother and child together, the sweet touch of grace upon them both.

Now Shelton breathed in the musty air of the nearly empty bus as though he were taking his first breath. He breathed again and thought of those happy stories. He thought of his mother, thought of how he'd left her in that bed, run to the park, chosen and climbed that one great withered oak. He thought of the shape he'd seen through the leaves the moment before he fell. Had it been his mother there, just his mother, swinging back and forth in the sky like a bird or an angel, come to tell him she was watching, she was there to save him? But she hadn't saved him, had she? She hadn't stretched out her thin twig arms to catch him and hold him and set him down on the ground. She hadn't kept his legs from winding up as twisted and bent as her own.

Shelton breathed again and tasted magnolia and heavy cream and the coarse threads of sugar cane, tasted the sweet taste of freedom — here she was now, here she was, having sent someone to save him — then he touched his tongue to his lips and found the taste gone, found his hands trembling then as they tremble now in the telling. There it was again, the Milne Home, its windows a hundred bulging eyes, its doorway a great sharp-toothed mouth ready to open, ready to swallow him.

But this is a child's story, isn't it? So it should be asked if in fact a thirteen-year-old like Shelton is capable of such thoughts as those I've given him. Can a child step back from the noisy clamor of circumstance? Can he take a moment of blind, silent fear and transform it into an accurate account of his thirteen-year-old life, finding in one single instance the dim glimmer of recognition, the familiar pattern?

If not, then I don't know this child half as well as I claim, and I might as well end my story here.

But if so, if one so young can indeed hold his own life in his small hands to measure and sift, sort and stack, save and throw out, then that's precisely what the child did in that moment when the Milne Home loomed before him. The bus screamed and stopped. The driver swung his arm out, and the bus door opened. Shelton's whole body shook. He was certain that he'd blink and find his body dragged from the bus and across the great green lawn and through the great white doors of the Milne Home. *Here he is,* the man would say, smiling. *Here he is.*

And here was the familiar pattern the child detected: lost and found, lost and found, another trip who knew where. Here was the story of his life, of his falling and running and being transported here and there with no certain destination except one sure to offer a fall from the sky, then the quick slap of impact.

So while he'd stepped onto this bus willingly, of his own accord, Shelton now found himself afraid of the man beside him, the dark devil who'd watched him escape the Milne Home, who'd grabbed his arm and held him upright when the bus shot forward but only to deliver him back to where he'd started or, worse, after some great distance, to a new place he'd never seen or heard or known, to some worse fate than being swallowed by an angry whale, cooked and eaten by an old hag, shot between the eyes with some poison-pointed, feather-tipped arrow.

Shelton couldn't look at this man, couldn't speak.

Niggers is as niggers does.

Whose voice was that, drifting front to back on the bus?

Daddy says in two weeks' time he'll come wandering back, holding out his hat, saying I's sorry, Mr. Johnson, I'll make it up to you, I's come on back. And he will, I bet. Niggers always does.

And Shelton watched the man next to him cock his head, squeeze his eyes shut, listen.

Niggers always does, don't they?

Shelton watched the man's grip on the bar tighten. He looked to the front of the bus to find out who was talking.

Then, just like that, a tottering old white woman, legs thick as hams, took her seat up front. The driver's arm swung out and the bus door closed. The bus lurched again and roared and spat, and the Milne Home was swept behind as if it were nothing more than a shimmering stray white speck of a boat in a calm sea of green. Now Shelton turned again to look at the man beside him, at the magic eyes that could see even when they were shut, at the skin nearly as dark as his own, at the smile that had left him smiling too.

Here was the man who'd come to rescue him, who'd followed his every awkward step, who'd led him to this bus to leave the Milne Home as far behind as the bus would take them.

Shelton let his thoughts spill forth like unwinding thread: Maybe this man had been sent by his mother; maybe she'd found her child after all this time. Maybe the man himself, with those magic eyes, had woken that morning to remember how he'd seen a young boy step forward in his dreams, a strange and silent child staring back at him, asking him please to take him home.

In that moment of wild imagining, Shelton concluded, and why not, that he'd fallen into the hands not of some black devil but of his very own flesh and blood, fallen there as surely as he'd fallen from that tree, only this time landing not in dirt and oak roots and leaves but in a saving and warm embrace.

Look how the man's skin was nearly as dark as his own. Look how he smiled at Shelton.

Do I belong to you? Shelton wanted to ask.

Where's my home? he wanted to know.

Where's my mother?

Where's Mr. Edward?

Where's all of it?

Did he ask even one of these questions?

Don't you already know?

What was it, then, about this child that didn't allow him to give voice to what tossed and turned inside him? That's the true question, isn't it?

So Shelton's heart rattled against his ribs. It pounded and

shook. It screamed its great swelling questions. No one heard, though, and the child couldn't find the words to say what he felt inside him.

Yes, he'd left the Milne Home; he'd put away his refusal to speak when spoken to, to answer when offered a question. But there was a certain dangerous, defeating silence in the child, a silence that lingered on and on, that felt embedded in his body the way he'd imagined the shards of glass embedded atop that wall at St. John Bercham's, a silence that cut through his muscle and bone and skin, that tore at the heart beneath.

It's a silence, I'll confess, I've remained familiar with on up to this very day. It's the silence that comes over me when I look and look for hours and hours at nothing but some still-life arrangement on an old wood table. I'll look and look, and somewhere in all that looking I'll find the flowers and books and the bowls of fruit talking back to me, whispering, *Just listen.*

I am listening, I'll think. *What do you think I've been doing?*

No, I'll hear, quieter and quieter. *Just listen.*

And so I'll stop answering those whispers and pick up my brush to see if I can paint not just those flowers and books and bowls of fruit but something else, something more, something much better and much worse: the things they're all saying, the things I know I'm meant to hear but can't or just won't — all the million things that are there to be seen if I keep looking and looking, the whispers and mutterings, the secret, quiet murmurings, listening and listening for the ways that every tiny speck on this earth, alive or not, can speak.

Well, that child looked over at the man beside him and did finally speak: "Where's this bus going?" Simple as that, but for the child that question contained just about the whole universe.

The man grabbed the bar of the seat in front of them again. "Where's this bus going?" he said. "Well, I'll tell you. This is the South Claiborne line. So we've got another bus to catch and then another. We're going South Claiborne to Louisiana to Tchoupitoulas." He turned his hand back and forth on the steel bar as if trying to twist it. "How's that?"

"And then what?" Shelton asked. *What's to become of me?* he meant, and he looked out the bus window and saw, first, the city's bright morning bustle, men in their sharp suits and jaunty hats, women in skirts pinched tight at their waists, children kicking up dust. Then he saw, in the window itself, his own sad reflection and behind that the man's, a ghost of a face shadowing his own, both heads bouncing to the bus's movement like they were bobbing up and down in the blue water of Lake Pontchartrain.

"Look here," the man said, and Shelton turned his head to see the man slide forward and reach into the back pocket of his pants. He pulled out a blue handkerchief. "Not that," he said, stuffing the handkerchief back in and pulling out a faded, tattered, folded map.

"Look here," the man said again, and he spread the map across his own and Shelton's lap, running a finger in a line across the dusty paper until the finger suddenly stopped. "Here," he said, finger tapping. "We're going over here, by the river, to Foucher Street."

"What's there?" Shelton asked.

"Four walls and a roof," the man said. "The house where I live."

Shelton looked at the grid of crisscrossing streets, at the marks drawn on the map. He saw the wide, curving line of the Mississippi, the robin's egg of Lake Pontchartrain. He wondered if were he to look long enough, the map would show his own house too, if it would show the street where he'd lived or even just the park with the tree where he'd fallen. That would be enough, wouldn't it? He could find his way from there.

The child looked and looked until the man folded the map, slapped his leg with it, and held it up in front of the child. "How about I get you one of these?" he said. "They're a good thing to have."

"I'd like one," Shelton said. "I would."

"Yes indeed," the man answered. "You'll have one, too." He slipped the map back into his pocket. "I took to carrying this what must be three years ago now, when I was handed a job with the WPA. You know what that is?"

"No," Shelton said.

"Well, it was President Roosevelt's idea, God bless him. You know who the president is, now don't you?"

"I've seen pictures of him," Shelton said. "He's got glasses like you."

"That's him," the man said, laughing. "That's the president for sure."

But the president, Shelton thought, was all tight-lipped stares and forever folded hands and a crackling radio voice. Shelton had seen his form sputter and shake for two whole minutes at the Negro motion-picture house, the boys quieting for just the trumpet blast that began the reel, shouting and shoving in their seats the hour after that. But Shelton had learned the voice well enough to recognize it when he heard it again one Sunday evening in the Milne Home infirmary, where he'd gone with an upset stomach. A radio Shelton couldn't see was broadcasting a speech, the president's voice resolute, calm, reassuring. What had he said? Shelton couldn't remember.

"Here's what he said," the man told Shelton now, as if he'd heard Shelton's thoughts, as if he were answering Shelton's question. "'Each and every man deserves a job.' Each and every man, you understand, Shelton. Even when there were no jobs to be had. So what did they do? They went and made things up."

"Like what?" Shelton asked.

"That's what I'm set to tell you," the man said. He closed his eyes, and Shelton stared at him, stared at the red cuts on his chin and the gray streaks of hair and the fluttering eyelids. Then Shelton remembered the magic of those eyes and looked away, down at his own hands folded in his lap.

64

"I don't know your name," he said, as close as he could get to asking all he wanted to ask.

"No, you don't," the man said, opening his eyes, turning to Shelton. "It's Minou," he said, and he spelled it for Shelton. "My given name's Lawrence. Lawrence Parrain. But I'm called Minou."

"Minou," Shelton said.

"That's it," the man said. "I've been called it since I was a toddling child."

"How come?" Shelton asked.

"Well, I'll tell you. An old gray tomcat I tried to pet went and scratched my face instead. *Minou* means cat, you see. My father's the one who gave me the name. He said the tomcat had lived clear past the nine lives he'd been given and now he'd left his mark on my face to give me his good luck. My father said that was something cats did just before they died, and you know what?"

"What?" Shelton asked.

"That's just what that cat did, the very next day. He curled up in the cold kitchen sink and breathed his last breath. My father acted as if we'd been paid a visit by the Lord above, along with an army's worth of angels. He was what the white folks call country colored, born and bred in the bayous and raised to believe all manner of such things — ghosts and angels peeking through the cypress trees, blessings or curses delivered by which direction a dog curls to sleep or how the moon shows through a patch of clouds or doesn't. But here was one time he'd seen firsthand his belief turn true before his very eyes. So after I got scratched and the cat passed, my father wouldn't let my given name be spoken in his presence. 'Minou,' he said to one and all. 'Mon minou.' Now isn't that something?"

"I guess so," Shelton said, thinking of the woman with the shaking hands and croaking voice in the infants' ward. "Carencro," she'd called him once, waving her hands in his face. "Fly away, Carencro."

Old toad, he'd said back, though he hadn't spoken, had called her that name only in his head.

"Carencro," he said now, hearing that croaking voice.

The man looked at Shelton, put his arm across Shelton's shoulder, and shook his head. "Someone call you that?" he asked.

"Someone did," Shelton said. "I don't know what it means."

"Well, it's funny how such names go, isn't it?" Minou squeezed his hand into Shelton's shoulder. "For a while my mother, when my father wasn't home, still called me Lawrence, which had been her own father's name. I guess she was sorry to see it go, but my father kept up and soon she couldn't help but call me Minou too. And with the passing of time, just about everyone did. I sometimes forget now that my true name's Lawrence. It doesn't feel like my own, you understand?"

"I do," Shelton said, thinking of all the names he'd been called, running them through his head.

"In any case, I was telling you about acquiring this map. You still want to hear about that?"

Shelton nodded. Never in his life had anyone spoken to him the way this man, Minou, was speaking, words flowing from his mouth as smooth and easy as a waterfall, crashing over Shelton as though his ears were the rocks down below. Shelton thought of the times he'd spied on Mr. Edward in the library with a handful of other men, their talking a great indecipherable roar that swelled and subsided, then swelled again. The men grew quiet only when Mr. Edward raised his hands and spoke, and his voice sounded to the young child's ears the way Minou's voice sounded now — as if contained in the rush of words was some secret message, hidden like the bright white flash of light at the lagoon's murky bottom.

"Well, I'd stood in line at the federal office for months and months," Minou told him, "just waiting to be given something to do. But there's a process, you see, something they won't exactly say outright but is certainly true. It's a process where each and every day they've got to hand out jobs to white folks first before they move on to us Negroes. You see?"

"Yes," Shelton said. Didn't he know this already, know it from Mr. Edward's speeches, know it from his mother's gentle warning?

Behave.

Minou looked at Shelton. "If there's enough white folks waiting in line to take all the jobs, they tell the Negroes to come back tomorrow, and that's that. After a while, tomorrow starts to sound like never, you see, like the two words mean the same damn thing. But when you've got a family to feed, you go back."

"You've got a family?" Shelton asked.

"I do," Minou said.

"Who?" Shelton asked, meaning *Where?* Meaning *How?* Meaning *Show me.*

"Who?" Minou said, and he laughed. "Well, that's a story unto itself." He held a hand up and raised his fingers one by one. "There's my wife and our two girls, not much older than you. There's my wife's sister and their widowed mother. That's five, not counting me, which none of them think to count anyway. It's a full house, you could say. One king and five queens, though that king is most times treated like a one-eyed Jack." Minou stopped. "You understand?" he said.

Shelton nodded.

"That's enough, wouldn't you say, Shelton? That's a full house?"

Shelton looked at him.

"You sure you're following me?" Minou asked. "You hear me?"

"I do," Shelton said. "They all live in the same house as you?" he asked.

Minou looked at Shelton and shook his head. "Here's something else my father said. He said the rabbit doesn't stop to give his thanks for being saved from the mouth of the fox. You understand now?"

67

Shelton shook his head. He was lost. He thought of the voice he'd heard from the front of the bus: *Niggers is as niggers does. Daddy says. Daddy says.*

Minou laughed. "That's just what he meant, I guess. As to your question, last time I checked, they all lived in my house. But that was five o'clock this morning. We'll see how things stand when we get there."

Maybe Shelton did understand now. Maybe it occurred to him that he might not be wanted in that house, that taking him in was not what Minou had in mind. And for that brief moment he wished, despite everything, that he was headed not to this man's house and family but back to the Milne Home, back to his bed and rusted metal desk and the boys' bodies pressed near his own as they sat and ate, stood and painted, woke and slept, shoved and taunted.

"Should I get on with my story?" Minou asked, and Shelton nodded.

"You sure?" he said, and Shelton nodded again and saw Minou smiling down at him. He forgot his longing then, forgot again what lay behind him, forgot that white voice shooting front to back on the bus like a flashing knife, forgot the voices of the boys at the Milne Home.

"Well, I will," Minou said, "and just listen. One day, after waiting like so many other days in that line, I decided I'd had enough of waiting. So I started cursing under my breath at the man behind me, telling him how there was nothing good and true in this world, how I'd been down to the St. Julia wharf at dawn that very morning. 'The biggest boat I've ever seen pulled up,' I said. 'It had bananas spilling over its sides like they'd gone and stripped the whole jungle clean.' I said how I'd stood an hour in that employment line but left when I stepped forward only to be told that the one hundred jobs they had unloading that ship were all reserved for white folks and white folks alone. They were paying too much for Negroes to have them."

Minou laughed again. He shut his eyes and shook his head. "Well, you should have seen me, Shelton. I pitched the awfullest cursing fit, though I kept it quiet, you see, like I meant it just for the man next to me, like we were two men just sitting in a corner bar, like I was just talking into my empty glass. You see?"

"Yes," Shelton said.

"The truth, of course, was there weren't any such jobs and no banana boat," Minou said. "At least not to my knowledge. But I had to do something, you understand? And just as I figured, a few of the white folks in line were listening the way they always listen, their heads turned away like they're smelling something awful but their ears big as a rabbit's. And one by one, the white folks spread that story around and started peeling out of that line like they were overripe bananas, which I guess they were. They'd been peeled and eaten, yes sir."

Minou smiled down at Shelton. "Maybe you're hungry yourself?" he said.

"No," Shelton answered. "What happened?" he asked, and he heard his words as though they were the echo of the words he would ask his mother when he held up a book before her and she paused to catch her breath, always pausing just before the very moment when a life was set to change or the storm was about to strike or the truth was going to make itself known.

"Well, I'll tell you," Minou said. "All that was left at the federal office was a long line of poor, hungry Negroes. And guess what? Every last one of us got handed a job. I stepped right up to the desk and they gave me this very map. They marked it with a big black X and said I was to report to a Mr. Morrison on Poydras Street, which is just what I did. He looked over my papers about as long as blinking and said, 'You can read and write?' and I said I could. I told him how I'd gone to Dillard University for a year but had to quit when the first of my children came along.

"The man snorted like he'd recently been changed into a man

from a pig. 'Well, it don't matter none,' he said. He told me I'd be assisting another man named Mr. Morrison, same as him.

"'What is it I'll be doing?' I asked.

"'You'll be doing whatever he tells you to do,' this man says, and he asks for my map and makes another black X and sends me off in search of this other Mr. Morrison, who turns out to be the man's own son. Well, the son is cut from the same cloth as his father, because he makes another black X and says, 'Here's where you'll be,' and by the time I get to that last black X, which is over at Audubon Park, it's the end of the day and time to go home.

"'I got a job today,' I tell my wife and children. 'What is it?' they want to know, and I say, 'Well, I couldn't tell you. Following X's all around the city, it seems.' And they all look at me like I'm speaking out-and-out gibberish.

"The next day, though, I found out what that job was to be. I'd be shoveling dirt in the park. 'We're making a levee?' I asked, but we were nowhere near the water, so that wasn't it. 'We're making a hill,' one of the men tells me, and I look at him just like my wife and children had looked at me the night before. 'It's for the children to run up and down,' he says. 'It's for children who've never seen anything their whole lives but the flat land of this city.'

"'Like me,' I said, and the man laughed, though it was just about true. I'd taken a train to north Louisiana two times as a boy because my mother's brother worked a farm in Floriene. They've got hills there, Shelton, a thousand of them. But making one of them down here seemed to me the foolishest thing I'd ever heard or seen."

Minou shook his head. "We did it, though. We worked on that hill for ten straight months, twenty men shoveling and shoveling that dirt, filling it with kitchen scraps and old boxes and whatever else we could find to make it rise higher and higher before our eyes. We sweated like cotton-picking slaves in the blazing sun, but not one of us wanted to be done, I assure you. It was a job, you understand, a job that was putting food on our tables and clothes on our backs. Then one day, when we'd shoveled and carted and poured so much dirt you'd think we'd gone out west and were building one of those WPA dams, we were told to go and put our shovels down. 'That's enough,' they said, but that wasn't it. We spent another month planting seeds. We put those grass seeds in the ground one by one, just taking our time. You don't rush something like that, Shelton, when all that's waiting for you when you're done is being hungry again and standing in some other line. So we covered every inch of the hill we'd made, and we took our time. Well, that was some kind of way to feed twenty families, don't you think?"

"I guess so," Shelton said, thinking of how the boys in the Milne Home painted and painted each summer, the paint they were covering just as shiny and white as the paint brushed on top of it. It didn't need all that painting, he realized now, and just the thought of it made his hands and arms itch as if they were still covered with that paint.

"Wait a minute," Minou said. "Here's where we change buses." He reached across Shelton and pulled the cord stretched above the window. A bell clanged at the front of the bus. "Well, I'll say this. I've gone back there time and again since then, and there was someone in Works Progress who understood what I didn't. You should see the kids running around up there. Not just the Negro children but white ones too. They all look out over those trees and it's like they're looking out over the promised land. It's as if those children, the colored ones, know who built this hill. Ask my girls and they'll tell you I've gone there a time or two. I'll take my shoes off and let that tall grass tickle my toes like I'm a happy child."

Minou took Shelton's arm as the bus stopped, and he led him up to the door. When they'd stepped back out into the bright sunlight, Minou said, "You ever seen a hill, Shelton? You ever stood on top of one?"

Shelton shook his head.

"That's what I mean," Minou said. "I'll show you sometime."

Sure enough, and just a short time later, the child would see that hill. And years after that, memory slipping into the touch of my hands, I'd paint it, giving the painting the name that Minou said the men, feeling like damn fools for all their digging, had named what they'd made. *Monkey Hill*, where two girls stand in cotton dresses, bows untied and streaming behind them like white cloth kite tails. The girls' faces are strong and sure and wild as they stand side by side and look off into the distance, into nothing but clear blue sky and the tops of the giant oaks and down to the great wide arc of the Mississippi, where the tiniest of figures, a child, sits at the edge of the river, shoes off, feet dipped in the rushing, stump-strewn, muddy water.

That child, of course, is Shelton, who when the day came, as it soon did, for him to climb that hill had rolled rather than tried to run down the steep grassy slope, a happy Jack next to two rolling Jills, three children laughing at the way the sky flipped itself over into the earth, the earth into the sky, both earth and sky flipping over again and again until there was only the sweet sting of their brush-burned elbows and knees, the yellow-green strokes of grass stains painted on their clothes, the bluest blue filling up their laughter as though they were breathing in and out the whole great wide stretch of sky above them.

Monkey Hill, passing years ago from my hands to another's for one hundred dollars, for the price of a couple of Galatoire's lunches or two pairs of leather shoes. Gone, never seen again, though for that one I looked and looked, as I've done with just a few others, wishing to have again what's mine, what my own hands made the way Minou's hands and the hands of those other men made that hill.

I've never found those works, though, so all I can do is close my eyes and then open them to see my two raised hands, imagining not the painting itself but the work of making it, the shape of two girls' bodies rising from these fingertips, the scratch of black that can become a solitary child on a riverbank. *See,* my hands say to my eyes. *There it is again.* And that's enough, isn't it?

 ❧   ❧   ❧

Well, it was those two girls the child saw first after he and Minou stepped off the third bus at the corner of Tchoupitoulas and Delachaise and walked the two blocks over to Foucher Street. The girls, both dressed in white dresses, with their hair pulled tight behind their heads, stood outside on the porch of a mud-gray shotgun house, hands raised to shield their eyes from the sun, which angled down between the tree branches, beneath the porch roof, to strike just their faces and shoulders. The girls looked to Shelton like they were offering their father some kind of military salute.

"That's my girls," Minou said. "The older one's Olivia, the younger one's Elise. Olivia's a good girl. So is her sister, though you better watch out."

"How come?" Shelton said.

Minou laughed. "Truth is, there's more sweetness in her than she'd ever care to admit. You've just got to find it. You've just got to dig and dig. You'll see what I mean soon enough."

He took Shelton's arm and helped him up the porch steps. "Olivia. Elise," Minou said. "This is Shelton. Come shake his hand."

Elise stepped behind her sister but leaned around her to keep her eyes on Shelton, to look him up and down. "He's a cripple," she said.

"Hush, child," Minou shot back, and turned to Shelton. He shook his head. "Well, I told you, didn't I?"

Olivia pulled Elise forward, then reached out to shake Shelton's hand. "It's nice to meet you, Shelton," she said.

"You too," Shelton answered. He looked straight into the girl's dark eyes. He marveled at the touch of her soft hand.

"I've got to go inside a minute, Shelton," Minou said; then he turned to his daughters. "Make Shelton feel at home out here." He leaned over near Elise's ear and whispered, though loud enough for Shelton to hear, "Watch what you say, girl. I'm warning you."

Elise laughed and turned her head to kiss her father's cheek. "You think I don't know that?" she said.

"I'm just reminding you," Minou said, and he pulled open the screen door and stepped inside.

Left alone with these two girls, Shelton felt worse than uncomfortable, his legs and body more awkward than ever. He stepped back to lean against the porch railing. "It's hot," he said, and he raised his hand to his face to hide the fear he was sure was showing there.

"I'll get you something to drink," Olivia said.

"No, I'm fine," Shelton said. "I didn't mean that."

"How's lemonade?" she asked, and Shelton looked at her.

"That would be fine," he said.

Olivia went inside, and Elise sat down on a wicker chair in the corner of the porch. Shelton looked out at the street, at the long row of shotgun houses, all of them resting atop blocks of concrete, clamshells scattered in the dirt underneath.

"You're from the orphanage," Elise said, and Shelton turned to her. She tapped the toes of her shoes on the porch floor.

"I am," he said, and he felt his chest and shoulders and arms tighten as if he were bracing for one of the boys' beatings.

"What's it like?" she asked.

"It's okay," Shelton said, looking down at her feet, listening to their tapping on the wooden floor, the sound it made, like a stick on a skin drum.

"How old are you?" she asked. "Same as me, I bet."

"I'm thirteen," Shelton said.

"I'm fourteen," Elise said back. She looked down at Shelton's legs. "How come you're crippled?"

Shelton tried to but couldn't answer. *I fell from a tree* was what he wanted to say, but his lips stayed shut. He looked at the girl's face.

"I already know," the girl said.

"How?" Shelton asked.

"I just do," she said. She turned her head as if she'd heard something behind her. "There's a lot I know. You want to find out about something, come ask me. I know a million things more than my sister."

Shelton tried to decide whether she was teasing him or not. "If you know so much," he said, "tell me why I'm here."

"My grandma asked for you," she said, smiling, eyes now staring straight at Shelton's own. "She knows you. Mama said no, but Daddy said why not, and Daddy does whatever he wants."

Shelton pushed himself off the railing and took two steps forward. "How's your grandma know me?" he asked.

"She just does," the girl said, still smiling, still tapping her feet on the porch floor.

"How?" Shelton asked.

"She knows that family, the white one."

Shelton's legs, thin as two matchsticks, shook beneath him.

"Where is she?" he asked, his voice shaking too. "Where's your grandma live?"

"She lives here," the girl said. "She mostly has to stay in bed." She tapped her feet again. "How come you're asking?"

Shelton couldn't speak.

"What lie did my daddy tell you? He's full of them."

Shelton tried to steady himself, tried to stop his legs from shaking.

"Go on and ask him why he went and got you. You'll see how he lies."

But Shelton walked to the screen door and pulled it open just as Olivia was walking out bearing a tray, three tall, shining glasses filled with lemonade on one side, a plate of sugar cookies on the other.

"Here," she said, but Shelton pushed past her.

"What did you say to that boy?" Shelton heard her ask her sister, but he didn't hear Elise's answer. He tried to shoot through the room, but one knee bumped a chair, which then struck the edge of a table. A stack of books fell before him, and he tripped.

Face down on the floor, he heard footsteps, felt them shake the floor beneath him. He looked up at the walls, saw all the faces there, pictures of Olivia and Elise drawn with pencil on yellowed paper curling at the edges, a drawing of a beautiful dark woman, of the dark woman again but now with a bright scarf tied over her head and her shoulders bare, another of an old woman with lips pinched closed, sorrow swimming in her milky eyes, deep lines cut into those eyes' corners and down from the sides of her nose. Genevieve.

Then Minou was standing over him, his hand reaching down to grab Shelton's arm. "I know where I am," Shelton said, angry, confused, and Minou let go, left him crouching there.

"Where you are is on the floor," Minou said. "Just why that is is what I'd like to know."

"I want to see her," Shelton said, and he pushed his legs behind him, kicked the books on the floor, kicked air. Then the toe of his shoe caught something, caught the edge of a floorboard. Hands spread and arms stretched, he managed to stand.

Minou shook his head. "You'll see her in a moment, Shelton. She just wanted some warning. She wanted to look her best."

Shelton's eyes burned. *Why didn't you tell me?* he wanted to say, wanted to shout. But here instead was the sting of tears, the first in longer than he could remember. No, the first since he fell from the oak tree and with blood and spit on his lips called out for his mother, called out *Please.*

Minou stepped forward and wrapped his arms around Shelton. "She wanted to surprise you, that's all," he said, as though Shelton had indeed spoken, had asked his angry, accusing question.

You should have told me. Not said out loud, of course. His body shook and shook, and Minou held on, pulled him tighter, pressed Shelton's face into his chest, then lifted him, held him in his arms as though Shelton were a tiny child, as though Minou were Mr. Edward turning a corner and running straight into Shelton, sweeping him up, holding him. Minou carried Shelton back outside.

"It's okay, child," he said. "She's feeling ill. She's not well. She just wanted some time to receive you properly. Let's wait here."

Even in Minou's tight grip, Shelton's body shook. Face buried in Minou's chest, he heard Minou tell Elise to go inside, heard him tell both girls to go through that door right now and help their grandmother get herself dressed. "If you're not the devil's child," he heard Minou say to Elise, then heard him sigh as the screen door slammed shut and the heels of the girls' white shoes clicked on the wooden floor inside. Elise was shouting, "We're coming, Maw-Maw." And Minou was holding Shelton tight, whispering, "It's okay," whispering, "You're no carrion crow, Shelton," whispering, "My little kitten, mon minet."

6   THE NURSEMAID

WHAT WERE THE CHILD'S MEMORIES of his mother's nursemaid? Hadn't she always, when he turned to her, averted her eyes, found somewhere else to look — at the mop or broom gripped in her hands, at the white washcloth she dipped in sweetened water and swirled in circles across his mother's body, at the two steaming plates of food she carried in through the door?

"How'd you pass the night, Miss Margaret?" she'd ask each morning, folding down his mother's blankets once and then again, pressing them into a thick, smooth line at the foot of the bed. All the while she ignored Shelton's presence nearly beneath her feet, his bundled body stretched out in his own small bed, picture books or wooden trains or painted blocks scattered across his blankets.

Then Genevieve and his mother would pass the time in conversation, would speak of the flowers blooming outside in the patio garden, of visitors come and gone or still expected, of the weather's never surprising shifts. They'd discuss Mr. Edward's travels here and there, the important business that took him away for weeks on end. They believed their talk didn't interest Shelton but it truly did, for what child isn't taken by talk of travel and adventure, and especially Shelton, nearly as much a shut-in as his mother.

Yes, Genevieve talked and talked with the child's mother, but had she so much as spoken a single word directly to him in those eight years? Hadn't she maintained, when her eyes fell by chance on him, a strange and frightening silence, much like the one he himself came to keep at the Milne Home?

No, she did speak to him, didn't she, saying his name, looking into his eyes, touching his body from time to time with the business of keeping him, as she called it, shipshape and squeaky clean. Her hands scrubbed his hair when he bathed, brushed biscuit or bread crumbs from his fingers and face and the folds in his shirt, straightened his black-buttoned coat before they stepped outside together.

Yes, she'd treated him with an affectionate, abiding interest, but never in his mother's presence, as if Shelton Gerard Lafleur were not a single child but two: one who deserved her every kind attention, the other a child who didn't.

That's not a conclusion, of course, that the child himself, gripped in Minou's arms, waiting to see this woman again, was able to reach. He just wondered how one moment he could remember one thing and the next moment another, as if it were his own memory that couldn't be trusted.

He remembered Genevieve's cold silence. He remembered her warm embrace. Which one was the true account?

Well, from time to time didn't she take him with her to buy groceries? The old woman and the child would ride the St. Charles streetcar together, side by side, then walk the four blocks over to Magazine Street. Didn't she wrap her hand so tight around the child's that her fingertips pressed into his palm, leaving the imprint of her nails there for a moment or two when she let go? And strolling in and out of the bell-clanging shop doors, she would fill two cloth bags with fruit and vegetables and meat, with flour and coffee and sugar that Shelton then hauled back home, the bags thrown over his shoulders, heavy as coal.

"You can manage?" she'd ask, wouldn't she, and Shelton would nod and groan and hoist the bags up higher.

"You sure, child?" she'd say, smiling, and he'd say back, "Yes, ma'am."

But it was riding on the streetcar, there and back, when she'd spoken most freely, as if the car's rocking and swaying shook the words out of her frail body the way a child shakes a few coins free through the thin slot of a piggy bank.

And my own words now are like those freed, falling coins, for just saying such a thing shakes my own memory too, and gives me this: The child had possessed one of those banks himself, though it was not in the shape of a pig or some other creature. Instead, it was just a glass jar, the tin top sealed with wax, the slot in the top made with an icepick he'd poked through the metal. He'd kept the jar beside his bed for the coins Mr. Edward gave him, coins from foreign countries like France and England and Italy that Mr. Edward visited time and again. He'd return home with a tired smile and a kiss for his daughter and a pocketful of shiny silver and gold pieces bearing pictures of palm leaves and half-moons and kings' and queens' faces and words the child couldn't read.

Mr. Edward, as if he were a lost, lonely boy who by accident had become a man, understood the child's mind, didn't he? I look and see, so many years later, those thick fingers flipping a coin in the air as if the heavens had sent the full moon tumbling, Mr. Edward cupping the coin in his hand only to make it disappear, then pulling the coin out of the child Shelton's ear. *Look what I've found, Shelton. Look what I've got here.*

Then Shelton would drop the coins one by one through the jagged slot in the jar's top, making them ring and clatter like the shop doors on Magazine.

At night, his mother asleep, Shelton sometimes picked up the jar, picked it up gently so the coins would keep quiet, and held it up before his eyes. He'd see, in what little light there was, the shimmering gold and shining silver. What were the things he'd buy on the cobblestone streets and in the bustling, busy squares and great towering buildings that Mr. Edward had seen and wandered through and described for him, saying, *I'll take you with me one day, Shelton?* Well, he didn't know what he'd buy, but there must be something — feathered caps or gleaming swords, suits of chain mail, magic lanterns with genies inside who'd grant him three wishes, whatever they might be.

He'd set the jar down and pull the covers up over his head and, eyes shut tight, wish for everything. Though he couldn't give his wishes names, couldn't say where his longing came from or belonged, he wished anyway, wishing until those wishes took over his dreams, forming unnameable, unsayable pictures in his head, pictures not of this or that particular thing but just of *having*.

Those pictures, when they did manage to take on a shape, were the ones he'd seen in the stories his mother read, the ones her curled fingers pointed to with the turning of pages during the thousand and one nights, or thereabouts, they'd spent together reading: lightning bugs parading through a dark forest, rickety rafts afloat on calm blue water, a child on a speckled circus horse, rabbits and turtles and lions who could talk but in such a way that only a child could hear them — those pictures just black ink on yellowed paper but taking on, in the child's mind, every imaginable color.

When Genevieve told her own stories to Shelton, she spoke as if there were pictures in front of her that only she could see, and her words rang out in his ears like those precious coins dropping into the jar.

What was it that she told the child when she spoke? Not stories of blooming flowers or Mr. Edward's travels. Not the comings and goings of visitors through Mr. Edward's door. What she told him instead was of the world she knew, a world beyond his Garden District home — a world guided, she made clear, like all else was guided, by the Lord's powerful, unflinching hand, by the sweet mystery of his giving and taking, his redemption and retribution, his mercy and condemnation. It was a world filled with characters whose lives, she believed, were sordid and sad and heroic and thus worth relaying to a child for the lessons contained in them.

Like what? the child wanted to know. *Like who?*

So she told him. Eyes wide open, her body rocking from side to side to the streetcar's swaying, she presented and passed judgment on those lives as securely as she held in her lap her black pocketbook, inside of which was an envelope containing Mr. Edward's money.

"Like that William and Eva Hawkins's girl," Genevieve told Shelton, the streetcar swaying. "Named her Mayelle, after Eva's mama, raised her so spoiled she kicked and screamed to have at least one if not more of everything she'd seen. And comes a time when she's sitting pretty as a picture in church, just five or six years old, and the collection plate comes passing by. Why, she thought she'd just reach in and grab hold of all those hands could get, and it took her mama and daddy both holding her down to pry those fingers open, one and all standing up to watch, the men all laughing and laughing like they'd been waiting weeks to hear this joke. The girl did the same thing again the very next Sunday and the next, and finally William and Eva decided they'd no longer bring that child to church. I can't say out loud, for fear of the Lord, what that child made of herself when she was grown, but she fell as far as one can fall, I will say that, and it's easy finding who's the ones to blame."

And Shelton watched Genevieve nod and nod her head, as if she meant to signal agreement with the harsh judgment contained in her own words, and he felt that maybe she was speaking directly to the Lord now, in some quiet language only the two of them knew.

Once Shelton and Genevieve had made the walk from St.

Charles to Magazine, the characters of Genevieve's stories would appear before Shelton's eyes as if she had blown the breath of life into their bodies, had summoned them to stand before her and speak. She'd say her polite and dignified hellos, pass a few moments in idle chatter, then stroll away and look down at Shelton as if to say, *I told you so, didn't I?*

So it was that Shelton met the once proud, now pitiable reverend who'd claimed to heal the sick with the touch of his hands but who couldn't save his own daughter from returning to dust after the flush of scarlet fever.

"Who might your handsome companion be this morning, Sister Genevieve?" the reverend asked. His coat stretched open at his waist like two dark wings as he crouched to take a look, his white shirt so white he looked to Shelton like an angel with smoke-stained wings.

"Only a child," Genevieve said, trying to push past him, her very posture suggesting she had somewhere to get to, business that had to be done.

The reverend, though, remained crouching in their path, his lips twitching out to a smile. "A young member of our congregation?" he asked.

"No," Genevieve said, "he's not."

"Well, is the child blessed with a name?"

And Genevieve, her voice fueled by a strange anger and impatience, pronounced Shelton's name as though it were the final thunder and lightning sent down from heaven. And the reverend did indeed stumble back as though he'd been caught in a storm. He stretched his body up, wings folding in, and stepped off to the side — struck dumb, Shelton guessed, by the dark eyes of this woman glaring at him.

The reverend offered a quick blessing and hurried off. Genevieve laughed and said, "That's the last man in the world you want knowing your business, Shelton. What reaches his ears is sure to reach a thousand others. He's got the gift of gab, that's certain."

"What's that?" Shelton asked.

"The gift of gab?" Genevieve said. "It's what it is. It's not knowing which words to speak so going ahead and speaking every last one of them." She shook her head as if she were shaking off the reverend's voice, and she laughed. "Come Sunday, I guarantee, you'll find my name on his lips, and what I don't need is him speaking of me from his pulpit, saying how he's thought long and hard on his encounter this week with Genevieve Simmons and here's all he learned."

Shelton met that same day another man whose story he'd heard, a chimney sweep, Genevieve had told him, who'd nearly eaten himself out of house and home and occupation. He'd filled up so on root beer and beans and rice and lemon pies that he'd fallen one morning through a roof and down to an attic room that served as a young child's bedroom. The Lord had been kind enough, Genevieve told Shelton, to use the fall more as lesson than as punishment, since the man's body had bounced first off the soft mattress of the child's wide, feather-blanketed bed before tumbling to the rug-covered floor.

Shelton marveled at the man's size, at the folds in his neck and the doughy fingers, which completely enclosed his own when the man shook his hand and said, "How are you and yes, nice to meet you and goodbye, my friend," and lumbered off down the street.

"Looks much like a turtle, doesn't he?" Genevieve whispered to Shelton, shaking her head and laughing despite a clear effort not to.

Shelton laughed too, but Genevieve stopped him with a gentle squeeze of her hand. "He's a good man," she said. "He provides for his family." She walked on but then turned to Shelton. "You should see all those children of his, climbing over him like he's a mountain."

"How many children?" Shelton asked.

"Lord knows," Genevieve answered. "But if his wife's not hell-bent on becoming a widow, she needs to teach her serving hand the difference between gluttony and hunger."

"What's the difference?" Shelton asked.

"You're full of questions, now aren't you?" Genevieve said and stopped to look at him. "That's a good thing, I suppose. You know what gluttony means?"

"No, ma'am," Shelton answered.

"Well, hunger's what you need," she said. "Gluttony's just what you want. You understand?"

"Yes, ma'am." Shelton thought then of his nighttime wishes, his million unnameable, now shameful longings.

"You remember that," Genevieve said. "If you've got any measure of good fortune on this earth, there'll be occasions for you to recognize the difference."

"Do I have a good fortune now?" Shelton asked, thinking of the coins in the sealed-shut jar, thinking of Mr. Edward's voice saying how a fortune was what he'd nearly accumulated there.

"Not yet, you don't," Genevieve said. And for no reason Shelton could discern she put her hand on his face, thumb on his chin, fingers underneath, then lifted his head up so he'd look at her. "Not yet," she said again. "But let's just see what plans this world can arrange."

There were others, weren't there, whom Shelton met, the sons and daughters of Genevieve's friends. Once Genevieve pointed out to him, her voice quivering with rage, the good-for-nothing nephew of a woman she knew, a woman named Annabelle Fougère. This particular young man, she said, would sell his soul before performing a day's honest labor. He survived only by the good graces of his poor aging aunt, who was all but blind and made her meager way polishing silver for the mayor of New Orleans and doing piecework in the evenings.

"How's your aunt, son?" Genevieve asked as they stood before the porch step where the man was seated, a newspaper folded in his lap.

"She's fine," the man said, squinting up at Genevieve as if he wasn't sure who'd spoken.

"You're looking after her?" Genevieve asked.

"I am," the man said, and he looked down and laughed as if he'd seen something funny in the paper.

"You better be," Genevieve said, and she pulled Shelton on.

"That boy," she said, shaking her head. "That boy thinks his spit's too fine to shine his own shoes."

And later, as they stepped out of the butcher shop, where Shelton had nearly retched at the sight of the pigs dangling on their hooks, they crossed paths with the daughter of the woman who worked as a maid next door, a girl who'd been so smart and quick, Genevieve told Shelton, she'd gone off to a teacher's college in Alabama, but who had lived up to her word that she'd come back to look after her mama and younger sister and brother, bringing along with her the nicest boy you'd ever wish for a daughter to marry.

"Good morning, Miss Genevieve," the young woman said, and she leaned down a moment to smile at Shelton and then stood back up. "Mama said you weren't feeling well. I hope you're better."

"I am," Genevieve said. "Can't you tell?"

The two women laughed.

"You've got news, I hear," Genevieve whispered, as if she were confessing a secret. Then she put a hand on the front of the woman's dress and smiled. "Yes, you do. Marcus proud of himself?"

"Too proud." The woman smiled. "He's shaking hands here and there and getting his back slapped, acting like his job is over and done."

"You tell him to talk to me," Genevieve said. She tugged at Shelton's arm. "We need to get going, but you tell Marcus we've got to have ourselves a word or two."

The woman said goodbye but then turned and called back to Genevieve. "Could you tell?" she asked.

"It's too early," Genevieve told her. "But you tell that young man of yours something else. Tell him he might start considering how he likes a baby girl."

The woman smiled, twirled around, and twirled back. "I will tell him," she said. "I'll tell him straightaway."

Genevieve looked down at Shelton. "Isn't that the Lord's greatest blessing?"

They turned the corner and headed back toward St. Charles Avenue. "Well, it is," Genevieve said, and she stopped and leaned down and touched Shelton's forehead. "That's the one and only joy, pure as the morning light," and Shelton heard but didn't understand the sorrow in her voice, the sorrow lingering there despite her smiling down at him.

Shelton would come to understand, of course, what that sorrow was, would come to think of Genevieve as the rickety footbridge between knowing the truth of his life and not, the sorrow in her voice like a quiet, steady stream beneath that bridge.

I'd even tried to paint it, tried again and again until I'd wound up not satisfied, not finished, but at least over and done with: an old woman leaning over a child, smiling that sorrowful smile, her hand on the child's head, behind them the trash-strewn street and peeling-paint and rotten-wood storefronts the child hadn't reason to notice, the slightest suggestion of the woman and child's reflection in the dark puddle and patch of cracked pavement at their feet, pitch-black lines in the folds of the woman's white dress, as if it had been torn and sewn time and again.

I'd tried to find a name for the painting, something that said what I'd tried to show. But I couldn't find it and, when I was tired of trying, settled for simply *The Nursemaid*, cursing and cursing myself for what I still, so many years later, couldn't name.

Can I name it now? Can I find words for the place of that woman in the child's life, the good deeds she performed on his behalf, the plans she made, the sorrow and longing she caused, the secrets she swore herself to keep, the things she knew but wouldn't say, waiting and waiting, then never getting the chance to speak?

I can't, can I?

I'm an old man, but I still tell myself that if I just wait long enough, surely the answer will come, sweeping down from the sky as slow as that leaf which Minou, his eyes shut, still managed to see as it fell and came to rest at the child's feet.

※ ※ ※

What can I do then but return to the safety of my story, to the child who still squirms on that front porch, wrapped as before in Minou's strong arms? Somehow the child manages to stop his crying. Maybe he sees and understands enough to consider that those tears should by all rights be joyful ones, not sad. This is the first time since he fell from that tree, isn't it, that he's taken a step anywhere near the direction of home. Maybe in a few moments' time Genevieve will summon her strength and lead him, the way she led him down Magazine Street, back to his one true home, back to his mother.

With that thought he manages to calm himself, and Minou sets him down, keeping his hands on the child's shoulders until Shelton has found his balance and can clearly stand on his own.

"That's over now?" Minou asks, and Shelton nods and twice runs his arm across his wet face.

How is it, I'd like to know, that the child held back his tears when faced with all manner of mistreatment at the Milne Home but couldn't manage to do so this moment? I don't know, though I hear Genevieve's voice answer as if my question has been put directly to her, as if I'm hearing, like the chimney sweep heard those voices, a mutter and echo in my head: *There's a million kinds of pain in this world, dear Shelton, more kinds and colors than form a lifetime's worth of sunsets and rainbows. Watch out for them. Learn to tell one from the other. Learn just that and you'll have learned enough.*

But that's not the child hearing a voice, that's me. What the child hears is Minou saying, "It won't be long now." What he sees, leaning away, is Minou lifting his eyes up, looking out over his head.

"Well, look what we have here," Minou says, "and just soon enough."

Shelton turns. Two women, he sees, are heading toward the house, their faces lit as if by the quick flash of a struck match when they pass through the angled rays of the sun. Their mouths are turned up in wide smiles, their dresses billow out as they start to run. Shelton hears their heels clicking on the pavement, same as the girls' heels clicked on the floor inside.

This is Minou's wife and her sister, Shelton knows, though he doesn't know which is which, who is who. They have the same dark eyes and the same bony shoulders and the same curved, soft-looking arms. Even their dresses are much the same, tied at the waist, gathered beneath like the folds of a fan, as smooth as if they've just been ironed. One dress is the pale green of new spring leaves, the other an even paler blue, an icy stream.

The one in the blue dress, the one whose face he has just seen on the drawings inside, steps up onto the porch and says to Minou, "That's him? That's Shelton?"

"Yes, it is," Minou says.

"My, my," she says, and she leans down and kisses Shelton's cheek. "It's good to finally meet you," she says. "Welcome, Shelton."

Shelton smiles but looks away, looks down at his feet, thinking of how Elise said her mother didn't want him there, didn't want Minou to go get him.

"I'm Isabel," she says. "Minou's wife." She turns and looks at the other woman, who is still standing on the walk up to the house. "That's my shy sister over there."

Shelton looks over at this woman, sees her smile and wave.

"Come meet Shelton, Adrienne," Isabel says.

"I will," the woman answers, but she doesn't move. She brushes at her dress with her hands, sets its pale green shimmering.

"Well, come on, then," Minou says, and the woman steps up onto the porch now to stand before Shelton. She reaches out her hand.

"How are you, Shelton?" she says, and Shelton nods. He takes

89

two steps forward to shake the woman's hand, but she lets the hand fall to her side.

"What's wrong with your legs?" she says. "You hurt yourself?"

"I did," Shelton says, and he looks over at Minou, hoping to be saved from this moment. Minou, though, stands with his arm around Isabel's back, his hand tight on her waist. He just looks at Shelton, smiling, so Shelton turns back to Adrienne. "I fell from a tree," he says.

"Just now? Today?" she asks.

"No," Shelton says. "When I was eight. That's how I got lost."

"Lost?" the woman says.

Shelton looks again at Minou, tries to plead with his eyes, feels the tears beginning again.

"You see a doctor?" Adrienne asks.

"I did," Shelton says.

"They couldn't fix it?"

"Adrienne," Isabel says, stepping over to her sister, putting a hand on her shoulder. "That's enough. I imagine Shelton has had some kind of morning."

"Yes, he has," Minou says. "He did all the freeing himself. I just watched."

Shelton hears the screen door open. He turns to see Olivia and Elise standing in the doorway. "Maw-Maw says she'd like to see Shelton now," Olivia says.

"Then let's go," Minou says, and he walks over to Shelton to lead him inside.

"Maw-Maw said she wants to see him alone." That's Elise, her voice all sunshine and venom the way it was when she spoke earlier to Shelton. "She said for all of us to just keep busy outside."

Elise steps out, and Olivia follows her, holding the screen door open for Shelton.

"It's straight back," Minou says, fingers pressed gently against Shelton's back. "You'll find your way." The fingers push, the slightest touch. Shelton's legs move, carry him forward. "Watch out for the furniture, though," Minou says, laughing. "It likes to grab you."

Shelton steps inside, one hand stretched back to the screen door so it won't slam shut, won't announce his presence. He turns and looks through the mesh of the screen and sees everyone gathered there, each of them looking at him. He's afraid now, afraid of what he'll find when he comes before Genevieve, afraid of what she might say when she looks him over, sees his crippled legs, waves him nearer, reaches out to touch his face, moves her mouth to speak.

He tries but can't make his legs move. Minou presses his face against the screen. "Time's wasting, Shelton," he says, and the child looks at his face through the screen. Minou is smiling, but there's something else there too. It's fear or worry. It's a sorrow like Genevieve's.

"No," Shelton says.

But Minou, angry now, impatient, taps his fingers against the screen. "Wasn't it just a moment ago," he says, "you were in the worst kind of hurry? Now go on."

Shelton backs away as if he has been threatened.

"Minou," Isabel says. "Gentle now."

Shelton turns and starts walking, heading through one room, then the next, as if he is walking through a dark tunnel, hands stretched out before him as if suddenly he can't see, as if any moment he might trip, fall, and keep on falling, striking not the wooden floor but branches and leaves, his body tumbling and turning, the dirt and oak leaves and roots, the whole earth itself rising up to greet him, to say its awful, familiar hello.

"That you?" Shelton hears, and though he doesn't want to, he steps forward, legs shaking, and follows the voice through the darkness.

"That you?" the voice says again, then says his name. "Shelton Lafleur?"

7 COME CLOSER

SO SHELTON CARRIED his body through the dark house and stepped into the doorway of a room lit by a single shaded lamp. He saw a circle of light cast down to the floor and in the center of that light Genevieve's swollen, slippered feet, ankles and calves swollen too, big as the limbs of that round chimney sweep.

"Buzz, buzz," Genevieve said, and laughed, and Shelton looked up to the spit-soaked mouth of a swollen-out face that both was and wasn't the one he remembered from five years before.

"Genevieve?" he said.

"Buzz, buzz," she said again, still laughing. "But, dear Lord, I won't sting." Her laughter quieted now, and her mouth swung open as if the hinge of her jaw had locked, the two rows of teeth like two leaning rows of once-white fence.

Shelton watched as that mouth tried to take on the shape of a smile, then barely did.

"Yes, it's me, dear Shelton, become a bumblebee. I know I look frightful. Come closer."

Come closer? Shelton thought. *This is close enough.*

Years later, I'd think to paint the child's memory of the butcher shop on Magazine where pigs had dangled from shiny silver hooks. From outside the butcher's plate-glass window, a child peers in, the sunshine bright against the smudged and smoky glass, the pig's skin the palest shade of purple, nearly translucent, the hooves marked by four gray W's that look like a doctor's stitches.

Come Closer, I named that work, as if the dead pig were calling out to the child, but when I looked at what I'd done, I saw not the dangling pig but Genevieve's swollen face and frame, saw the child's stricken body trying to push against the brick wall of his repulsion.

That was an ugly work indeed. It was downright spooky, one and all agreed, wondering what had come over Shelton Lafleur to allow his hands to make such a work.

I could have done worse, I thought to say but didn't, for who'd understand that this pig in the window took the place of what I wouldn't dare paint and didn't want to — the old woman sitting in a chair and calling to the child?

And finally that child made his body listen. He summoned the strength and courage, more than he'd thought he possessed, to swing one leg and then the other out and around. He looked down at his own broken body so Genevieve would see what he was showing her.

"My legs . . ." he started to say, wondering now how he'd ever find the strength to tell that story. Hands raised in the air, fingers fluttering, he said again, "My legs —" but Genevieve stopped him.

"You think I don't know?" she said, lifting her arms from her lap, pulling him, once he was close enough, up against her chest. "You think I haven't been watching you like a hawk since the day you left? You think I haven't counted the days until it was safe to bring you home?"

"Home?" the child said, and tried to push away. But Genevieve kept him squeezed against her and rocked the way the women in the Milne Home rocked the infants in their care, her voice like theirs humming some quiet song, her swollen feet marking time on the floor, Shelton marking the time too, holding his breath and counting: *One. Two. Three. Four.*

How was it that she'd been watching him through his five years in the Milne Home? If she'd seen him, if she knew he was there, why hadn't she come to get him, why hadn't she taken his hand the way she'd taken it when they took the streetcar to Magazine Street and led him straight away to his mother in her bed?

Magazine Street. Had she ever mentioned, on those trips, her own family, her two daughters and two grandchildren, the man Isabel had married? Had she ever said, *Be patient, child, for one day I'll send someone to get you. It'll be my daughter's good husband, a man named Minou. Keep an eye out for him. He'll come get you?*

Home, she'd said. *Home.* He wasn't home yet.

"Oh, it's been so long," she said and squeezed him again, still rocking. "Times I thought I wouldn't live to see it. Oh, the story I had to tell that girl, telling her again and again and then Mr. Edward. I nearly believed it myself. Poor child."

Then she stopped. "Just look at you, Shelton. You're so strong."

Strong enough to pull away, though he didn't.

Strong enough to say, "Where's Mama?" which he did, though his voice was just a whisper, just a rush of air.

Genevieve didn't answer, so he asked again.

"Where's Mama?" he said.

"Shelton Lafleur," she answered as if that was and would be her only reply, and squeezed a final time, then released him. "Stand before me now so I can get a good look up and down. You've grown so, haven't you? Hardly a child at all."

Her eyes swept a circle over him, the lamplight in the white of her eyes become a glaring, blazing sun.

"I want to know —" Shelton said, Shelton pleaded.

94

"Yes, these five long years," Genevieve went on, eyes coming to rest on his own eyes. "I've been mighty sick, child, but I'm on the upswing. I'm feeling fine now. I'm feeling fine now you're home."

"I want to know," Shelton said again, but he could see that Genevieve wasn't listening, was lost in her own swirling thoughts.

"Five long years, and they've about made you a man," she said. "That's what I prayed for, you know?"

"Please," the child said now.

"Didn't I get down on my knees most every night?"

"Please," he said again.

"Didn't I ask the Lord to keep you safe?"

"Please, please."

"Didn't I put my own complaints aside? And you should have seen me, big as an elephant then, bigger than this buzzing bumblebee I look like now."

"Where's Mama?" he said, louder now, as loud as he could shout.

"Quiet, child." Her eyes shut like two slamming doors. "It's all right."

"Where is she?"

"Oh, Shelton Lafleur. Yes, you are. You're a flower for sure." Her hands, scabbed and trembling, reached out, clutching air.

"Where?" the child said.

"Now, now." Not tears but some sign of her sickness, yellow bleeding from the crusty creases of her eyes, oozed out the way the yellow cream had bled from beneath the gauze on that boy Emanuel Jackson's hands.

The child waited for the woman to speak, for her to tell him, his hands gone to fists at his side to quiet their shaking. How could she have been watching him those whole five years? Where was she watching from, and how come? How come she hadn't told him, hadn't called to him, hadn't given him some sign?

"Where's Mama?" he said again, crying now.

95

Eyes still closed, Genevieve drew in her breath. "Hush, child. Hush. That's the very reason."

"What?" Shelton said.

"That's why I sent Minou now to get you."

Again Genevieve drew in her breath, a rush of air as if she meant to suck the whole world in, suck him in as well, the way the infant he'd been had sucked and sucked on his own balled, banana-smeared hand. "That's one reason," she said. "There's others too. You'll see."

Now Shelton waited, and Genevieve's eyes peeled open, looked away from him.

"Tell me," he said, voice and fists and body shaking. "Tell me, please."

"Miss Margaret," she said and breathed again. "The poor girl," she said.

"Tell me."

"She's passed on, Shelton."

"No," he said.

"I'm sorry, son."

"Please," he said again. "Please." Then said, then called out, "Mama!" as though he were lying again in the dirt and oak leaves, lips bruised and bleeding, feet and legs and hips burning — this time, though, the burning turned to rage, to a stinking flash of flame.

"It's a mercy, Shelton."

And the boys' curses, all the child had heard but never spoken, now became his own. He sent those curses shooting straight up to darken heaven's door, sent them spiraling down and down through earth and root and rock, digging deeper than fiery hell, beyond.

He'd take his hands, wouldn't he, and put them on her, put them around her neck, squeeze them tight. Five years, and now his mother was dead. He'd take this woman's life in his hands and end it.

Instead he said, sobbing, "I knew."

"Dear Shelton, dear Shelton." The old, bloated woman, a stranger now to Shelton, put her hands on the chair's arms as if to stand. He stepped back, stumbled, fell.

Again, he thought, going down, falling backward.

His elbow struck the floor, and the pain shot through his arm and shoulder and neck. Then his head struck the floor too, and he lay there, the bedpost square against his cheek, the frayed tip of a blanket scraping his lips and nose like dusty feathers. Suddenly he sneezed, his head jerking up and then slamming down against the floor. He wanted to scream now, didn't he? He felt like a fool.

Why'd I say I knew?

Sneezed again, and his head jerked up and slammed down, and now he did scream, he did, and his fists rose before his eyes with not his own strength but the boys' and so bloodied his mouth that the blood pooled in his throat and he choked, gurgled, spit. Then the fists made of his eye sockets two plum-colored slits. Again and again.

Again.

Did I know? Did I?

Punched. Kicked. Squeezed his hands into tighter and tighter fists.

Then he heard Genevieve's raspy, choking scream in his ears as if he were standing over her, but he wasn't, was he, and heard the scream become a cough, then a wheeze, then a cough. Then she was quiet and he saw, as though he were looking again through the warped wood panels of Mr. Edward's dressing closet, a strip of light, a dark shape — Minou standing over him, Minou's fingers wrapped tight around his wrists.

"Quit, Shelton!"

The child broke free and with his fist, with another quick punch, caused his right eye to swell closed.

"Quit, Shelton!"

But he broke free and punched at his left eye until it too had closed.

"Goddamn it, now. Quit!" Minou called out, and Shelton's wrists stung as if they were bound with rope.

"There now. There," Minou said. "There now, child." And finally Shelton, unable to see anything at all, gave up.

8 THE AWFUL SILENCE

HIS FACE BRUISED and swollen by his own fists, Shelton felt as if he could not see again until he'd been led inside the One Holy Church of the Innocent Blood. Minou held one of his hands, Isabel the other, Olivia and Elise and shy Adrienne following close behind. They walked the whole length of the shoe-scraped aisle, past faces and faces turned to watch the grieving family and the orphan child whose crippled presence had become the second breath of news to spread across Foucher Street, over to Antonine and Amelia, down to Annunciation and Tchoupitoulas, on up to Magazine.

The first breath, carrying a secret sigh of relief, contained the message that Genevieve Delery Simmons had finally passed after her long, bedridden, body-bloating illness. *What's more,* Shelton all but heard the voices say, *she'd called from the orphan home that very morning the child, you know the one, our own child, a Negro son, raised by white folks, rich as kings, the one who fell from a tree as if he'd fallen from the sky and wound up uglier than ugly, wound up crippled and abandoned and shy.*

And here was the pine coffin, thrown open for all to see. Genevieve's body lay stretched out as if on a bed made up with bleached and freshly ironed sheets, her head sunk square in the center of the same lace-edged, embroidered pillow she'd been sitting on when Shelton came upon her a day before in that dark room lit by the shaded lamp. Shelton looked now at Genevieve's body, looked just long enough to see that it was thin again, as if someone had drained from it a hundred gallons or more of whatever it was that had left her swollen like a bumblebee.

Then his swollen eyes drifted down to the floor, to the line of gladiolas and daisies and satin-bowed berry wreaths whose pin-sharp leaves nearly touched the tips of his new black shoes. Minou had purchased the shoes for him at a secondhand shop on Magazine just yesterday, the evening following the morning Genevieve had died, along with the black coat draped from his shoulders, the black pants squeezing at his waist, the white shirt whose buttoned collar choked his neck.

Minou had stood beside him as Shelton pulled and tugged and leaned to try the clothes on, feeling the way he'd felt when the nuns had watched him dress near his bed in the charity hospital, feeling as if his body weren't exactly his own but had been given to him as some kind of unanswerable question, a tricky riddle he couldn't for the life of him comprehend.

Why'd she leave him five years in the Milne Home only to summon him now, once his mother was gone? What had she done to him? What had he done in return?

And after he'd pulled and tugged and leaned and was finally dressed, Minou assured him with an approving whistle and nod, just as he'd assured him earlier with gentle words, wiping a washcloth across Shelton's blood-soaked face, that it had just been Genevieve's time to go and nothing more, that the Lord had granted to an old woman the long, peaceful rest she'd earned.

Why'd she leave him in the Milne Home?

But Minou's voice was soothing, as if Genevieve's passing were cause more for relief than sorrow. "Not now," Minou had said. "There'll be time. Now's the time for quiet, for calming down."

What had he done?

"Quiet, quiet," Minou told him. "Quiet, child."

And when that proved insufficient to calm Shelton's nightmare vision, Minou told him that his being there, his standing before her, hadn't mattered at all one way or the other, that she'd died from a heart choked into stillness by its own body, from lungs that the medical doctor said had filled to overflowing with blood and water, and not — though Minou didn't say it, maybe knowing that saying it might make it seem so — from the fright Shelton might have given her, falling and hammering at his own body so, not from the real or imagined grip of Shelton's fingers around her throat.

"I'm sorry," Shelton had managed to spit out from where he lay on the floor when Minou let go of his wrists and stepped away to stand before Genevieve's slumped silence. He'd lifted her hand in his own and called out to his wife so loud that not just Isabel but the rest as well, Olivia and Elise and Adrienne, came running and stepped right over Shelton as if he were a sleeping dog. Seeing the old woman's open but empty eyes, they set about their weeping.

"I think I killed her," Shelton whispered, through the blood and spit. "I'm sorry."

Only Olivia, crouched at her grandmother's feet, turned to look at him. Through her tears she smiled a smile that Shelton, behind the throbbing pain of his own hands' beating, took as an offer of forgiveness, an offer he returned not with a smile of his own, for his mouth was too bruised and swollen, but again with a gurgling of blood and spit that he meant to be words of gratitude.

Was it in this moment the child Shelton, thirteen years old, decided that if the question formed by his loneliness and longing were to have an answer, it would be contained in this other child's name, in the bright flash of her dark eyes, in the smooth skin of her limbs, in the great good grace she showed to him just by turning her head now, smiling through her tears, forgiving him? That's how it felt, it did, and wasn't it this moment and no other in which Shelton sensed he'd long now only for this girl to keep him company, to sit still before him for hours and hours the way she must have sat for whoever had done that pencil sketch of her he'd seen on the wall with the others, the lines of her chin and nose and ears, the smooth skin and the bones beneath them, taking shape somewhere behind his eyes, running like a river down through his neck and shoulder and arm to his hand, which he raised now to Olivia because there was nothing else he could do, the words wouldn't come.

Or maybe that's just an old man applying sentiment to his memory like it's liniment, healing his oldest, deepest wounds by the sweet trick of remembering not what was but what might have been, creating out of ragtag, scattershot circumstance a world as simple as a child's picture puzzle: Match and fit the pieces on the board. Look and see how it all becomes clear.

So maybe there was no one moment when the child found himself drawn to this sixteen-year-old girl who'd been granted her father's good heart and quick smile and magical eyes along with her mother's beauty and grace. Maybe there was no such moment but only should have been. If that's the case, then this, I swear to heaven, was the moment it would have been.

This is only a child's story, I've said, and maybe this isn't the time or place to leap forward through the years, but I can't return to that first moment of tenderness between a thirteen-year-old boy and the bright girl of sixteen without seeing the line that stretches, like a kite string going up to the sky, straight from that moment to the present day. If the child's eyes, while he lay bruised and bloody on the floor, were filled with gratitude and devotion, imagine those eyes now, having seen what they've seen, the face of that girl changing with time into an old woman's, a face that contained, even in its final moments, every bit of its beauty and grace and more — the certainty of love, my own.

Listen: Any day now my lungs will fail me or my heart will simply quit. I'll go to bed one evening and never wake again, or I'll linger on, pale and emaciated, in some hospital bed for weeks on end. What use is there, what relief, to speak of love and such a loss in the same breath? There's not much I know of prayer, of casting my words up to heaven, but I'll do it now: *Make it quick, Lord,* I want to say. *Don't you hear me? Make it quick.*

❧ ❧ ❧

That's enough, isn't it? So I'll just say again that the child lying on the floor, three steps from a dead woman's body, was caught in the wonder and gift of a girl's smile even while he wept at the thought of what he just had or hadn't done. Then Minou stepped back over to him and lifted his body from the floor as if he were lifting it up from the ground beneath the tree where he'd fallen. He carried him to the girls' bedroom and placed him on one of the soft beds, shaking his head and saying, "No, no. Quiet, child. You didn't."

Even so, a day later Shelton stood in the church before the coffin and didn't want to look long enough at the body of Genevieve Simmons to see whether or not her neck bore the imprint of his hands, the way the palms of his hands had borne the imprint of her clutching fingertips when they'd walked side by side from the St. Charles streetcar over to Magazine.

Eyes cast down, Shelton waited until Isabel let go of him to wipe her eyes, and Minou led him back to their seats in the first row of long wooden pews. Adrienne stepped up to take hold of her sister, and the two of them wept again at the sight of their mother's body, at the thought of her being gone.

In the balcony at the back of the church, the white-robed women rose, songbooks gripped in their hands, gold crosses gleaming against their chests. Shelton was too far away to make out their faces, but he knew for certain that these women were the very ones who looked after the infants at the Milne Home, and he wondered if they'd seen him too. They had, hadn't they?

They wouldn't mistake, even from such a distance, Shelton's bent frame and awkward step for someone else's, some other injured child's. And weren't they singing with the knowledge of his presence when they sang, first one voice and then the rest, *Wonder where is my brother gone? Wonder where is my brother John? He's gone to the wilderness, ain't coming no more. Wonder where will I lie down?*

Shelton lowered his head and listened. *Wonder where will I lie down?* they sang. *In some lonesome place, Lord, down on the ground.* And Shelton longed to race back down the aisle and climb the balcony stairs, longed to let these women enclose him in the folds of their white robes, longed to tell them he never should have left the Milne Home and never would again.

Then Minou, as if his shut eyes could read Shelton's thoughts, put a hand across the child's back and pulled him close. "You're not lost," he said, leaning down to speak in Shelton's ear. "Just because she's gone, and your mother too, doesn't mean you're lost. You understand?"

Shelton nodded and let the tears roll down his face and drip to the floor the way the sweat had dripped from his face when, a morning ago, that was all, he'd run from the Milne Home. Maybe Minou had guessed what Shelton felt — that he was attending not one funeral but two, his own mother's as well as Genevieve's, the two of them being laid to rest together, side by side.

Hadn't his mother spoken to him about this very moment, about her passing away, about leaving him behind? Hadn't she pulled him close and said, "Daddy's always going to look after you"? Wasn't that the promise she'd made?

He could feel the touch of her hands as though she were holding him now. How was it that his own ruined body felt so strange to him, as though it had been twisted by the hands of some mighty beast, while his mother's, worse than his own, had felt so familiar, such a comfort, so perfectly formed?

He'd known, though, that her body hadn't always been pinned

to the bed. She'd told him about the time when she could still walk and run, when she could do what other young girls did — ride horses, swing on swings. She had learned to dance by placing her bare feet on top of Mr. Edward's, the two of them swinging through the house, crashing here and there, while her own mother stood by and laughed.

Her own mother. "Where's she gone?" Shelton had asked once, and his mother had lifted a hand from the bed and reached for him, had held his head against her head while she told him. "Daddy says it's just the soul that goes to heaven," she'd said, "but I see her up there wearing some fancy dress, the blue one she liked with a hundred pleats that she'd twirl around in to make me laugh. That's what I think. And listen, Shelton. When I'm up in heaven, when I've gone there with her, I want you to think of me that way, wearing a beautiful dress like that and twirling around the way my mother did. That's how you should think of me. That's how I'll be."

Now Shelton did try to think of her that way but couldn't. He saw the shape of her curled, twisted body, and it felt like his own.

Shelton kept his head bowed as the women sang "The Sun Will Never Go Down" and "I'm Crossing Jordan River." He listened as the voices around him joined in, became louder and louder. Then the reverend, the same man he remembered meeting on Magazine Street, stepped up to Genevieve's coffin and leaned down to kiss her face.

When the reverend raised his head, he lifted his arms. His black robe stretched out so he looked to Shelton not like the angel he'd been before but like a small-headed, big-bodied bat. "Lord knows that's the first time she let me do that," the reverend said, smiling, shaking his head, lowering his arms so that his robe folded in to become a black curtain. "Any other time, don't you know, I'd have had my face slapped."

The voices behind Shelton laughed. Hands clapped against the wooden pews. Feet tapped.

Then the reverend's face grew somber. "That means our beloved Genevieve Delery Simmons is gone, don't it?" He looked out over the crowd as if looking for someone to answer his question. The reverend's eyes met, for just a moment, Shelton's own. Shelton saw the reverend's look of recognition, the acknowledgment he made by letting his eyes pause, his head nod, before turning up and away.

"By the good Lord's word, it don't," the reverend said. "She's not gone. She's right here. Look." And he peered down again at the body in the coffin. "No, those hands can no longer raise up to defend her honor, but that's not from death taking hold of them. It's because Jesus himself has taken up this woman's honor. He's taken it in his own gentle, abiding hands. He's taken hold of her body, taken hold of her soul. He's secured them both in his heart. Tell me, hasn't her name been written down in gold? Is there any man, woman, or child can erase it? There's no one, I tell you, not one."

The reverend paced before Genevieve's coffin. He stretched his arms out again over her as if he'd call upon her to rise up and walk. "The devil had his chance with this woman," he said, "like he's got with each one of us. And though that battle may be carrying on full-scale and still burning bright in the region of my body and yours, though our souls may remain for the claiming of one side or the other, for good or bad, for the Lord's bright hand or the devil's sharp cloven hoof, here's one battle the devil's lost. Here's one battle that's over and done with."

Then the reverend lifted his arms again, looked out at the faces before him, and let his eyes sail up above them as though he were following the flight of some strange and glorious bird. "Here's a passing that makes a victory from defeat. The body rests, dear Lord, but the soul takes flight."

❦ ❦ ❦

There was a time, not long ago, when I gave myself over to a single work, what was meant to be my last. I went from family to

106

family, one death to the next, expressing my sympathy, lying about knowing the woman's late cousin, the man's best friend, the child's great-uncle or aunt. What I looked for in those homes again and again was what happens to faces and hands and the covers on a bed and the curtains and most of all just a room's light and darkness when a family has been touched by death and that death's still got a firm hold of everything.

The Awful Silence: It's a body under the pulled-up patchwork blanket of a slanting bed, five pairs of women's hands set atop that blanket, five bowed women's heads, the light of dawn just about to touch the pane of a shut window, about to clip the knees of the men who stand along the dark walls to stare out at their wives' and daughters' grief, the men's shirttails untucked, their pants' waists sagging, their shoulders slumped from the long night of not sleeping. Any minute they'll step forward to lead away their wives, lead away their sobbing daughters. Any minute these men's passing thoughts of how enough's enough will become conviction. They're ready to move, these men, ready to turn grief into action.

I won't admonish myself for having such reasons as I did to intrude on those families and their grief, for on each occasion comfort was taken from my presence, wasn't it? There was pride in the simple fact that Shelton Gerard Lafleur had thought to creep up their stairs or walk through their houses and down their halls and steal into their sickrooms, given over now to death. There was pride that I was willing to expend all manner of effort to witness what, expected or not, after a long illness or quick accident, had overtaken these families, what they were eager to share.

It's Shelton Lafleur, they'd say, they'd whisper under their breath and through their tears. *Come in, come in.*

And I felt, I confess, as though I were a mighty angel of the Lord who'd swooped down from on high to visit them. They were my people, were they not? They were my old age's neighbors, the folks whose houses I strolled past when I felt strong enough to walk, the folks whose children gathered round to watch me paint. The lucky ones got to help clean my brushes for a quarter apiece, leaning over a coffee can of turpentine the way the child Shelton had leaned over that giant drum behind the Milne Home's kitchen.

These children were no different from their hard-working, sweat-soaked parents, their grandmothers and grandfathers who'd lost memory and sight and hearing as surely as they'd lost their teeth. But I was altogether different, wasn't I? Didn't I know everything? Didn't I remember it all? Couldn't I tell them when this neighborhood was something special to see, Magazine Street full of thriving shops and stores and the bright, happy faces of well-to-do Negroes: Negro lawyers, Negro doctors, Negro teachers and preachers and undertakers?

I could tell them more, I could, but what they wanted to hear were the stories of how there'd once been a time when all was well, a high time here as elsewhere, a time when Magazine Street down to Tchoupitoulas and on over to the banks of the Mississippi River was nothing but grand and glorious, so grand and glorious that these houses and streets and whatever wind was blowing through the trees could take a crippled child like me and make something equally grand and glorious of him: a man who paints great canvas pictures, an artist named Shelton Gerard Lafleur. Now wasn't that something to see?

That's why you never left, isn't it? they'd ask me. *That's why you call these same streets home?*

"That's why," I'd tell them, taking their hands in my own, smiling and smiling.

I did leave, of course. I did. I left and came back and left and came back, not for the grandeur and glory these children imagined but for something else, for the hard work and pain and simple joy and terrible sadness that I needed, for my own sake, to see.

Olivia was already sick, already planning everything. She

wanted to be near her childhood home. She wanted, she told me time and again, just to remember.

What do I do now with such memories as this place has given me?

Go on, say my hands.

Well, folks believe, right or not, that one such as me has a special sympathy to offer, that the work of my hands proves it. It doesn't, of course. That's just the game that artwork plays and plays. But that's a gift in any case, isn't it? That's a gift I can give, so why not?

And the gift that I've received in return, that I've asked for from grace and gotten, is the one that now lets me go back and watch the child I was, that lets me — through all those paintings, through my memory of every one — follow that child step by step. That's all I've wanted, isn't it, though now I've asked for something else — to be given the voice I need to speak of that child's life, to put words, not just pictures, to his every thought and act.

Go on, my hands say again.

I will, my voice says, and I wonder if maybe the day will come when I will pick up a brush one more time to paint a final self-portrait, one that shows the ugly creases and folds of my weathered face but not just that, something else as well, something more: the dark beauty of remembering, all the other faces that old face once was.

But my face isn't enough, is it? I'd have to show this sunken chest, this bent back, all four of these shoestring, twisted limbs.

The Wrecked, Blessed Body of Shelton Lafleur.

And that body, as sure as all the others it's known, as sure as his crippled mother's, would be dancing in the clouds, twirling this way and that, arms become a windmill, fingers become ten streaks of bright white light.

That's Fred Astaire? No, that's Shelton Lafleur. He's passing over to the other side, happy as happy can be to be joining all those others, happy to be leaving his wrecked body behind, happy to find sprouting from his bent and broken back these two bright white wings.

Can you see me? Can you hear me?

That's a voice. That's my own voice, and it's singing. It's singing long and loud and clear, singing, *Here I am. Reach out your hands, one and all.*

༝ ༝ ༝

Singing and singing. Voices raised to heaven. And when the Church of the Innocent Blood finally began to quiet, the voices swinging low, the reverend stepped up and closed the lid of Genevieve's coffin, leaving his hands resting on top of it, fingers pressed against the wood. Then he sighed and hung his head and said, "This doesn't get any easier, Lord, let me tell you, sending home to you our loved ones. There's not one I send on his way doesn't remind me of my own dear girl, Ruth Ann. There's not one I deliver to your loving hands doesn't remind me of my dear wife, Rebecca. You know, Lord, how it makes me weep."

And Shelton shut his eyes, only to see Emanuel Jackson, that boy from the home who'd lost his mother and father and two sisters, who'd scrambled through a window only to wind up standing in some church to watch four bodies prayed over like this.

How'd he manage to smile again after such a sight? Shelton wondered. *How'd he manage ever to open his eyes or listen with his ears or speak so much as a single happy word after seeing what he'd seen?*

"Now there's not going to be one, from here on in," the reverend said, "doesn't remind me of Genevieve Simmons. Seventy-four years, dear Lord, she called your name. Seventy-four years she walked the long walk of faith. Now you've taken her, and we shed our tears. She was a blessing on this earth, a blessing to her husband, the good man you saw fit to take in the prime of his life. She was a blessing to her daughters, Isabel and Adrienne, to her granddaughters, Olivia and Elise. She watched over them, Lord.

Now you've left it to us to watch over them for her. We will, Lord. We will, now won't we?" Shelton felt more than heard the rising murmur, the hushed, whispered call of the congregation. *Amen.* "And she was a blessing to another child, dear Lord, yes she was. It's a child by your grace stands with us here today. Many of the good folks gathered around don't know, dear Lord, don't know the first half or second of the good works our own good Miss Genevieve performed. Many don't know all she'd set about doing for this child, a child she'd waited years and years to give a home. A thousand days it was and then a thousand more, dear Lord. But he's got a home now, don't he? He's got a true home, don't he, Minou?"

And Minou squeezed Shelton's hand, looked down at Shelton, up at the reverend, and nodded.

The reverend smiled. "Yes, he does. And his life will forever be a testament to that good woman's name. May the Lord bless the pure soul of Genevieve Simmons, which he's already taken. May he bless the body we deliver over to him now. May he bless you all as you fight the one great battle the Lord Almighty is bound and determined to win."

The reverend nodded now to Minou, and Minou stepped past Shelton and out to the aisle, where he was joined by three other men. They walked up to Genevieve's coffin and lifted it, and the women in the balcony began singing a song that contained not words but sounds, a jumble of sounds shaped by their voices into music, a rising and falling of moans and shouts and wailing that washed over Shelton, that rocked against his ears like a boat rocking in a storm on a dark night or a door slamming shut again and again to frighten him from sleep, and he saw not just Genevieve's face pressed close to the top of the pine coffin, surrounded by the unrelieved darkness of earth, but his mother's face as well, twitching and grimacing as it took its last breaths, as her mouth tried but couldn't call out Shelton's name.

Isabel took Shelton's hand now and led him out to the aisle, where they marched together behind the coffin, Olivia and Elise and Adrienne beside them, Shelton scrambling forward again and again to keep up. Ahead, Minou and the three other men, arms straining, shoulders square, bore Genevieve forward to be buried in the cemetery beside her long-dead husband.

Shelton turned away, shut his eyes, when they went to lower her body into the earth. He raised his hands over his ears rather than listen to what he feared would join that awful silence, rather than hear what he was sure he would hear — his own mother's twisted legs and curled arms knocking at the side of that box, her voice screaming out his name now, not in fear or love or longing but accusation.

What have you done? that voice said.

I haven't done anything, Shelton wanted to answer but couldn't.

And returning to the church after the burial, Shelton looked back, stumbled, looked back again. Trailing behind was the procession of mourners and behind them the white-robed choir of women, singing again their wordless song, arms raised high in the air, moving back and forth. Their arms looked to Shelton like the slow, swaying branches of a hundred bare trees, the robes beneath those arms like a bright new covering of snow.

It was as if Shelton had just imagined the summer's heat on his face and chest and legs, as if the truth were he'd stepped through the creaking cemetery gate to discover that the weather had turned in an instant, in a single shallow breath, from summer's heat to the biting chill of winter. And Shelton, arms like tree branches blocking the sun from his head, felt the cold, felt his body shiver.

9 THE BLIND MAN
OF JACKSON SQUARE

BUT NEVER MIND what the child felt at that moment. Let it go. The seasons, after all, would go on to do what they always do, changing places not with the blink of an eye or a child's shallow breath but with the inch-by-inch caterpillar crawl of one day to the next to the next.

Look: There's the green and tumble of Monkey Hill, the black scratch of a child on the riverbank below.

Look: There's proud Isabel and shy Adrienne in their steaming, sun-streaked kitchen, late summer's swollen tomatoes gleaming on the countertop like Christmas ornaments of painted glass, a square splash of light on the stretched-to-bursting skin of every one.

There's a fall evening's shimmering and shadow on Foucher Street, the line of clapboard above clamshell shotgun houses set aglow with candlelight through cloth-covered windows.

There's the wind-whipping, bone-chilling freeze of a night that's hunched every shoulder, tilted down every head, slapped closed the shutters of each and every house, and sent trails of swirling smoke up through squat chimneys to the clear winter sky, hiding the moon and stars.

It was all this that the child Shelton would come to see and know and one day, with the work of his hands, try to show, the brittle shell of the child's body replaced by something new, a change so slow and steady he couldn't have said how or why that change had come to be.

I'll say it now, though: Shelton was happy, wasn't he, in the house of Minou. Forget what he did and didn't know. Forget that he carried with him, as if they were thrown across his back, not just the slumped figure of Genevieve Simmons but the curled form of his mother. Forget the questions that swirled inside him like that swirling black chimney smoke. Forget how Minou brushed all the child's questions aside with stories and lies, with the trick of his shut eyes, with laughter meant to hide the truth.

Look, and there are the faces the child came to know: Elise's, O-mouthed in sneaky merriment, eyes sparkling with devilish fire, her dark, coiled hair snaking down to her shoulders, swallowing every speck of shining light. And Olivia's face, quiet and radiant, smooth as sanded wood.

And there's Adrienne, eyes turned toward Shelton, hands fidgeting at her side. She wants to say something, doesn't she? She's got something to say.

And Isabel, proud, unforgiving.

And Minou. Yes, keep looking and you'll see the shut-eyed Minou in a work named *The Blind Man of Jackson Square*. Minou's face is seen straight on, as if he's eager for some confrontation. His mouth is smiling at the simple magic of his blindness, the red scratches and dark lines of his face declare how he can see as much with his eyes closed as others see with their eyes open.

And it's true, isn't it? He may well be, as Elise told Shelton on the porch, full of lies — more than the night sky could hold if every one of those lies were bright stars — but this much is true: Minou knows men and women in every dark corner and secret square of the city. He's shaken hands with them, nodded his thanks, traded stories, shared a bottle or streetcar ride or bed. He's found out from all that talk and riding around and drinking just about everything a man, even a blind man, needs to know — what's what and who's who and how, when you're telling lies one after the other, you can still circle nearer and nearer and finally wind up at the truth.

And listening to him, holding his hand, following just behind: that slow-changing, twisted-limb child who still stands before me as though I've made him a promise he knows I can't keep. The child's hands, just like my own, are raised and trembling. His face is black as black, dark as Minou's. But look again, look close: That face is also, in one work or another, a hundred thousand other indecipherable hues. Yes, here's that child finally scratching a pencil across some paper to make one poor excuse for a picture, what's meant to be a leaning fruit and vegetable cart pulled by its stocky, sullen mare, but no one else would ever be able to make out what's wood plank and what's the mare's shank, what's vegetable or fruit or the mare's glassy eye, what's the cart's spoked wheels, what's the early-morning sun.

Even so, the child discovers there in that picture what he'll make of his long life, what it is he feels he has no choice but to do, since any hope for words has left him.

He'd rather speak, you understand. He'd rather sit down, leave his hands in his lap, tell his story straight out, not with pictures but with words, but he can't.

I'm trying now, though. I am.

So let the seasons slip back to where they belong, to the summer evening that followed Genevieve Simmons's body finding its home in the ground. Watch how the child sits in the front room of Minou's shotgun house. Watch how one visitor after the next enters through the swinging screen door to offer heartfelt condolences and gifts of food the likes of which the child has never seen: just-caught pompano and red snapper, a giant bowl of

Gombo Zhebes, red beans and rice and banana fritters, clunking oysters in a burlap sack, crabs scrambling in a wire-tied cane basket — so much food it would feed for a week, the child Shelton thinks, all the boys in the Milne Home.

The visitors offer their gifts and embrace Isabel and Adrienne. They embrace Minou and Olivia and Elise. They turn to Shelton then and pat his head or shoulder or knee, say *Poor child,* say *You're home, yes you are,* say nothing at all but smile a sorrowful smile like Genevieve's and, heads shaking, turn to leave, blessing house and family, offering their prayers for the care of Genevieve's soul, their sympathies to the family, their well-wishes to poor crippled Shelton.

The boys who arrive with their mothers or grandmothers or aunts — *Where's their fathers?* Shelton wonders. *Where's their grandfathers and uncles?* — these boys stand in a corner of the front room beside Olivia and Elise, leaning close to speak into the girls' ears, making them smile a quick smile or slowly nod their heads or reach out to slap a hand or shoulder gently. Both girls turn from time to time toward Shelton, eyeing him, and the boys turn too, shaking their heads.

I'm the one who killed her, the child wants to say, eager to turn all that pity around until it becomes as sharp and accusing as blame. *Just lead me over,* he wants to shout, *to St. John Bercham's.* But he can't say it, can't speak, so he's still sitting on that front-room sofa when the last visitor has come and gone, when the food has all been tasted and what's left has been sent by Olivia and Elise and Adrienne up and down Foucher Street, over to Antonine and Amelia, down to Tchoupitoulas and up to Magazine.

"You've found your bed, I'm afraid," Isabel tells Shelton as she gathers up the dishes, pinches three and four glasses between her fingers, then carries them all off to the kitchen.

"In time," she says when she returns, "we'll find some kind of better arrangement."

Then she sits down next to Shelton as if she means to enjoy

this moment of quiet. Elise and Olivia and Adrienne are off delivering food to neighbors. Minou has gone out too, though Shelton doesn't know where.

Isabel puts a hand on Shelton's leg. "You don't want to go back there, do you? You didn't like it, Mama said. Is that true?" Shelton nods, then looks up at Isabel. "Why'd she ask for me now?"

Isabel stands. "You talk to Minou," she says, looking around as if searching for dirty dishes she might have missed. "You ask him that." She reaches out her hand and touches Shelton's forehead. Shelton looks at her, tries to tell her just with his eyes all the questions he wants to ask.

And Isabel understands. She understands, doesn't she? "Listen to me," she says. "Minou and Mama were the ones who came up with this. I'm glad you're here, Shelton. Don't think I'm not. But you talk to Minou. You ask him all you've got to ask. It was two weeks ago when he saw the notice in the paper. He showed Mama and said wasn't that Edward Soniat's child who'd passed. Mama set to crying but seemed more happy than sad, like the woman's dying was a relief. Then she called Minou in and asked him to shut the door like this was their business and no one else's. So you go ahead and talk to Minou. I've tried, Shelton. Believe me. No matter what he says, though, I want you to know you're welcome to stay. I don't care how it is or why you've wound up here. I want you to know you're welcome to stay."

Then Elise and Olivia and Adrienne step through the door and the two girls place themselves at their mother's side, their arms like ropes around Isabel's waist.

"You're both tired," Isabel says, and she tells them to march off to their rooms. "Go on," she says. "Say your goodnights to Shelton."

The girls say goodnight and follow their mother from the room. Adrienne, holding a dishtowel in her hands, says goodnight too, moving toward Shelton but then backing away, shrugging her shoulders, smiling, patting her head as if to make sure it's still there where she left it.

"It's been nice to meet you, Shelton," she says, "even considering." And starts, but just like that stops, weeping. "What I mean is, I'm looking forward to your being here." She shrugs again, steps forward and back. "I am."

"Me too," Shelton says, and he's sure there's something else Adrienne plans to say, but Minou walks in through the door, looks at them both, shakes his head, and calls out for Isabel. She doesn't answer, and he calls again; then he leaves the room without saying another word.

Shelton keeps watching, as if he'll see Minou moving through the house. Then he turns back to Adrienne.

"He's been drinking," Adrienne says. She pats her face with the towel. "Watch out."

Then Minou comes back into the room. "Goodnight, Adrienne," he says, smiling. "Now you've got the whole bed to yourself."

Adrienne smiles at Shelton, then turns to Minou, her face changing to a frown. She raises her hand toward him as if she's set to speak, but he raises his own. "Careful," he says, his smile gone. "Don't be thinking I need more than one woman telling me what I should and shouldn't do."

Shelton watches as Adrienne shakes her head and walks away. "Go on to sleep now," Minou calls to her. "Go on." He turns to Shelton, stretches his arms up in the air so that his white shirt pulls out of his pants at the waist. "What did I tell you, Shelton?" he says. "Every one of them's a queen. Well, it's only four queens now."

He looks down at Shelton and yawns, running his hands across his arms. "You tired?" Minou says. "Too tired for an evening stroll?"

Shelton stands. "I'm not tired," he says, but that's a child speaking, for his legs burn and ache. He can feel his eyes trying to swing down and close.

"Let's go, then," Minou says. "You can smell it, can't you?"

"What?" Shelton says, and Minou laughs.

"Yes, you can smell it," he says. "I'm in need of fresh air."

Outside, Minou leads Shelton down Foucher Street to Tchoupitoulas, Minou's steps slapping up against the dark houses, Shelton's scraping. They walk a block down Tchoupitoulas, then Minou stops at a small park on the corner. A rusted iron fence surrounds it, and old newspapers and leaves and trash blow up against the fence, catching in its iron railings. They walk in through the open gate, Minou's hand on Shelton's shoulder as if to guide him along the dark path.

"Adrienne," Shelton says, for he's still seeing in his mind her strange manner with him, her stepping forward and back, her starting to speak but then not, her looking at Minou with anger and warning in her eyes, her mouth turned down in a frown.

"Adrienne, Adrienne," Minou says. "She's a little lost, that one." He stops and stretches his arms up again, and the leaves of the trees rustle above their heads, as if that's what Minou has asked them to do. "Yes, a little lost, and sleeping all those nights in my house right beside her mother, listening to the woman's every breath and wondering, I bet, which one's to be the last."

Shelton thinks of his own mother, of his bed next to hers, of her curled body. Dead.

"She wants to like you, that's all," Minou says, and he starts walking again, Shelton behind him, his feet scraping as he tries to catch up. "She wouldn't know to say it, of course, but that's it. Don't let it worry you, no sir." Minou stops and turns back to Shelton. "You know what I think?" he says. "I think she sees something of herself in you. There are some that sadness seems to hunt down, Shelton. She's one of them."

"I'm one too, you mean," Shelton says.

Minou puts his hand on Shelton's head. "I guess I do. But maybe that's wrong. Maybe it's happiness trying to hunt you down. Maybe you've had enough of sadness and now that's behind you. What do you think of that?"

"I don't know," Shelton says.

"Well, you'll do fine," Minou says. "And maybe Adrienne will too. There's a man about ready to marry her. He's a decent man, I guess, though his father's nothing more than the wrong half of a jackass. You might have seen him today." Minou holds his hands out before him. "Fat as an elephant," he says.

"The reverend?" Shelton asks.

"No, no," Minou says, and he laughs. "Samuel Warren. He's the undertaker. Makes his money off others' misfortune."

Minou takes a seat on a concrete bench, and Shelton sits down too. He leans forward to look at the base of the bench, which is made of two pigeons, their beaks touching the ground, the bench resting like a block on top of their backs and the tips of their tails.

Shelton looks up at Minou, who points across the park's curving walk to where there's another bench, the legs of that one some animal, though it's too dark for Shelton to see what it is — two crouching lions, maybe, or two sleeping cats.

"This whole long day, Shelton," Minou says, "there's not been opportunity to ask all you've been thinking." He reaches into his shirt pocket and begins rolling a cigarette. And in the flash of his match, Shelton sees that beneath the far bench, forming the base, aren't lions or cats but two fat squirrels. "I'm asking now," Minou says. "Tell me your thoughts."

"I don't know what," Shelton says, and the warm night seems to close in on him. If he were to shut his eyes for the shortest moment, he thinks, he'd find himself in bed in the Milne Home, Minou nothing more than a dark ghost waiting to join him once he's asleep and ready to dream.

Why'd she leave me there? Shelton wants to ask, but he sees Genevieve slumped in her chair, feels his fingers curl as if they've taken hold of her neck.

"Maybe you're wondering why you're here and not back at that asylum," Minou says. "Maybe you're wondering why I was there to fetch you."

Shelton nods. Minou looks at the child, then looks away. "Well, I don't know," he says. "How's that for an answer?" Then he turns back to Shelton, raises his hand toward him. "Maybe you were thinking I could tell you everything?" he says. "Maybe you figured I'd just sit you down and spell it all out clear as day."

Minou raises the cigarette to his mouth, and Shelton sees his face set aglow, sees the anger there despite his smile. "Here's one thing worth remembering," Minou says. "Most folks know a whole lot less than you think they do. Well, I'm no different. I wish that wasn't true. It's not just you who could have used another word or two from Genevieve Simmons before she took her leave. I had my own questions for her too."

And Shelton thinks of what he'd said when she told him that his mother had passed away. *I knew*, he'd said. *I knew*. And I can say now, though the child surely couldn't have said such a thing, that this answer was nothing more than a body giving voice to its last particle of trust and faith and hope. What the child meant by that answer, I suspect, was something along the lines of this: *I knew, because otherwise, if she were breathing and alive and able to, she'd have come to get me or sent someone over, wouldn't she?* But she had been alive, hadn't she? She'd been alive all that time he was at the Milne Home. So why hadn't she sent someone over?

"I'll tell you what I do know," Minou tells Shelton. "I know there's wrong things that have happened to you. Not just unlucky, not just falling from that tree. Worse than that."

"What did she tell you?" Shelton says.

Minou turns to look at the child.

"Isabel said you talked to her," Shelton says. "She said you closed the door and talked to her."

"That's true," Minou says. "That's true enough. Listen now. I'll tell you what she said. Understand, though, how she was these last few months. 'The child was dead,' she told me, 'but now he's not. He fell from a tree and died, that's what, and I told Miss Margaret so. I told her I'd see he was looked after. With Mr.

Edward gone abroad for another month, I said I'd make all the proper arrangements.' That's what she said, Shelton. That's it. She said, 'The child was lost, but now he's found. Go get him, Minou,' she said. 'Go get him now.' So I did."

"She lied," Shelton says, fingers curled into fists. "Why'd she lie?"

"Well, it wasn't as easy as all that," Minou says. "It's never as easy as all that. It seems Miss Margaret said she wanted to see you, Shelton. She wanted to hold you in her arms a final time."

"Why?" Shelton says. "Why'd she lie?"

"Those white folks had no business raising you," Minou says, and he shakes his head. "That's her words, Shelton, not my own. 'I'm going to steal a child from an asylum just for that?' I said to her, and I'll tell you what she said back. She said, 'You going to grant a dying woman's wish or not?' Well, we went around and around like that, and what else could I say? You want me to go ahead now and take you back?"

Shelton looks at Minou, shakes his head.

"I made that woman a promise," Minou says. "I might not have had much room in my heart for her, but I did and do for her daughter, and that's enough. I said I'd look after you, and I will. That's my promise. What can I do beyond that? You tell me, and I'll set my mind to it."

Shelton looks up at the leaves of the trees above their heads. "I don't want to go back," he says.

"What's your wish, then?" Minou asks. "Just go ahead and tell me."

Shelton hears the leaves in the trees rustle as if something is up there he can't see. He'll have to say it sometime, won't he? He'll have to say it straight out — that he's lost not one mother but two, that it would take less time to name what he knows about how he came to be than it took for him to fall from that tree.

"What?" Minou says. "Anything. You just name it."

"I want to see Mr. Edward," Shelton says.

"Not that," Minou says.

"You said anything," Shelton says, and he stands up. "You said anything," he says again, and he hears his voice carry up into the trees.

"Listen now," Minou says. "That man thinks you're dead." Then Minou shuts his eyes and laughs. "You could give him some kind of start, though, couldn't you now? You'd be a ghost scaring him whiter than white."

Minou opens his eyes and reaches for Shelton. "Sit down now," he says, and Shelton does, though he looks off into the darkness, away from Minou.

"You're right in feeling you've been mistreated," Minou says. "You're right in feeling you've been done a terrible wrong. I'll do what I can for you. That's my promise. I understand that's not enough. Nothing's enough. But right now that's the best I can do."

Shelton is still staring off into the darkness, hearing the wind in the trees, imagining his body falling, not from the tree but in Genevieve's bedroom.

"Look at me, Shelton."

Shelton turns.

"This is a hard time," Minou says. "It's been a hard time about as long as anyone can remember. Not just you but me too. But I'm going to look after you. You understand?"

Shelton nods.

"Good," Minou says. "That's said and done." He stands up, and Shelton stands too. "We should go home now. This is one day, if there ever was one, that deserves its coming to an end. I've got work in the morning, bright and early."

"What do you do?" Shelton asks.

"What do I do?" Minou says. "Maybe I'll just show you. Maybe I'll take you over to the Vieux Carré."

"Where's the Vieux Carré?" Shelton asks.

"The French Quarter," Minou says. "Jackson Square."

"What do you do there?" Shelton asks again, so tired now that even standing up he feels as though he's falling asleep, as though a dream is coming on.

"I make pictures," Minou says. "I draw and paint." He puts a hand on Shelton's back, and Shelton feels his eyes swing open, not realizing that they'd been closed, that he'd been watching not anything real but just the specks of light inside his own eyes.

"There's something more to it than that, though," he hears Minou say, though Minou's voice sounds as if it's reaching him through a thick brick wall or a lake's worth of water.

"I'll just show you," Minou says, and now Shelton feels his legs moving, feels them steering him out of the park and along Tchoupitoulas Street.

"It's one long, sad trick," he hears Minou say, and Shelton feels his legs following Minou's, feels them turn at the corner, carry him down one block and the next of Foucher Street.

Shelton can't keep his eyes open, he's so tired. He sees Genevieve's slumped body. He sees the dark arms wave in the air, hears the singing voices, feels again the chill he felt earlier.

His legs, though, keep following Minou. They take one step and the next and the next until finally, as he climbs up to the porch, Shelton's eyes open and he sees where his legs have carried him.

"Home," Minou says as if he has heard Shelton's thoughts. Then Minou stomps his feet on the porch, says, "Go on, now. Get away. You've had your day."

Shelton looks at Minou.

"Never mind," Minou says, laughing. "I'm just talking to the devil. I'm just scaring him off from my home."

Home, Shelton thinks and he lets his eyes close, lets Minou take him by the arm and guide him inside. *I'm already asleep*, the child thinks, and his body feels now as though it's swimming through water. *I'm already asleep*, he thinks, *and this is already a dream.*

10 A GOOD FORTUNE

IT WASN'T the next day or the next or the next that Shelton went to work with Minou. Instead, each of those mornings at the break of dawn, Minou slipped quietly out the door while Shelton curled as if in sleep on the front-room sofa, a tattered quilt Adrienne had sewn as a girl thrown over his body.

In fact, all three of those mornings Shelton was awake. Just the creaking of Minou's feet on the floorboards was enough to lift him out of sleep, to call him back from the fitful dreams that had sent him sailing all three nights over the clear blue water of Lake Pontchartrain, winding up at that place he'd been told was on the other shore: that asylum in Carville, Louisiana, the one filled with peeling-skin lepers who spent their days, in Shelton's imagining, like monks behind high stone walls, their bodies covered head to foot by dark robes, their faces hidden beneath sagging hoods, their knee joints crackling like dried branches lit on fire as they knelt down to pray in a great stone church, asking again and again for a cure.

In his dreams Shelton kneeled with them, and one by one the

other lepers, though they didn't turn their heads, whispered questions Shelton knew were meant for him.

What's your name?

Where'd you come from?

Where's your mother gone?

Why'd you leave her?

Why'd you run from home?

What happened to twist and knot and bend those limbs?

Each time, Shelton tried to speak but couldn't, though he finally shouted that he'd fallen from a tree, that was all. He didn't deserve to be there among all that diseased, peeling flesh. He'd not done anything wrong.

Then the others turned to him one by one and their skeleton hands leapt like string puppets', the fingers twisting now around the coarse dark cloth, pulling back the heavy hoods: his mother, Genevieve, Emanuel Jackson, one boy after another from the Milne Home, boys whose names he'd never spoken but that sounded out now in his head like the ringing of a bell — Delfree and Thomas and Skeeter and Paul, Marcel and Joseph and Roland and John. It was an unveiling that went on hour after hour. There was Emanuel Jackson's mother and father, his two sisters, the reverend's wife and daughter. There was the fat chimney sweep, his hundred starving children, his widowed wife. There was the not-yet-born baby of the kind woman he'd met on Magazine Street, the baby curled in a circle inside its dark robe like the moon in a pitch-black sky.

To each Shelton said, screamed, pleaded, *I fell from a tree, that's all,* though even in his dreams he knew there was more, knew that his fall had gone beyond just setting fire to his knees and hips, had gone beyond just ruining the way he walked. *That's all,* he said but heard the echo in his head, an echo that took on the same rising intonation he heard in his own name. *That's all?* the voice said. *Shelton Gerard Lafleur?*

Then the child opened his eyes to see what he first took for a

126

ghost but then realized was not — it was Minou's shape looming in the dim light of the doorway, Minou creeping his way out.

The mist from outside slipped into the house around Minou's head and shoulders as if sometime during the night, during all of the child's dreaming, the clouds had fallen from the sky or a hurricane wind had lifted the house in the air and left it there, tottering and tilting side to side.

That was memory, not a dream, taking hold of Shelton now. He remembered the turning pages, his mother's voice. He remembered how the rich farmer's house, swept up by a storm and set atop a curving rainbow, had tottered and tilted until the farmer's gold spilled from the cabinets where he stored it and the coins rolled out the door and down the rainbow, spilling like moonlight on sparkling rain through the chimneytops of the peasants' houses down below.

Yes, that was memory. His mother had held that book up before his eyes, and Shelton had looked and looked at the pictures, thinking of his own precious coins stored in the tin-top glass jar. Could such a thing really happen? Could he wake up and find their house in the air, the glass jar broken, the coins all gone?

"Oh, it can't," his mother had told him.

"How come?" Shelton had wanted to know.

"It's just a story," she'd said and proved it by closing the book and setting it aside, sweeping Shelton into her arms.

From where he lay on the sofa, Shelton looked at the shape before him. He could make out the old paint-splattered shirt and pants Minou wore, clothes that looked to him much like the ones he'd worn himself when he ran from the Milne Home. He saw the dark wooden case Minou held in one hand and swung out before him, his shoulder sagging with its weight. He saw the long, twisted stick Minou squeezed under his arm as he reached back to shut the door, as he leaned in to glance at Shelton the way Shelton had glanced at his mother that final time before he'd run off.

Maybe she'd been the same as he was now, Shelton thought — not asleep but only pretending to be, watching him all the while his back was turned, closing her eyes just as he thought to take a last look at her face. Maybe she'd sensed what he sensed now — the value a wordless leaving can have for the one taking leave, going off with the notion that there's not been a moment's disturbance to the peace and quiet in one's home.

Then Shelton closed his eyes and slept without any further dreams. He was glad to be left behind, glad not to start right away on what he feared would be nothing more than a dust-sweeping, stone-lifting, backbreaking job, a job that would make clear every single moment, as all that painting at the Milne Home had done, what his body couldn't do without enduring the pain that was less an ache in his muscles and joints and bones than it was — well, what?

Just name it, my hands say.

The child's shame, I answer, though maybe the child couldn't have said as much. *I fell from a tree*, he'd say time and again, only to hear his echoing question: *That's all?*

Well, here in this house was what he wanted, what he waited for the next two mornings after having it the first — falling back asleep so Adrienne could wake him with a whisper that he'd have to get up now or his breakfast would be cold. Olivia lingered over the last bites on her plate for no reason beyond courtesy, just so he'd have some company at the table while he ate.

As fast as he could so he wouldn't be seen, he'd slip on the clothes left out for him in a neat stack by the sofa — Minou's clothes, swallowing his body more than his own clothes had swallowed him, but feeling a better fit somehow — and he'd walk back to the kitchen, where Isabel directed kisses to every cheek, including his own, as she prepared to leave for her long day. She was a nursemaid just like Genevieve had been, though not to children or a bedridden young woman but to an old couple, a man and woman whose children had all grown.

The old couple had been at Genevieve's funeral. Shelton had seen them. They'd taken a seat at the back of the church, and Elise had pointed at them. "Look," she'd said, right out loud, "there's the Dried Bones."

Fast and fierce as lightning, Isabel had said, "Shush your mouth, child," and she'd raised her hand to Elise as if she might slap her.

The old couple's true name, Shelton would learn later from Olivia, was Hyde-Jones, and they were from across the ocean, in England. "You should hear how they sound," she told Shelton. "Like they're talking not from their mouths but from the back of their throats. 'Hello, hello, my dear.'" And Shelton laughed at Olivia's imitation, less at the sound of her voice than at the way she tilted her head up and scrunched her eyes shut and shook her head from side to side.

They were sweet, Olivia went on to say, and gave her whole family gifts, not just for their birthdays or for Christmas but also out of the blue — beautiful china dolls in linen dresses for her and Elise, a string of pearls for her mother, another for Adrienne, stacks of books for her father to read.

Minou, Shelton learned, liked to stay up with those books late into the night — so late that late became early, Olivia said, and he never did lie down to sleep. She said she'd crept up on him a time or two but never managed to scare him as she'd meant to do. He'd smile, wave her off, give her a kiss, then send her straight back to bed. And he'd go on sitting still at the kitchen table, his glasses slipped down on his nose, one of the books the old couple had given him opened up like it was the Holy Bible, the reflection of a candle's flame leaping in the glass of water he'd set down within his reach but never seemed to drink.

Shelton wondered what Minou learned from those books — maybe the trick of seeing with his eyes closed? of knowing others' thoughts? — and one evening he switched on the lamp by the sofa and paged through the books sitting on the table. They were the same books he'd scattered when he'd tried to run through the front room just after Elise, tapping her toes on the porch, had told him Genevieve was waiting inside.

As soon as he'd opened one book and then another, Shelton discovered that they weren't at all what he'd thought. They weren't about mystery and magic or how to do this and that. They were just stories of men and women who talked and talked about who had money and who didn't and who would marry whom. "It is a truth universally acknowledged," one of the books began, "that a single man in possession of a good fortune must be in want of a wife."

A good fortune, Shelton read. That's what he'd thought he'd collected in the glass jar. That was what Genevieve had said he didn't yet have but maybe one day would. Did he have it now? Shelton wondered. He thought he did.

And he'd thought so even on that first morning, before he'd taken a look at those books or knew the first thing about the old white couple except what Minou had leaned over at the funeral to tell him — that they'd come as a sign of their feelings for Isabel, white folks stepping among black to show that loss was loss no matter who'd been visited by it.

A Good Fortune. Couldn't you guess that I'd find a use for those words, that I'd put them to work naming a painting I'd done? And what else would that painting be except a jar of coins on the floor beside a child's empty bed, the coins shining in the glass as if they've been caught by the bright light of a morning sun? It's a simple work, happy as can be, the glass jar as inviting as a piece of rock candy, the bed's blankets warmed by the bright rays of the sun. There's not a single one who has asked why that bed is empty, where that child has gone. *A Good Fortune.* That's what it was, wasn't it?

A Good Fortune. In Minou's house, in his family's embrace, that's what the child had found.

❦ ❦ ❦

130

"You'll keep Shelton company?" Isabel had said that first morning to Olivia, who nodded and smiled and returned her mother's hug. Olivia's raised arms, the child Shelton thought, looked like the delicate frames of a butterfly's two wings, with her hands hidden behind her mother's neck.

"I will," she said.

"Not too far, though." Isabel lifted herself, brushing her hands across the ironed front of her white dress. "Just show him around. Maybe there's boys his age he could meet. What are the two Curtis children up to?"

"They're in the country again," Olivia said. "Berry-picking all summer. Dawn to dusk, Wendell said, but he likes the money that the white family pays him. You should see his hands when he comes back, all cut up and stained."

Elise laughed, and everyone in the room turned to her, which was exactly what her laughter was meant to have them do. "Why don't you go ahead and tell us how those hands feel?" she said, pushing past her mother to put her own hands on Olivia's back, rubbing them there in a manner that made Shelton turn away.

"You going to tell us or not?"

"Mama," Olivia said as if she were angry, though she laughed too. "Come get this groping pest off me."

"Elise," Isabel said. "Come here." She wrapped her arms around her daughter. "You be good."

Elise squirmed away. "I always am," she said. "And besides, I'm not the one talking about Wendell Curtis's fine scratchy hands."

"There's no one talking of such things in my house," Isabel said.

"There's not?" Elise said, hands on her hips in imitation of her mother. "Last night, maybe midnight or so, when you'd think everyone was sleeping —"

"Watch yourself," Isabel said.

"Didn't I hear you and Daddy —"

"You just hush right now," Isabel said, wrapping Elise in her arms again, putting a hand over Elise's mouth. "Hush, child," she said, laughing now as if it weren't just Olivia and Elise but she as well who was a young girl full of happy secrets.

She put Elise down and kissed her. "You do make me laugh," she said. "At a time like this, I'll thank you for that."

"Just look," Olivia said, smiling and turning to Shelton. "She tries causing trouble, says she's going to tell some secret, and she winds up with a kiss. You think that's fair?"

"I don't know," Shelton said, smiling back. "Don't I have to hear the secret first?"

"No, you don't," Isabel said, still holding Elise.

"Besides," Olivia said, "that girl's got a secret of her own. There's some boy she's seeing herself, now aren't you, Elise?"

Shelton looked at Elise, who glared back at him as if he were the one who'd spoken.

"If I was as nosy as you," Olivia said, "I'd know who it was."

"No, you wouldn't," Elise said.

"Then maybe I'll make myself that nosy. I'll put my mind to it."

Isabel let go of Elise now. "Stop it, you two." She walked around the table to Shelton. He pushed back his chair to stand, but she stopped him by placing her hands on his shoulders. "Don't get up," she said. "Just have a good time today, you hear?"

Shelton nodded and felt Isabel's lips brush his cheek. He smelled the clean smell of soap on her face or in her hair or on her white dress, he couldn't tell where. It was a smell that made his eyes close, it was so sweet.

Then Isabel called to Adrienne, who stepped into the kitchen carrying an oil-stained paper bag, which she set down on the counter. Isabel asked Adrienne if she'd see her out, and the two of them left the kitchen, headed for the front of the house. As soon as they were gone, Elise looked at Olivia and Shelton. She quickly reached into the paper bag on the counter. "Potatoes," she said. Then she smiled, turned, and followed her mother and aunt.

Olivia pushed her plate away and looked at Shelton. "She's going to go snoop," Olivia said.

"What's snoop?" Shelton asked.

"You know," she said.

"I don't," Shelton answered.

"It means she's going to listen in on all of what Mama and Aunt Adrienne are saying. Then she'll march back in here and tell us what they said."

"How do you know?" Shelton asked. He thought of his own actions as a child — watching Mr. Edward's visitors through cracked doors, seeing that woman and Mr. Edward's hands from the dark of the dressing closet, listening through the walls or, outside, through an open window. Was that snooping? He spooned his oatmeal into his mouth, careful not to spill it.

"I know because it's what she always does," Olivia said. "Maw-Maw'd tell her how her ears were going to turn beet red from such a habit, but Elise said if that's what they were going to do, they already would have. So that didn't stop her." Olivia waved her hand in front of her face to brush away a fly. "Just watch what you say. And it doesn't matter where. You can bet Elise is just around the corner."

"I will," Shelton said, finishing the last of his oatmeal. He set the spoon down in the bowl.

"You had enough?" Olivia asked.

"I did," Shelton said.

"You like it?"

"I did."

"I only like it with butter," Olivia said. "You ever had it like that?"

Shelton shook his head. Then he said, "Maybe I did. I don't remember."

"Well, that's the only way I like it. It's been a while since we've had some, though. Maybe Mama could bring some home. I could ask her. The folks she works for will give her about anything she asks for."

"How come?" Shelton said.

"They just will. They've been giving things away for years.

Mama says it's all that's keeping them alive. Lucky they're so rich, she says. She figures when they've run out of things to give away, they'll just die."

Shelton wondered if that could be true. What could he give away to keep himself alive? There wasn't anything.

"Why's she do it?" he said.

"Why's who do what?" Olivia said.

"Elise, I mean," Shelton said. "Why's she snoop?"

"I say it's just she's nosy," Olivia said, "but Daddy says it's because she's the youngest child. He says the youngest child's always feeling kept in the dark, like all the news of life has come and gone when she was just a baby."

"That's how I feel too," Shelton said.

Olivia looked at him across the table, and he felt he had to say something else, though he didn't know what. "I mean sometimes," he said. "Like there's nothing I've learned except by accident."

Olivia still just looked at him.

"I mean I snoop too, or did," Shelton said.

"Then maybe you were a youngest child too." Olivia stood up and carried her plate over to the sink.

"I was the only child," Shelton said.

"I mean your true family," Olivia said, running water in the sink, rinsing her plate.

"I don't know," Shelton said. "That's what I mean. I don't know anything."

"Well, maybe not knowing is the same thing as being the youngest child. You see?" She turned to Shelton, her hands holding a dishtowel.

"Maybe," he said.

"Maybe so," she said, and Shelton tried not to look at the way her dress swung from side to side as she dried her hands on the towel. He was sure his feelings for her were plain as day — the pleasure he took in her company.

Years later, Olivia would tell me that she had indeed noticed how I'd watched her those first few days, that she'd seen my eyes linger on her. I was just a child, though, she said, and she'd thought nothing of it. I was only thirteen and she was three years older. She just figured that living in a boys' home, I hadn't seen or been near or had the chance to talk to girls. "It was more," I said, stammering just like the child I'd once been, and Olivia looked away.

"You got any idea," she asked on that first day, "what you want to do today?"

"I don't," Shelton said.

"We'll think of something, then." She put the towel on the counter. "We could go over to Magazine Street. I've got friends working in some of the shops. You could meet them."

"That's fine," Shelton said. "Anything."

"Maybe I'll see if Aunt Adrienne's got a dollar we could use to buy you some clothes of your own." She laughed, then stopped. "I'm sorry, but Daddy's don't quite fit you."

"They don't?" Shelton said, smiling and raising his arms, flapping them like a bird's wings, the shirt's shoulderline down to his elbows. "I think they're just fine."

Olivia laughed, throwing her head back so that Shelton was left looking at her long, smooth neck. "Then you're as blind as my daddy pretends to be."

Shelton wanted to ask how her father did that with his eyes. He wanted to ask if she knew. But he laughed and said, "I'm not blind. I'm just crippled."

Olivia stopped laughing and looked at him, her expression the same as Shelton had seen on the faces of the Milne Home teachers when they called on him to answer some math or history question and he wouldn't.

"Don't say that," she said.

"I am," Shelton said. "It's true."

Olivia sat down again at the table. "Can I ask you something, Shelton?"

Shelton waited.

"What were the boys like where you lived? Were they tough?"

"They were okay," Shelton said.

"Elise says they beat you up. She says she heard Maw-Maw talking about it with one of the women from the choir who'd come sit by her bed. That true?"

Shelton looked down at his lap, at his hands folded there.

"Why'd they beat you up?" Olivia asked.

Shelton looked up at her now. "Because of what I told you," he said. "Because I'm a cripple."

"How do you know that's why?"

"I just do," Shelton said.

"Well, that's just cruelness," Olivia said. "That's all that is."

"I know," Shelton said, seeing his mother's face, hearing her voice. *Behave.*

"It make you mad?"

"It did," Shelton said.

Olivia stood up. "You ever see one of those boys, you tell me," she said. She took Shelton's bowl and carried it over to the counter. "I know ones who are tougher. They'd make those who hit you wish they hadn't. I mean it."

And Shelton imagined one of Olivia's friends, maybe that one named Wendell Curtis, taking hold of the Milne Home boys one by one, whipping them each with that bamboo switch, wrapping his berry-stained fingers around their throats and saying, *This is for Shelton Lafleur. This is on account of what you've done.*

"Can I ask you something now?" Shelton said.

"Of course you can," Olivia said, crossing her arms and looking over at Shelton.

"Why is it I'm here?" Shelton asked. "Why'd your father come get me?"

"Maw-Maw asked for you," Olivia said. "Daddy says she'd been feeling sorry for you ever since you were a baby. She didn't think a colored child belonged being raised by that girl. She said it wasn't the natural order of things."

"That's all?" Shelton said.

"That's all Daddy said, though Daddy and Mama and Maw-Maw talked on and on about it for days. But it was all mostly quiet talk, so even Elise couldn't hear. She tried, of course. You know she did."

And now, as if she'd heard Olivia speak her name, Elise ran back into the kitchen. Olivia put her hands on her hips and waited. Elise looked at her and then at Shelton.

"Just go ahead," Olivia said.

"Mama said —" Elise stopped and stepped back to the kitchen door to close it. Then Shelton listened as the words sprang from her mouth like a flock of pigeons taking flight. "Mama said how Mr. Samuel Warren is a no-good dirty stinking rat with not an ounce of goodness in his fat black body and she didn't care if Adrienne said as much to his only son because it was true and he ought to know it."

"What's he done?" Olivia asked.

"It's not what he's done, it's what he's asking for." Elise opened the kitchen door, looked out, and shut it again. "He wants the money for taking care of Maw-Maw. Her arrangements, Mama said he called it. He wants it this minute, she said. Twenty-three dollars for fixing her up like a wax statue and for the box they put her in and for the hole in the ground next to Paw-Paw. Mama says he had the nerve to tap Daddy's shoulder before they'd even finished the Lord's Prayer or started throwing the dirt back in. He said how he'd need it in a week's time though he'd rather have it sooner."

"What did Daddy say?" Olivia asked.

Elise laughed. "He was blistering mad, Mama said. He told Samuel Warren that for all he cared he could haul out Maw-Maw's box and place it at our front door. He said that would be a fine idea because it would leave a space for Mr. Warren to go right ahead and take her place."

"Then what?" Olivia said.

"Then Mr. Warren said, 'I don't suppose you're threatening my well-being, Minou Parrain.' And Daddy says, 'I don't give a damn about your well-being, Samuel Warren. What I'm threatening is your life.' Even Mama laughed telling Aunt Adrienne."

Elise and Olivia laughed too, but then the kitchen door swung open and Adrienne stepped in.

"What's so funny?" she said, but Elise and Olivia didn't answer. She turned to Shelton. "What's so funny, I said."

Shelton felt his body shaking. "Elise . . ." he stammered. "She was just this minute telling us a funny story."

"About what?" Adrienne asked, glaring at Shelton.

Shelton tried to think of something to tell her but couldn't. "I don't know," he said.

"I know what she was telling you," Adrienne said, leaning her face toward Shelton's, as if by doing so her words would be heard only by him. "Don't let that child make you into a liar, Shelton."

Shelton looked at Adrienne, wondering at the change in her manner, in her whole bearing, as if her shyness had marched off with Isabel to leave behind a different woman, one who threw her shoulders back and stomped her foot and shouted, one who scared him.

Shelton thought of how when he'd first seen Adrienne and Isabel walking toward the house, he'd known they were sisters, for they'd looked so much alike. Maybe the truth, though, was that she was as different from Isabel as Elise was from Olivia. With Adrienne still leaning near him as if she were waiting for an answer, Shelton wondered if all sisters were like that — one of them full of warmth, the other cold and brittle, frightening. She hadn't seemed that way before, but now she did, and Shelton wondered whether he needed to watch himself with her the way Minou and Olivia had said he needed to watch himself with Elise.

Shelton kept silent and wished Adrienne would back away from him, leave him alone. Finally she did. She stepped away and turned to Elise. "You've got some kind of nerve, child, don't you?" she said, grabbing the dishtowel from the counter and swinging it at Elise. "Your daddy's right. You're the devil's child."

"That makes you the devil's relation, now don't it?" Elise said, dodging around the kitchen and laughing as Adrienne chased after her. Shelton ducked his head when they shot past him, as if he were the one they were running after.

Then Adrienne stopped and caught her breath. "This is family affairs," she said, angry, defeated, raising the towel to her neck and patting it on one side, then the other. "The least you can do is not go blabbing it house to house."

"She won't," Olivia said.

"Besides," Elise said, "I got a way to take care of Samuel Warren."

"No you don't," Adrienne said, her voice rising in anger again. "You leave that man alone. That's for your mama and daddy and me to work out."

"Then I won't tell you," Elise said.

"That's just fine," Adrienne said, turning toward the kitchen door.

"You're just worried about Joshua Warren, that's all," Elise said.

Adrienne turned back to her. "You shut your mouth."

"You're just afraid he won't give you that ring he's got stashed in his drawer."

"You don't know a thing about that," Adrienne said. "Not one thing."

"You'll just see what I know," Elise said, and she ran for the kitchen door, trying to dodge a last swipe of the towel from Adrienne. But the towel struck her back like a loud clap of thunder, a slap that, Shelton could see, made Elise wince as if she'd been bitten by some sharp-toothed animal.

Then Elise was gone, the kitchen door slamming behind her, and Shelton imagined a small red mark rising on her back like the ones he'd gotten from the bamboo switch. He imagined her running to her room and turning her head to look over her shoulder, under her dress, and see it.

Olivia turned to Shelton. "That's life in this house," she said. "I'm sorry."

Shelton started to say that he didn't mind, that he'd seen worse exchanges every day of the five years he'd spent in the Milne Home, pointing and whispering and name-calling, fights on the dormitory floor or on the great green lawn or beneath the dining room's thick-legged tables, one boy winding up on top of another and shouting, *You take that back or I'll kill you.*

I'm grateful to be here, is all, Shelton wanted to say. But he turned to look at Adrienne and then turned back to Olivia and didn't speak. In his head he was still seeing Elise, her dress slipped off her shoulder to show the red mark on her back, her dress falling to the floor and forming a circle of cloth around her feet.

How is it that such a moment as this produced for the child such thoughts? Well, he was thirteen years old and, for the first time in his life, in the company of girls. But there was more to the moment than that, something else to it that the child couldn't name, something he'd see years later, when he spent his time paging through books showing works of art — Degas's bathers, bending down with a towel to dry their legs or twisting at the waist to dry their hair. And he'd try to use that same radiant, speckled light in his own work: a girl, a young woman, her head turned to look over her shoulder, a circle of cloth at her feet, the mark on her back just one stroke of color among a hundred others.

What had he named that work, which was not about the light or that girl or her injury but about his own quiet longing? I don't remember. I swear I don't.

What I do remember is Adrienne turning to Shelton and saying, "Nothing's easy right now," Shelton looking at her and nodding and feeling his fingers curl and touch his palms, feeling them stretch out again as if his hands were reaching of their own accord to touch that mark on Elise's back, to touch the remembered marks on his own.

"I know," he said. "I do." And he closed his eyes just like Minou to hold on to the pleasure of his imagining.

❧ ❧ ❧

Later that first morning, Elise disappeared, running from the house despite Adrienne's shouts that she had chores to do first, clothes that needed to be washed and hung out to dry. These were the clothes that Adrienne gathered in bundles from those in the neighborhood too old or sick to wash for themselves. They paid Adrienne a quarter for every bundle, which she returned to them in tall stacks tied together with twine.

Olivia took Shelton to Magazine Street, and they wandered from shop to shop. Shelton shook hands with Olivia's friends but backed away as quickly as he could to walk up and down the aisles while Olivia told how he'd come to be living with her family. She called him over from time to time to explain this or that, to answer her friends' questions about the Milne Home, which they all seemed to see as a place full of dark secrets and mystery.

Olivia added on to the story as they went along. She told how her father had gone three straight days and lingered near the home, wondering how he'd set about stealing Shelton, then lo and behold on the fourth day Shelton had just stepped up like a dog fetched by one of those silent whistles.

"No," Shelton would call out from wherever he was listening. "I ran out myself, that's what."

How come? Olivia's friends wanted to know.

"I was mad," Shelton said.

About what?

"About being there."

That's all?

"That was enough."

You weren't afraid they'd catch you?

"I wasn't."

And lock you up?

"No."

You've got some nerve, boy.

"They tried to beat me up."

You've got some nerve, child.

"I couldn't stand it another day."

You've got some nerve, I'll say that.

"Yes, I guess I do."

And from friend to friend, shop to shop, the story lengthened, grew more mysterious and grand. Morning became noon, hot as a house on fire, and now Minou was as clever and courageous as a spy, Shelton as brave as a soldier, his escape on the bus as daring as if he'd leapt upon a moving freight car.

His legs' sorry state, which couldn't be ignored, was left unexplained, as if that silence served to confirm rather than contradict the story — Shelton's awkward, swinging steps the high price of his great daring, his legs injured, the silence suggested, only during his escape and not five years earlier from his fall.

Olivia steered him from block to block the way Genevieve, holding his hand in her own, had steered him along Magazine Street years before. Olivia didn't take hold of his hand, of course, but it didn't matter to Shelton. She walked slowly enough for him to remain always at her side, letting him forget, for that short time, his strange swinging steps, the scraping of his shoes on the ground. He walked on the inside, away from the street, so he wouldn't have to see, when he looked at Olivia, his own reflection in the shop windows. Instead, he imagined how his back had in the course of that one day grown straight, how his legs had grown not just better but strong. The imagining felt, for those few moments, like enough to make it so.

And the second day, after another night of dreaming, another morning of breakfast, they went back to Magazine Street, Elise with them now. Shelton tried not to fear this girl's sharp, stinging tongue, tried to laugh like Olivia at the way she could spin circumstance into a complicated web of truth and lies, the two so intertwined you couldn't decide what was what and so were better off not trying.

She told them that the day before, when Olivia was off with Shelton, she'd gone to Samuel Warren's home. "Around back," she said, "to where he takes in the bodies."

"You didn't," Olivia said.

"I did," Elise said. "I stepped right up and knocked on the door."

"Then what?" Olivia said, already swept up, Shelton could tell, by the promise of Elise's story.

"What do you think I did?" Elise answered. "I offered him a piece of my mind. I said how my daddy would see him six feet under if that's what it took."

"That's a lie," Olivia said.

"It is not," Elise said. "His fat belly was shaking and shaking like a big bowl of jelly. And you know the way he talks. He said, 'I'm appalled a child would be sent to convey such angry sentiments.' So I told him there was more to it than that. 'What might that be?' he said, and I said, 'I'll just show you.' He put his hands in his pockets and jiggled the coins there to show how he was just waiting, so I went ahead and did it."

"Did what?" Olivia said, looking at Elise and then at Shelton, her eyes wide and shining and beautiful.

"I punched that fat belly of his," Elise said, throwing her arm out now and punching air.

"You didn't!" Olivia screamed, laughing.

"That's what you think."

"I do."

"Well, I did and I can prove it."

"How?" Shelton said; he couldn't help himself.

Elise turned to look at him the way Emanuel Jackson had done

143

that time on the bus when Shelton had put his silence aside to speak. Then she turned back to Olivia. "You take a good look at him sometime. Take a good look and tell me whether or no Samuel Warren wears a woman's corset."

"Go on," Olivia said, bending over in laughter.

"Got it off some poor white woman's dead body, I'll bet you," Elise said.

"There's the lie," Olivia said. "No white woman, dead or not, is going to land in Samuel Warren's hands."

"Some do," Elise said. "You know who?"

"We don't," Olivia said, and Shelton nodded to show he didn't know either, but wanted to.

"The ones who take money to lie down with Negroes," Elise said. "I heard Joshua Warren tell Adrienne it was so. No white undertaker, he said, will touch those women. And anyway, I felt it there. I did. It hurt my hand."

"If that's all true, and I don't think it is, Mama's going to kill you," Olivia said. "Daddy too."

"Samuel Warren's not going to say a word, I'll bet you," Elise said. "You watch. He's too scared."

"What about all Daddy owes?" Olivia said.

"I bet he won't mention that either. He thinks it's true, I'm telling you. He thinks Daddy would kill him."

"He wouldn't," Olivia said, turning to Shelton as if this were something she wanted to make sure he knew.

"But I might," Elise said, smiling and turning her head away. "I just might do it." And though he couldn't see her face, Shelton thought he knew what expression was showing there — the same one that appeared when the dishtowel popped against her back. He felt sorry for her now.

But Olivia was laughing, so Shelton laughed too. He pictured Elise raising her arm to punch that man, knocking him down and climbing on top of him the way the boys had fought, using their knees to pin the other's arms to the ground. He saw Elise putting her hands on the man's throat and squeezing tighter and tighter until that thing she said was around his stomach, the woman's corset, popped open and the man gasped for every breath, wheezing and coughing and spitting the way Shelton had heard Genevieve wheeze and cough and spit and then grow silent. Shelton saw Elise standing over the man's dead body, smiling the same way she was smiling now, as though she were nothing but proud of herself for everything she'd ever thought or said or done. Even this. Even now.

Shelton looked at Olivia and Elise, turned his head from one to the other, knowing only that he wanted to feel inside him the great shining radiance and grace of the one and the fierce, satisfying power and rage of the other. He wanted both, he did, and just by their presence, by their standing next to him, speaking his name, he felt he had it. He was happy, wasn't he? So he laughed and laughed, his laughter good and strong.

❧ ❧ ❧

The third day, Adrienne gave them each a dime and they rode the streetcar to Audubon Park. Shelton looked for the tree where he'd fallen but didn't see it, didn't see anything familiar at all. The tree was an oak surrounded by magnolias, he remembered, but that didn't help. There were oaks and magnolias everywhere, and each one looked just like the others. He looked back across St. Charles Avenue in search of the street where he'd lived, the alley he'd run down, certain that he'd find, if he looked long enough, the exact path he'd taken to get there. But he didn't.

"Come on, Shelton," he heard the girls yell, and he turned this way and that as though he were lost.

"Here," Elise said, and Shelton looked to see her sitting on one of the two concrete lions that marked the entrance to the park. Did he even remember that? He didn't.

He walked over, and Olivia said to Elise, "You better get off. They'll make you wash and scrub it."

"I'd just paint it," Elise answered, reaching forward to run her hand along the lion's mane. "I'd paint it gold, that's what."

"Then you'd scrub it some more, girl," Olivia said. "Come on."

"Where are we going?" Shelton asked, and Olivia pointed.

"Over there," she said. Shelton looked. He didn't see anything.

"You can't see it from here," Olivia said. "It's too far."

So they walked through the park, Shelton reaching out as they passed one oak tree and the next to touch the rough bark, to feel it scratching at his fingertips as he went by, reminding him of falling. They passed old men and women sitting on stone benches just like the ones he'd seen in that park on Tchoupitoulas Street where he'd gone with Minou. They came upon white people, young and old, out walking their dogs, which strained against their leashes when Olivia and Elise, with Shelton following close behind, walked by.

"He don't like coloreds," one woman said, smiling, using two hands to drag her dog past.

"That's okay," Elise said, smiling back. "We don't like white folks."

Olivia grabbed Elise then and pulled her on. "You're just crazy," she said, but she was laughing, and Shelton thought he saw for just a moment in Olivia's eyes the wildness and daring that belonged to Elise.

Then Shelton did see where they were going — to the hill that Minou and all those other men had built for the WPA. It was smaller than Shelton had imagined, more like the Indian burial mound he'd seen a picture of in his history book at the Milne Home. The grass growing on it wasn't what he'd pictured either — not a smooth, rich covering of green but clumps and patches between the worn-down stretches of earth where, Shelton imagined, children had run up and down a million times.

"Monkey Hill," Shelton said.

"My daddy built it," Elise said.

"I know," Shelton said. "He told me."

"He tell you why?" Elise said.

"There wasn't a why, he said. He told me it was just for children."

"I mean why he was one made to dig it."

Shelton shook his head.

"He didn't mention his legs being in chains?" Elise said. "Or the men with guns tucked under their arms?"

Shelton looked at Elise. He laughed.

"He didn't mention any of that, did he?"

"He said the WPA —"

"I told you to watch how he lies, didn't I?" Elise said.

"Stop it now," Olivia said, shoving Elise's shoulder. "Don't listen to that nonsense, Shelton." Olivia ran ahead and then called back, "Come on."

"What?" Shelton said to Elise. He wanted to hear her story.

"You still want to know about Wendell's hands, don't you?" Olivia called to Elise.

Elise looked at Shelton. "Oh, I'll tell you sometime, I suspect."

Shelton watched her run ahead to catch up with Olivia, then watched the two of them start to run together, holding hands and gathering speed to make it straight up the hill. Shelton followed after them as best as he could, his body leaning forward, his hands touching the ground again and again as he climbed.

At the top, Shelton leaned over, his hands on his thighs, his breath straining at his chest, his heart pounding inside the way it had when he'd run from the Milne Home. "That was hard," he said.

"Now make a wish," Olivia said.

"How come?" he asked, standing up straight, feeling the muscles in his back tug and pull.

"That's what you do," Olivia said, shutting her eyes and throwing her head back. "You make a wish, then run down."

"I can't do that," Shelton said.

"Then I'll show you what," Olivia said. She sat down, and Elise sat too. "Come on, Shelton," Olivia said, and the girls slid apart to let Shelton sit between them. They took his hands. "Now the wish is no good," Olivia said, "unless you keep wishing it the whole way down. You ready?"

"I don't know," Shelton said.

"You better start wishing," Elise said, "because here we go," and she tugged on his arm and then Olivia did too, and the three of them rolled down the hill, Shelton's hands slipping free as he fell on his side and tumbled down, one shoulder and then the other striking the ground, his head snapping around over and over.

At the bottom, Shelton laughed and laughed as gray dust settled over the three of them. Olivia was stretched out facedown in the grass. Elise was on her back, her dress twisted around her legs.

Olivia lifted her head, turned to Shelton, and said, "Now, what was your wish?"

Shelton tried to sit up. "I couldn't think of one," he said.

Elise rolled over to him and reached up to slap his head. "So it's not just your feet that's slow, is it?" she said.

Shelton reached up and caught Elise's arm, grabbing hold of her wrist, feeling his fingers touch his thumb.

"Let me loose," she said, but she didn't pull away. Instead, she fell into him and they both rolled over onto their sides.

"Get up now, you two," Olivia said.

"I can't," Shelton said. "Everything's spinning."

"You have to get up," Olivia said, standing now, leaning down to take Shelton's hand, pulling on his arm as if she meant to break it.

"Let go," he said, still laughing.

"No," she said. "We've got to do it again or else we'll all have bad luck."

"It's true," Elise said, standing and grabbing his other arm. "You better find a wish quick, boy."

So Shelton stood and walked up the hill, the two girls still holding his arms, keeping him from falling.

"What's your wish, Shelton?" Olivia asked once they'd reached the top of the hill.

"No," Elise said. "Don't say it." She pulled Shelton to the ground. "You can't say it except when you're done."

Then the girls pulled down on his arms again, and now they were rolling and tumbling and flying through the air, and as the sky and ground turned end over end Shelton could not, no matter how he tried, wish for anything.

11   THE STRONG MEN

THE NEXT MORNING Shelton woke not to Minou's figure slipping through the doorway but to a voice, Minou's voice, whispering in his ear: "Time to wake, mon minet."

Mon minet, the child Shelton heard in his head, and his other voices joined in: *Carencro*, one said. *Pigeon Foot*, said another. *Creampuff Sissy. Eightball. Silent, Stupid Shelton.*

The child opened his eyes and pushed himself up on the sofa. The quilt was still wrapped around his waist and legs as though he were a hunter's bagged bird, a dove or quail. He struggled a moment, then pulled the quilt free.

"Come on now," Minou said. "We've got to beat the light of day."

Minou folded the quilt and set it down in his lap, staring at Shelton as if he still weren't certain the child was awake. Shelton stared back at Minou. What had he been dreaming? Not about the lepers again. Not that.

Then what? Then who?

Mr. Edward.

Mr. Edward, yes. About Mr. Edward. In his dream he'd heard a knock on the door and opened it to find Mr. Edward standing there, his hair a tangle of weeds falling down over his face, his clothes tattered and torn. "I just found out," Mr. Edward said, leaning on the door frame and panting as though he'd just run some great distance to find Shelton. "I just found out," he said again, and Shelton took Mr. Edward's hand, his nails long and sharp and gray with dirt, black with blood or ink, and led him through the house, showed him Minou reading by candlelight in the kitchen, Olivia and Elise sleeping in their beds, Adrienne and Isabel whispering to each other in the darkness of the room where Genevieve's dead body still slumped on the chair in the corner, the lamp next to her gone out.

Then he brought Mr. Edward back to the front room and pointed to the couch. "Here's where you'll sleep," Shelton told him, and Mr. Edward lay down, pulled the quilt Adrienne had made over his body, and slept.

Shelton watched him sleep, watched his legs and arms twitch and fly out time and again as if to defend him from some imagined attack, and Shelton kept watching, made himself stay awake though he was tired, sure that at any moment Mr. Edward would sit up and tell him about his mother, tell him where she was, how he could find her.

Shelton looked at Minou now. "Where are we going?" he asked. "I'm sleepy."

"Sleeping's fine so long as you can walk while you're doing it," Minou said. "Can you?"

"I can," Shelton said.

"Then all's well," Minou said, pointing to the table where Shelton's clothes lay. Shelton reached for them and saw that they were the ones he'd worn when he left the Milne Home, folded and washed now but still stained with turpentine and paint.

"Come on, child, skittle-scat. You won't need any fine attire today. The worse off they are, the better," Minou said.

"I'm going with you to work?" Shelton asked, pulling on the pants while he sat facing Minou, pulling the legs over one foot and then the other.

"Going to work? Yes, you are," Minou said. "Get yourself dressed. We're running late."

Shelton moved, tried to stand, but he felt the pain shoot through him. His body was sore from rolling down the hill, from laughing and laughing in the grass and dirt. One of his hips, he saw now, was marked with a bruise, a green and purple circle. Minou reached out to touch it, as if that touch were meant to heal him.

"How'd you get that?" Minou said, pulling his hand away, watching Shelton cover the bruise with his pulled-up pants.

"Monkey Hill," Shelton said, dull fingers buttoning the brown rusted buttons.

"You tripped and fell?" Minou asked, but Shelton shook his head.

Minou leaned near, as if he could see the bruise through the cloth of Shelton's pants. "The girls made you roll down, didn't they?" he said, and Shelton nodded.

"Well, how'd it feel?" Minou asked, sitting up.

"Good," Shelton said. "I had a good time."

"I'm glad," Minou said. "I've told them they're too old to still be doing that, but they don't listen."

"We went by the river too," Shelton said, pulling on his shirt now, tucking it into his pants. "We saw a riverboat. A real one, white and red."

"Did you now?" Minou said, standing up. "I'll have to tell you about that sometime."

"About what?" Shelton said. He sat back down to put on his shoes.

"My father served as captain's boy on one called the *Dixie Queen*. I was just a young boy, but he took me along once. They put me to work like I was earning a grown man's wage, though I wasn't, so I didn't go back."

When Shelton had finished tying his shoes, he followed Minou to the door. "Where'd you go?" he asked.

"On the water, you mean?"

Shelton nodded.

"Just up the river to Baton Rouge and back," Minou said. "Here." He handed Shelton the long wooden stick. "Could you take that?"

They stepped outside, Minou carrying the wooden box. He shut the door behind them.

"What's this stick for?" Shelton asked.

"It's for walking," Minou said.

It was nearly light now. The houses along Foucher Street appeared before Shelton as if they were stepping forward one by one through the mist. "If you can't see," Minou said, "you need one of these."

"Who can't see?" Shelton asked.

"I told you," Minou said. "Didn't I say how there's a trick to my work?"

Shelton nodded.

"Well, that's it," Minou said. "I play the part of a blind man. I make my pictures keeping my eyes closed, like I couldn't open them if I tried."

"Why?" Shelton asked. Even carrying the heavy box, Minou was walking too fast. He set the box down and waited for Shelton to catch up.

"It makes my living," Minou said. "It gives folks something in return for their kindness. The worse off you are, the better they feel. You understand?"

Shelton looked at Minou, thinking about the riverboat, about Minou riding on one to Baton Rouge and back, looking out over all that swirling, rushing water, tracking the swimming fish or broken tree limbs or whatever else shot past.

"Well, you'll see," Minou said. "They come from near and far. Hearts full of pity and pockets full of change. The Blind Man of Jackson Square, they call me. They say how the Lord has reached out and touched me, how he's given me a special kind of sight that comes not from the eyes but from the heart."

"Is it true?" Shelton asked.

Minou laughed. "Truth's not the issue here," he said. "Making my living's the issue. Feeding my family. Putting clothes on their backs." Again Minou stopped and set down the box to let Shelton catch up. "Now, if truth was the issue, Shelton, I'd say it's more true than not. In fact I can see, so that part's not right. But the other? About having a special kind of sight? There are times when I think it's so. Other times I think I'm more like a circus clown than what I'd hoped to be."

"What did you hope for?" Shelton asked.

Minou shifted the box from one hand to the other. "When I was coming up, Shelton," he said, "you mostly gave your attention to what you didn't want to be, like a captain's boy on a travelers' boat or a sharecropper or a nigger migrant. The thing you didn't want to do was whatever you'd seen your mama or daddy doing. You didn't want to wash white folks' clothes or work their fields, because you saw where that got you."

"Where?" Shelton asked, breathing hard now from trying to keep up.

"It got you more clothes to wash and more fields to work, that's where."

They reached St. Charles Avenue, and Shelton followed Minou as he crossed over to the neutral ground. They stood by the streetcar tracks. "I draw pictures," Minou said, looking down at Shelton. "Folks hand me money and hang my pictures on their walls. What's that make me?" He set the box down at his feet.

Shelton thought about the time when a white-haired woman had come to paint his mother's portrait. His mother had sat up in bed, let her hair fall across her shoulders, straightened as much as she could straighten her curled body, stretched out her fingers one by one in her lap. And Shelton had watched for hours and hours, for more days than he could count, sitting behind the white-haired woman so he could see both his mother's face and the way it took shape on the canvas. When the woman began painting a dark red dress, as if that were what his mother was wearing, Shelton had stepped up and said, "That's not right. There." And he'd shot his finger toward the canvas and touched it. A circle of the dark red paint stuck to his fingertip, as if someone had pricked it.

What had the woman done then? She'd smiled at his mother and then turned to him, her smile disappearing. "Oh, it is right, dear," she'd said. "It's precisely right. You'll see." And she'd grabbed his hand and with a white cloth wiped off his finger. "There," she'd said.

The child turned to his mother.

"She's not taking a photograph, Shelton," his mother said. "She's an artist. That's what artists do." And the child had felt embarrassed, betrayed somehow by his mother.

"An artist?" Shelton said now to Minou.

"Well, you said it, not me." Minou stretched his arms up in the air. "That case feels heavy this morning."

"You did those ones in the house?" Shelton said. "The ones of Isabel and Genevieve. I saw them."

"Yes, I did," Minou said.

"They're good," Shelton said. "They look just like them. Or did, I mean." The dead, swollen face of Genevieve flashed through the child's mind as if that were the picture Minou had drawn.

Minou reached out and put his hand on Shelton's head. "That's kind of you, Shelton," he said. "Maybe it's a sad state of affairs when one is grateful for a child's praise, but I am."

"They *are* good," Shelton said, thinking of the sorrow in the lines of Genevieve's face, the dark beauty of Isabel's.

"Well, they're nothing much," Minou said.

Through the mist, Shelton saw a light shining in the distance. Minou took off his glasses and put them in his pants pocket, then

155

he took the long stick from Shelton. "Here's where it starts," he said. "Most times, he lets me ride for free. Here." Minou handed Shelton a nickel. "Just hold on to that," he said. "You make those legs of yours perform a little worse and you just might get the same treatment."

When the streetcar screeched to a stop before them and its door swung open, Minou reached out with his stick and struck the car's side.

"Over here, blind man," the conductor said. "Step's over here."

Shelton watched as Minou tapped the stick along the car until it landed on the step.

"That's it, now," the conductor said.

"I got family with me today," Minou said, his head turned up, his eyes squeezed shut.

Shelton stepped onto the car behind Minou. He tried but didn't know how to make his legs worse than they were, so he put one hand on his hip the way he'd seen old people with bent backs do, and he made his face twitch as if he were in pain.

"That's a relation?" the conductor said, pinching his fingers on the brim of his black hat. He pushed the hat back, revealing a thick red line across his forehead. "You got some kind of sad family, blind man," he said.

"Poor child," Minou said, tapping his stick as he stood in the aisle. "My sister's boy. Was an automobile accident crippled him and just last month." He swung around and the long stick struck Shelton's leg, a slap that made him think of Elise, made her bare back flash in his mind the way Genevieve's dead face had just done. He thought of the dark red circle on his fingertip, which wasn't paint now but Elise's blood. Shelton felt his body flinch, not from Minou's stick but from what flashed through his mind — that Elise had taken the place of the woman in that photograph passed around the Milne Home. It was her body naked, sprawling on a giant bed. It was her legs stretched open, her mouth shaped into an inviting O, calling out his name.

156

"Seems I was the one driving but shouldn't have been," Minou said. "Didn't see that man's Ford coming, though I heard it. It's just I took all that honking for a goose."

The conductor laughed. "Get on," he said. "Least you can still tell a joke."

"I can sing too," Minou said, and as he walked to the back of the streetcar, Shelton walking behind him, he started singing, his voice deeper and stronger than Shelton would have guessed it would be. "Ever since my woman been dead in her grave," Minou sang, "rocks been my pillow and crossties my bed."

"Blind man, you sing about as well as you see," the conductor called back to them.

"I wish I did," Minou said, and Shelton saw Minou open his eyes and smile and then close his eyes again. "Yes, I only wish that was true," he said. "I'd go sing for the Duke. I'd send off that woman he's got. I'd send her off, though first, of course, I'd give her my home address. 'You just wait for me, sweetie,' I'd tell her. 'I'd sure wait for you, but first I've got to show these folks a thing or two about singing.'"

"Go on," the conductor called back to Minou. "You'd wait a long time, that's what."

"I got a long time," Minou shouted. "Time's one thing I got in aces and spades."

"Well, I don't," the conductor said, and the streetcar jerked forward, sending Minou tumbling to the floor. Shelton, though, was holding on.

"Now it's me," Minou said, standing and smiling and dusting himself off, slipping past Shelton to take his seat near the window. "Can't show a blind man a moment's courtesy, now can he?"

"No," Shelton said, and because Minou was laughing, he laughed too.

The streetcar moved from block to block, and the giant wood and brick houses on St. Charles Avenue were replaced by buildings four and five and six stories high. Shelton leaned over Minou to see out until Minou stood up and let him slide over by the window. "I guess I don't need a window seat, now do I?" Minou said.

By now the streetcar was nearly full, and Shelton saw how everyone turned and looked at Minou. It was the same look people trained on him, Shelton knew — a look half of feeling sorry, half of fear and disgust.

"People are looking," Shelton whispered, hand covering his mouth as if he might cough.

"That's how it works," Minou said back. "That's how the game starts. Don't let it worry you."

Then the streetcar swung around a wide circle with a statue in the middle, the pedestal too high for Shelton to see who the figure standing up at the top was. Shelton imagined looking down from such a height, seeing the whole city, searching and searching until he found his own house. He thought about the map Minou had showed him, about how Minou had promised to get one for him.

"Where are we?" Shelton asked. "Can you tell?"

"Indeed I can," Minou told him. "We're making the turn at Lee Circle."

"Who's that statue of?" Shelton asked.

"It's General Lee," Minou said.

"It is?" Shelton said, thinking of the streetcorner near the Milne Home, of the tiles embedded in the pavement.

"Yes, it is," Minou said. "You know what they say, don't you?"

"No," Shelton said.

"They say he's up there to keep an eye on us, making sure we keep our place."

Shelton turned around in his seat as the streetcar passed the statue. One of Lee's legs, he saw, was in front of the other at the pedestal's edge, as if at any moment he might step down. Maybe it was here and not at that other streetcorner, Shelton thought, where this man was buried. He turned back to Minou. "Where's our place?"

Minou laughed and shook his head. "I wonder if it's good or

bad all you don't understand," he said. "Think of it this way and you got one chance in a million, which is better than none. We've got to make our own place or else we won't have one."

Shelton didn't understand what Minou meant, or he understood just enough to hear again his mother's voice: *Behave.*

"There's a place up in New York called Harlem," Minou said. "You ever heard of it, Shelton?"

"No," Shelton said.

"I didn't think you had," Minou said. "That's our place. That's how we make one."

"What's there?" Shelton asked.

"Negroes," Minou said. "Thousands and thousands of them, and of every kind. Doctors and lawyers and artists. Black folks sweeping those streets but with a smile. Black folks teaching the children how to count. Black folks driving their own cars, singing their own songs, making a living without a fat white hand reaching into their pockets." Minou turned toward Shelton and opened his eyes, then closed them again. "Just picture that."

And Shelton did try to picture it, and later, of course, when the child had grown, the man he'd become would go see it for himself. Yes, I'd walk those noisy, dirty streets and look hard at each and every one of the faces I passed, looking the way the child had looked from face to face in the St. Louis Cathedral, looking this time for one that looked like Minou's, feeling certain that if he'd wound up anywhere on this earth, it would be there, one man among thousands who could tell a story like his own, of pretending for years a certain blindness just to put food down on a table, of finally winding up with no choice but to open his eyes and run.

And I'd take a circle of men on 116th Street, let them wear their suits and neckties, their white shirts and navy-blue suspenders. I'd let them hold their hats across their chests or slap them against their thighs, let their mouths open wide in wild merriment. That's *The Strong Men*, and couldn't one of them be Minou?

"Yes, that's one place too far, you can bet, for old General Lee,"

Minou told Shelton on the streetcar that morning. "It's there, child, where we ought to be."

And maybe Shelton should have known at that moment that Minou was as good as holding a map in front of them, spreading it across their laps, pointing to a black X. But he just watched as Minou nodded his head and slapped his hand against the seat in front of them.

The streetcar turned off the circle and now it was traveling down a narrow street of even taller buildings, their stone sides slick and wet as though it had been raining but only on this one street.

When the streetcar turned one more time and pulled to a stop, the conductor shouted, "Canal Street! Canal Street! Final stop!"

Shelton watched as the passengers filed out. When everyone had stepped off except Shelton and Minou, the conductor stood up and walked down the aisle, stopping at each row and pulling at the chairs until their backs gave way and they faced what had been the back of the car.

"This is Canal Street, blind man," the conductor said, and Minou stood up and reached down for the wooden case.

"I was sleeping," Minou said. "I dreamed I could see."

"Did you now?" the conductor said. He stood in the aisle and Shelton had to squeeze past him. The man's white shirt, where its buttons were, caught on Shelton's shoulder.

"Yes I did," Minou said, squeezing past as well, bumping the conductor, then tapping the stick from side to side as he slowly made his way up the aisle. "Guess who I saw?" Minou said.

When the conductor didn't answer, Minou turned back and said, "Don't bother yourself guessing. I'll just tell you. It was you."

"And how'd I look?" the conductor asked.

"Well, let's say I preferred being blind."

Minou laughed, still slapping his stick from side to side, and the conductor laughed with him. "You're one funny nigger," the conductor said. "Go on."

The conductor followed Minou and Shelton until they stepped off the car. "I'll see you tomorrow," he said.

"Not if I can help it," Minou said, and the conductor's bright laughter disappeared when the streetcar's door slammed shut. Shelton watched Minou's face change, watched his smile disappear, replaced by something else, by a look that frightened Shelton. Minou cleared his throat, turned his head to the side, and spat. He opened his eyes, looked at Shelton, then shut his eyes again. He let his back fall forward as he started to walk, as if the case grew heavier and heavier with every step.

"What's wrong?" Shelton asked.

"Nothing's wrong," Minou said, tapping the stick on the pavement. "Nothing's wrong at all. You heard the man. I'm one happy nigger. You'll see."

❧ ❧ ❧

What the child Shelton saw, once they'd made their way from Canal Street down Chartres and over to Jackson Square, was the way Minou's shut eyes left him so fully changed that even Shelton, knowing what he knew, would have sworn that this blindness was real, was an affliction that through the years had altered, inch by inch, Minou's entire body, taking the sure movements a man is meant to have and making a joke of them, full of spasm and confusion, full of halting, uncertain sorrow. *Any minute*, Minou's body seemed to shout, *I'll be struck by some object or person I can't see. Any minute I just might fold in on myself, shrink to nothing, cease to be.*

Outside the iron fence surrounding Jackson Square, Shelton watched Minou lower the case to the ground as if he didn't know when the two would meet. He watched Minou's hands grope, trembling, darting this way and that, as they unlatched the case and swung it open, as they assembled the rickety wooden easel inside, then pulled out the yellowed, dusty paper and broken charcoal squares and the soft cloth that looked as if it used to be white but was now a gray square streaked and smudged with black. Shelton watched the way Minou's hands shook, the way his body shifted from side to side as if he had to work and work just to keep his balance, to keep from falling to one side or the other like a chopped-down tree.

Then Minou began drawing, and Shelton watched his body change again, a charcoal square gripped in his hand like a ball, the hand raised to the easel, moving back and forth in swift, sure strokes. Minou's back straightened. A line of muscles appeared in his arms as if he were lifting some great weight.

"What are you going to draw?" Shelton asked, watching Minou sweep the cloth across the paper, leaving only a gray shadow of the egg-shaped circle he'd just made.

"I'm going to draw you," Minou said. "That's what. I'm going to show how this works." He raised his hand to the paper again. "But first you've got to talk."

"How come?" Shelton asked.

"Because that's what I tell folks when they want their likeness drawn. I tell them I can see but only by listening to their words, by hearing the way they speak."

"Is that true?" Shelton asked.

"It is now," Minou said. "I tell them that every one of our mind's thoughts contains not just words but pictures too, and those pictures tell how a person looks. Not just the face, I say, but from the top of the head to the tips of the toes and all points in between."

Shelton felt tired and wanted to sit down, but there was nowhere to sit.

"Well, they think I'm crazy, of course," Minou said. "They think I'm crazy until they see what I've done. Then they believe it. Yes, they do. They think there's a miracle going on. So that's why. Just try it."

Shelton did try. He tried to think what he could say. He thought about the dream he'd had of Mr. Edward. He saw, clear as day, his shameful imagining of Elise. He turned his head to look around Jackson Square. Strolling in and out the great iron gates were men in loose white shirts and neatly pressed pants and women in bright dresses and wide straw hats. Covered with pigeons, the statue in the center of the square was a soldier riding a horse whose front legs were thrown up into the air. The man and horse faced a giant church with spires and stained glass windows. Shelton squinted his eyes and looked at the church. He hadn't recognized it at first but now did. It was St. Louis Cathedral, where he'd gone that time with the other Milne Home boys, where he'd searched the great sea of faces, looking for one that would recognize him and lead him home.

"I've been here before," Shelton finally said, and just as he spoke, Minou began to draw, his arm shooting up as if just the sound of Shelton's voice had tugged on it. "They took us all here for Sunday mass."

"More," Minou said, his eyes squeezed shut, his hand raised in the air as if he meant to throw the charcoal square at Shelton. "You've got to tell me more, Shelton, or else I can't draw."

Shelton looked at Minou. "I can't think of anything," he said. "I'm sorry."

"Just say anything at all," Minou told him. "Tell me about the asylum you left behind. Tell me about Miss Margaret or Mr. Edward or anything else that comes to mind. Tell me about rolling down that hill. Tell me all you think of being a child left on that white family's doorstep. I bet there's folks watching already, Shelton. They've got to see how it's done."

Shelton looked around and saw that Minou was right. A group of men and women had stopped to look, waiting to see, Shelton guessed, what ended up on the paper.

"Elise," Shelton said, surprising himself.

"What?" Minou asked. "Go on."

Why'd I say that name? Shelton thought, and then saw her again, saw that bare back, saw her body. "I don't know," he said.

"Go on," Minou said, his voice impatient, almost angry.

"I was just thinking," Shelton said, knowing he couldn't dare put words to the thoughts in his head, to the picture he'd drawn there as if he were the one holding the charcoal and standing before the yellow paper. "I was just thinking," he said, "of something she said yesterday."

"What is it?" Minou asked, his hands working on the easel. Shelton stepped up to take a look, but Minou stretched his arm out again. "Just stay where you are, Shelton, and talk."

Shelton knew he was about to do what Elise herself had done, repeating something he'd heard and seen, making himself a snoop, but he couldn't help it. He had to say something, didn't he? So he told Minou about Elise going to Samuel Warren's back door and punching his fat belly and discovering he wore that piece of woman's clothing with a name he couldn't remember.

"She told you this or you saw it yourself?" Minou asked.

"She told me," Shelton said.

Minou let out a long breath. "That girl's full of such stories," he said. "I told you, didn't I, not to pay her any mind."

"She said something else," Shelton said, trying to make himself laugh to show he didn't believe it. "She said you were wearing chains when you worked on Monkey Hill."

Minou raised his head now and turned toward Shelton. Shelton was sure he was going to open his eyes, but he didn't. He went back to drawing, his eyes still closed.

"Go on," Minou said, and Shelton tried to think. He looked around again, saw Jackson Square filling up with more and more people. A man wearing clothes as old and worn as his and Minou's lay down on a bench inside the square. The man's face was covered with a tangled beard. He didn't move when a pigeon jumped up from the ground to stand on his legs. Shelton thought of his mother, of Genevieve, of Mr. Edward.

"My guess," Minou said, "is it's not that you've got nothing to say but just the opposite. You've got too much. Am I right?"

And Shelton, though Minou wasn't looking, nodded. "Can I just ask you one thing?" he said.

"Ask," Minou said.

"Is it true or not?"

"About the chains and digging that hill?" Minou said, stepping away from the easel.

"Yes," Shelton said.

"It's not true," Minou said, and he stepped back and began drawing again.

"But she said —"

"It's not true," Minou said again. "She wasn't out-and-out lying to you, though." Minou pulled a handkerchief from his back pocket and wiped it on his face. "Here's how it is. She just had her stories mixed up. I was put in chains once. That's true. But the girls were little. About four and five, I'd say. Too young to remember, that's certain, though I suspect their grandmother told them all about it time and again, thinking it was as good a way as any to put the fear of God into them."

Minou laughed and shook his head. "The long and short of it, Shelton, is that I was about as lucky as a man could be, because they didn't string me up or shoot me dead before finding out how they'd made a mistake. I came in for my share of mistreatment, that's true, but at least I wasn't dead. It was some other man, you see. It was a Negro of the same size and shape who did what they thought I'd done."

"What was it?" Shelton asked.

"Killed someone," Minou said, without a moment's pause in his drawing. "Killed another man. Was another Negro, not a white one, thank the Lord, or else I wouldn't be standing here."

"How come the man was killed?" Shelton asked.

"For reasons of jealousy, they said."

"So they just let you go?"

"They did," Minou said. "First they dragged me out to the Angola prison, then they dragged me back again. I'm not ashamed to say how much it scared me. I'd not care to be treated in such a way again. You want to know about getting the fear of God? That's one way, for certain."

"That's how you got those red scratches on your face?" Shelton asked.

"No, no," Minou said and laughed.

"Was it that cat? The one who died?"

"Not that either," Minou said. "It was just a woman, Shelton, though maybe she thought she was a cat."

"Isabel?" Shelton said, trying to imagine her provoked to such anger.

"Not Isabel. No," Minou said. "Now look."

Shelton stepped over to the easel. The face Minou had drawn looked back at Shelton as though he were looking into a mirror, registering the same surprise he felt now in his cheeks and the corners of his eyes, the lips turned up in the same smile he felt on his face now — a smile of gratitude, of thanks for being found, for being looked after.

"How's that for a likeness?" Minou said, laughing. "You think that deserves a place on the wall in my home?"

Shelton didn't answer but leaned into Minou's body, let Minou's arms sweep around him. He felt the charcoal square in Minou's hand scrape his shoulder, let it run down the length of his back.

"I'll tell you something," Minou said. "There wasn't anyone to teach me how to draw like this. There's not been one to say, 'Close your eyes now, Minou, because you've seen enough and all you've got to do is let yourself remember.' But it's true, Shelton. You can try it for yourself. Close your eyes now. Go on."

Shelton closed his eyes.

"Now tell me," Minou said. "Tell me what it is you see."

"I don't see anything," Shelton said.

"Come on now," Minou said. "You've got to let yourself."

"I can't," Shelton said, but before his eyes opened, he did see something. Or he felt something more than saw it, something passing through Minou's hand and that charcoal square straight into the child's shoulder, straight through his back, a feeling that was like a light shooting up into a dark sky.

I'll say more here: There has never been a time when I picked up a pencil to draw or a brush to paint and didn't feel again, in that very same spot, what the child felt in that embrace.

And something else, too: It was in that very moment of Minou holding him that Shelton felt for the first time that something was certain to happen, something to make him lose Minou. The child felt at that moment, knew it for sure, that there'd come a time when Minou would be gone and that the time wasn't far away, was closer than the child could stand to imagine.

So that's why Shelton kept his eyes closed, isn't it? That's why he wouldn't let Minou go. And though I'm not one and never have been to believe in great mysteries and magic, it still seems to me that maybe Minou already knew something of what would happen too — that the child would wind up taking a life the way he thought he might have done with Genevieve in that bedroom, though the life the child took would be Minou's own, not choking him, not leaving him gasping for air, but something else, something worse, stripping that life of all it had known, wiping it all out the way Minou's hands wiped across the yellowed paper to leave behind just a dim gray shadow.

How could I, once I'd grown, try to paint such a work, one that showed all those feelings, showed how they were true? I couldn't, I knew, and so didn't even try to. There are some places, no matter the gift in one's hands, that just can't be reached.

Well, a few moments passed in that man and child's embrace. Then Minou said, "You understand how there's times when you don't even need to hear someone talk to know what's inside them. You understand that, don't you?"

And Shelton nodded.

"Yes, you do," Minou said. "And now we've got to get to work,

Shelton." But Minou wouldn't let go either, as if he knew precisely the thoughts the child was thinking and knew how they were true.

      ☙ ☙ ☙

Later that day, the two of them covered with sweat, their clothes sticky and drenched, Minou told Shelton it was the busiest morning of drawing he'd ever had. He said that the child's presence had worked like a lucky charm, luring folks over who wanted to see the flesh-and-blood child and that child's likeness side by side. Minou had tied the portrait with string to the fence around Jackson Square, and Shelton stood near it, the portrait and the child smiling the same happy smile.

One after another stood before Minou and told him their stories, how they were from Omaha or Hattiesburg or St. Louis, how this was the first time or the fifth or the sixth that they'd come to New Orleans, come to see family or for Royal Street food or Bourbon Street drink or, with a wink and a shuffle and a secret smile, the low-down side-street women.

"They'll make a meal of your heart," Minou told one. "Chew it up and spit it out."

"That'd be fine," the man said. "That's just what I want."

"I guess there's no reason in want anyhow, is there?" Minou asked, handing over the man's portrait, which made his eyes look like they'd been set on fire, which they did seem to be.

Sometimes the ones who stood before Minou and let him draw them had children tagging along. The children squealed behind Minou or reached out to touch Shelton or paid neither of them any mind, running after the pigeons along the walkway in Jackson Square, scattering them, scaring them off, drawing shouts or smiles from their mothers and fathers while Minou, eyes squeezed shut, drew and drew.

Some didn't even stop to have their picture drawn. They looked at Shelton as he walked up and down by the fence; they looked at Minou standing by his easel. Then they pulled coins from their pockets and pressed them into Shelton's hand or dropped them into the open case at Minou's feet. *Poor colored child*, they said. *Poor nigger man.*

"Poor no more," Minou called out to them when he heard the coins sing in the case. "A mighty thank you."

And Shelton said the same, head bent down, eyes on the ground, as he slipped the coins into his pocket, thinking of Mr. Edward's outstretched hand and the glass jar he'd kept by his bed.

A good fortune, he heard in his head again and again, felt in his mouth as he tried to speak those words, tried to say them. But those words tasted as worn now as the coins themselves. They tasted of copper and dirt and smudged fingers and the slick pools of water that stood at the edge of the street, that soaked the feet of those who stepped up to him and reached out their hands, their path marked by wet footprints back and forth along Jackson Square.

A good fortune. By noon Shelton felt tired and sick. His legs ached. But Minou laughed and laughed. One child, a girl whom Minou had just drawn, at her mother's instruction muttered her thanks as Minou handed over her portrait. Mother and child stepped away, and Minou called to Shelton.

"Look," Minou whispered, leaning his head to the side and nodding, his eyes closed. "There," he said, and Shelton looked, saw in the distance a group of boys near the cathedral, the boys surrounded by dark women in white dresses, gold crosses gleaming against their chests.

"Come to pay you a visit?" Minou said, laughing, but Shelton heard the shaking in his voice. "Stay right here," Minou said, and he held Shelton close.

Shelton looked up at Minou, saw that his eyes were closed. But he was watching, wasn't he? His eyes were closed, but he was seeing just what Shelton saw. Shelton turned to the crowd of boys, saw them heading toward him, the women marching in front, the gold crosses swinging on their chests. And he heard his name, didn't he? He heard one of the women shout, or one of the boys. *Shelton Lafleur,* they cried out.

"Stay right here," Minou said again, but Shelton pulled away. He lifted his head from Minou's side, stepped back one step and then another. Minou dared to open his eyes for just a moment and must have seen Shelton's terror, must have understood what the child might do.

"Stay right here, child, I said." Minou's voice was filled with anger now, the anger that comes of desperation.

Shelton didn't listen. He didn't stop even when Minou called out for him. "That's nothing, child," he called. "They're not coming for you."

Now Shelton heard Minou call his name, heard the wooden stick slap the pavement as Minou shuffled back a step or two, as Minou let himself trip and fall, that fall one last call for someone's charity, for someone who'd say, *That's your child, is it now? Well, I'll go after him.*

No one did, though. And filled with his own fear, blind with the imagined picture of being surrounded by the dark women in their white dresses, of being swallowed inside the crowd of boys, of being carried back to the Milne Home, the child did just what he'd done before. He swung his legs out and around, threw his body forward, and started to run.

12 POOR NO MORE

I DON'T BLAME the child. I don't. He remembered those women, who had looked down from the balcony of the One Holy Church of the Innocent Blood on the day of Genevieve Simmons's funeral. They'd seen the child there, standing right up front. They'd heard the good reverend speak the child's name. They'd heard him say how that child had found himself a home.

Look here, the women must have whispered up in that balcony, *it's the cripple Shelton.*

Here's the one, they seemed to call out now at Jackson Square, *wouldn't so much as speak his own name.*

But how'd they know to find him here?

They knew, that's all. They had eyes and ears.

Found a home for himself now, hasn't he? they called.

Speaking up now, isn't he?

Speaking up now loud and clear.

But all Shelton knew to do was to run. And he knew, in that moment when Minou's eyes opened and then closed, that this man who'd taken him from the Milne Home couldn't run after him. No matter what Minou might feel for Shelton, he couldn't put his blindness aside, for all the others around Jackson Square — the shopkeepers and police officers and tourists and bums — they'd all see his trick, see how they'd been fooled, see that the years of kindness and pity and charity had all been wasted, had gone to one who didn't deserve it.

Minou had a living to make, a family to look after. He couldn't risk giving all that up for this strange, orphaned child who would come back anyway, wouldn't he, who couldn't go very far.

Yes, Shelton, knowing as little as he did, knew all that, and so he ran knowing that Minou wouldn't follow. He ran down a narrow alley, dark and wet like that street they'd gone down on the streetcar that morning. Pirates' Alley, a sign said, and Shelton managed to wonder, even as he ran, why it had been given such a name. Were there pirates who'd stepped into this dark place and leaned against the cathedral's slick walls to trade stories of their wild adventures, to make plans for which Mississippi River ship they'd ransack next? His mother would know, Shelton thought, and with his next step: *She's dead.* And he kept on running.

Then he stepped out of the alley to Royal Street, scattering the crowd of people walking up and down and looking into the shop windows filled with delicate carved furniture like the kind Mr. Edward brought back from across the sea.

What have you stolen, nigger boy? Shelton heard one woman cry as he ran. She put her arm out as if she meant to stop him. Dangling from that arm like a clock's stopped pendulum was the woman's pocketbook, and Shelton felt, as he had with Genevieve, the fear in him turn to rage, felt that rage curl his fingers into fists, felt it lift his arms as if to strike out. The woman stepped straight into Shelton's path, and though some other child might have been able to shoot clear around her, step to the side, Shelton couldn't. He didn't.

Instead, he grabbed the woman's pocketbook, kept running,

and behind him the woman fell, her arm wrenched around behind her, the pocketbook's two thin leather straps caught in her clutching fingers and then broken free, waving behind Shelton now like the tails of two tangled kites.

Pickaninny thief! Shelton heard the woman cry, and now hands reached out for him, tried to grab him, but he ran and ran as if he were not running but tumbling down Monkey Hill, his head bobbing as it had bobbed in Lake Pontchartrain, as he'd seen it do in the window of the bus he'd taken that first morning, just six mornings ago, with Minou.

Shelton turned off Royal Street into another alley, which smelled as rotten as that place behind the kitchen at the Milne Home, the place where he'd dipped his arms again and again into the turpentine to wash them clean. He saw rats scatter, saw roaches freeze and get trapped under his feet, saw a striped gray cat arch its back and dance sideways like a Halloween cat.

Where was he? Some strange place crawling with rats and cats and insects, with the concrete animals he'd seen holding up those benches, those animals come alive now, lurking behind corners, ready to pounce.

When Shelton couldn't run anymore he threw his body down between two damp brown boxes in the alley. In his lap, his hands wrapped around it, was the woman's pocketbook. He threw it down as if it were on fire, as if it would burn his hands like that boy's hands, Emanuel Jackson's. Was he one of the boys who'd been in that crowd? Was it Emanuel Jackson and not the women or the other boys who'd called out his name?

Shelton heard the clatter on the pavement, saw the contents of the pocketbook spill out — a fountain pen, blue and silver and black; a metal case with a mirror inside it, lying open; a glass bottle with its cap gone, spilling some sweet liquid into the alley in a thick, slow stream; an array of shiny coins; a black leather wallet; a folded card tied with a pink bow, numbers scrawled across the back.

Shelton crawled over on his hands and knees and picked up the coins one by one, pennies and nickels and dimes and three quarters. Then he made himself stand though his legs throbbed and ached, and he ran again, from alley to street to alley. The woman's coins rang in his pockets at every step, mixing with the coins he had there already, the coins handed over to him at Jackson Square just because he looked the way he did, because his back was bent and his legs were crippled. The coins — those given and those stolen — burned into the sides of his legs now as though they meant to scar him.

Then, when every street began to look exactly like the one before, when every house was smoky brick with green shutters on the windows and doors, Shelton stopped and wondered if he'd just been running a circle — he had been, hadn't he? — then knew he needed to find a place to sit down or his legs would collapse. There, between two houses, was an iron gate left open, leading through a narrow, brick-lined path to a shaded patio. He stepped inside, closed the gate. He crouched down between two thick bushes with wide dark leaves that felt to Shelton's touch like a cat's coarse tongue licking his face and fingers, like the rough wool coats in Mr. Edward's dressing closet. He rested his back against the brick wall behind him. His feet sank into the wet soil. He waited.

His every breath rustled the dark leaves that surrounded him. He felt the rush of blood in his wrists and neck. He closed his eyes and listened. Was that someone calling his name, shouting for him, pleading?

No. There was nothing but the sound of his breathing and his heart beating and a trickling of water as if he were crouched beside some clear stream and then a scraping and slap that became footsteps growing nearer and nearer, then a woman's voice: "They'll be late, dear. They always are."

And a man's voice, loud and impatient: "We've an obligation."

The woman again: "Oh, Henry."

Then Shelton heard the gate open and close. He heard the

voices and footsteps carry themselves down the street and, a moment later, disappear.

Shelton crawled out from between the bushes, slipping as he did so that his hands were covered now, as his feet were, with the wet soil. He brushed his hands against his pants, then rubbed his eyes and felt the wet grains of dirt smear his face. His legs still burned and throbbed and ached. Why had he acted like such a frightened child? But they were coming for him, weren't they? They were coming to take him back to the Milne Home, to beat him again, to name him anew.

He'd find his way back to Minou now, say how he was sorry for running, sorry for stealing the woman's purse, for knocking the woman down. If he was spotted along the way and sent to St. John Bercham's, then he deserved it, didn't he? He'd stolen. He'd done what they'd said at the Milne Home he'd do — he'd shown his true stripes, let his true nature loose on the unsuspecting world.

Shelton wiped his face on the shoulder of his shirt. Yes, he'd go back now, go back to Minou, but before turning to go back out to the street he looked around the patio and saw a door, the one the man and woman must have just stepped through. That door would be locked, Shelton knew, locked to keep out wandering thieves like himself, but there was a window too, and Shelton walked over to it.

Inside, the house looked just like Mr. Edward's, the room lined with soft fabric furniture and tables that gleamed. He should go home, he knew, go back to Minou, say he was sorry for running off. He had scared Minou, hadn't he? But where was Minou now? What would he be doing? Would he be wandering here and there, tapping his stick from side to side, eyes still closed, mouth calling out Shelton's name?

Shelton was tired. He stepped away from the window, turned to go. But there was an iron bench on the patio, and Shelton sat down. He hadn't slept in a bed, had he, since he'd left the Milne

Home. Six days ago, that's all. And now, this evening, where would he sleep — out on the street or strapped down at St. John Bercham's or once again safe and sound on Minou's front-room sofa, Minou and Isabel curled together in their bed, Adrienne stretching out now that Genevieve was dead, Olivia in her own bed, peaceful, maybe praying for Shelton, Elise naked, calling out his name?

He'd lie down now, lie down just a minute, that's all. He lay down, lifted his legs, swung them up and around onto the bench. He saw the mud, the garden soil, at the edges of his shoes, and he looked at the path they'd left on the patio — up to the window, over to this bench. He closed his eyes and decided that yes, here he was, once again on the patio behind Mr. Edward's house. He'd hear that voice soon, hear Mr. Edward call out his name, the name he must have given the child when the child was only an hour old. Shelton turned onto his side and slept.

※ ※ ※

The voice that woke him was a woman's voice calling not his name but another's. "Henry!" the woman called, and Shelton sat up. "Look! Look!" the woman said, and Shelton turned to see a man come through the patio gate. "Henry! Look," the woman said.

Then the man walked up to Shelton. He raised his hands. "What on earth —" the man said, then stopped.

"Henry," the woman said, and the man turned to her.

"It's just a child," he said. "It's just a child."

Now the woman stepped behind the man. She looked around his shoulder the way Elise had done behind Olivia when Shelton first met them. "It's a nigger," the woman said. "It's a nigger child."

"What do you think you're doing here?" the man said.

"I was sleepy," Shelton said. "I'm lost. I just —"

"You just wandered in?" the man said. "Thought maybe this was your house?"

176

Shelton shook his head.

"Where's your home, son?" the man said, and Shelton looked down at his feet.

"Your home," the man said again, louder now, and Shelton looked up at him, saw how the man's hair was silver. He was an old man, older than Minou or Mr. Edward, as old as Genevieve had been.

"Where's your home, I said. You understand me?"

But Shelton couldn't make himself speak.

"Oh, Jesus Christ," the man said. "Go on now. You've gotten mud everywhere, child. I could call the police. They'd give you a place to sleep."

Shelton didn't move. "Please," he said.

"Come on," the man said. "I won't hurt you."

"Henry?" the woman said. Shelton heard the fear in her voice.

The man turned to her. "It's fine," he said. "He's just a child." He turned back to Shelton. "Come on."

Shelton stepped toward the man. "You hurt yourself," the man said.

Shelton nodded. "You need a doctor," the man said, and Shelton shook his head.

"I fell from a tree," Shelton said. "I'm just crippled."

"Dear God," the man said, and he shook his head. "Well, come on."

Shelton followed the man down the path to the gate.

"Next time," the man said, "you try ringing the bell. There's a bell by the gate. We'll give you food. We'll find something for you. But you've got to ring the bell, you hear?"

Shelton nodded.

"Go on, then," the man said. "Go on home."

And Shelton walked through the gate and out to the street. He turned and tried to remember which direction he'd run from. He tried retracing his steps, this way and then that way and then this. But it was evening now and, except beneath the streetlamps, dark. He was lost. He tried to ask someone — an old woman standing on the corner, looking back and forth, clutching her pocketbook against her chest as if she knew what Shelton had done when he'd run down Royal Street. He asked her which direction was Jackson Square and could she show him, but the woman laughed a nervous high-pitched laugh. She looked back and forth again and said, "I'm lost myself, boy. I'm sorry."

Shelton tasted dirt in his mouth, so he turned to the side and spat the way Minou had spat when he stepped from the streetcar that morning.

And the woman said, "You run along now, boy," and Shelton heard the fear in her voice, saw it in her face, and he spat again and saw the woman step back, still clutching her pocketbook. "You go on now," she said.

This fear, the same fear the other woman had shown when she leaned around the man named Henry — this was something new, wasn't it, Shelton thought, and he looked and looked at this woman now. The woman was giving him something with her fear, Shelton knew. He didn't know what it was, but he knew it was something. He stepped closer and the woman just about jumped, the same way he had in the Milne Home when he woke to find the boys standing over him, frightened and amazed.

Now the woman fumbled in her purse and pulled out a folded dollar bill. "Here," she said, and Shelton reached out to take it from her, his eyes still searching her face. "Now go on," the woman said, so Shelton turned away, but then turned back again to say he was grateful.

But the woman was hurrying off now, her heels clicking on the pavement. She turned her head back toward Shelton once and then again, then she reached a corner, turned without looking, and was gone.

Shelton stood with the dollar bill in his hand and watched the spot where the woman had stood before him, watched it as if at any moment she might reappear, offer him another dollar, explain her fear to him. Then, just as he'd seen Minou do, Shelton laughed, and the voice in his head said something, what was it? *Poor no more,* the voice said and then again, *Poor no more.*

And I'll tell you the work of mine that very moment produced. Not a picture of the lost child on the corner but one of Minou the moment the child ran off. Painted in black and white, the way Minou would have done with his charcoal square raised to the paper, the canvas shows a falling man's body about to meet the brick pavement, a wooden stick in the air like it's one of old Moses' that came to life as a snake, the man's two hands open, reaching out. You can see the man's face, his squeezed-shut eyes along with a smile that in just an instant, though the man can't know when, will meet the brick against his legs and shoulder and head. And all around him, scattered on the pavement, are the rolling coins, gray and black but touched with gold.

Poor No More, a work understood by one and all as a story or allegory or fable of the ruin that comes of wealth.

That's Shelton Lafleur's account of the Great Depression, isn't it?

That's Shelton Lafleur doing more of his preaching, showing his people the promised land.

That's Shelton Lafleur himself about to greet the pavement. See the cane. See how dark he's made that man. See how the man falls, not like he has tripped but like he has tumbled from the sky. That's Shelton Lafleur, isn't it? That's a self-portrait.

And I would have laughed at those explanations if I hadn't known the pain I felt in showing such a thing as that, in knowing what I knew of this work and every other — that it's got its own sad, secret story. That there are things lost that can never, no matter one's trying and trying and trying, be regained.

Poor No More. That's a work filled with shame. That's the one work that I wished I'd never painted, that I'd never given myself reason to paint. But I did, didn't I?

I did.

❧ ❧ ❧

All evening the child wandered from one street to the next, trying to find his way back to Jackson Square. Each time he passed someone on the street, he looked up at that person's face to see if he'd find there what he'd seen in that woman's face, that gift that had felt like something new, something that had jumped from her eyes straight into his own to make him laugh.

But he didn't see it again. Most turned away as soon as they saw Shelton, and eventually the child stopped looking, kept his head turned down to the ground or raised it up high to read the street signs when he approached them: St. Philip, Orleans, Barracks, Ursulines, Burgundy, Dauphine.

I've tried to imagine myself, the old man I now am, standing at a distance and watching the lost child, dirty and exhausted and confused, making his way from one street to the next. What kind of sight was this even for a city where Negro boys of Shelton's age and even younger roamed the streets offering to shine white men's shoes or to perform smiling spasm dances in oversize steel-tap shoes, feet kicking up and down as fast as spinning spoked wheels, coins ringing on the pavement like bright drops of rain on a new tin roof? How is it that this child walked amid all the seediness and splendor of a centuries-old city and couldn't have said, ten minutes later, what he'd just seen?

Time and again I've set up a chair at some French Quarter corner to sketch a street where the child Shelton must certainly have roamed, and though I've put all of what there is to see down on paper — every brick and twisting wisteria vine, every shop window and painted sign, every drenched shadow and flickering of the fading light — there's not a time that my drawing did what I meant it to do, which was to bring back these streets as the child had seen them.

Here's the barber shop that was once the French Opera House. Here's a bar in a three-story home meant for Napoleon. Here's Madame John's Legacy and James Gallier's residence and the rooms where John James Audubon painted a hundred or more of his perfect birds. Here — and what if the child had known he'd walked straight past it? — here is the crumbling brick wall that once hid the Maison de St. John Bercham, a home that would become a high school for Negro children and then, as if the city were scrubbing at some old stain, a Catholic convent for nuns too old and sick and tired to do anything but lie down in their beds and finger their rosaries until their time came to meet the one whose lonely bride they'd been for so many years on end.

Instead the child walked and walked as though he were blind, and finally he wound up on Royal Street and followed it, first one way then the other, until he came again upon Pirates' Alley. He imagined the alley, which in fact was deserted, crowded with men dressed like those in the pictures he'd seen as a small child: scarves tied around their heads and knotted, striped shirts stained with gunpowder, rum, and blood, black boots that rose to bony and scissor-sharp knees. He imagined the men's toothless smiles and the squawking parrots perched on their shoulders, pecking at their ears. He imagined one of the men turning to him and saying, *So you want to set sail on the seven oceans? Come back tomorrow, son, and we'll see.*

Then he stepped out from the alley to Jackson Square. It was late evening now, and Minou was gone. The square was lit up by flickering gaslights atop high poles, and the light carried over to the cathedral, washing its stone walls clean like a fresh coat of paint.

It seemed to Shelton now that what he'd imagined was this whole day — imagined Minou's blind portraits, imagined the crowd of Milne Home boys, imagined his own running and stealing from that woman, imagined falling asleep for who knows how long at that house. He walked over to the place where Minou had set down the box and put together his easel, where he'd tied Shelton's picture to the iron fence. There wasn't a trace of him; there wasn't one thing to suggest that this day was anything more than something Shelton had dreamed.

Here, though, were all those coins in his pocket. Here were the rage and the shame of stealing that coursed through his body. Here was the feeling that he'd had with that woman on the corner, a feeling that said she was the one who was frightened and small, she was the one who was lost. He'd seen, hadn't he, his own reflection in the dark pupils of the woman's eyes. He'd seen how in her eyes he was immeasurably large, big as a giant, a terrible, menacing sight to behold.

Then his thoughts turned to his tiredness, his exhaustion, and Shelton walked around to the gate that led inside Jackson Square and sat down beneath the statue of the man on his horse. He sat on the bench where he'd seen the man lie down and let the pigeon jump up on his leg.

And as he shut his eyes, feeling that he might fall asleep, he was so tired, Shelton thought of the dream he'd woken with that morning, the dream of Mr. Edward knocking on Minou's door, of his leading Mr. Edward through the house, watching him fall asleep on the front-room sofa. Then it occurred to Shelton that it was now, at this moment and not any earlier one, that he was finally free. Since he'd run from the home, he'd had Minou holding him, watching him, steering him here and there. Now there was no one — not Minou, not Olivia or Elise, not Genevieve in that corner chair or the procession of people patting him on the head to say how sorry they were but wasn't he glad to have a home, not the arms like tree limbs swaying behind him, not the voices singing that wordless hymn.

Though it took all the strength he had, Shelton stood up and started walking again, guided now not by the tapping stick of Minou's pretended blindness but by the bright light of his own freedom. He retraced the steps they'd taken that morning and found Canal Street, found the corner where the streetcar had turned. He waited, standing with his hands in his pockets. "You're late getting home, child," Shelton heard a woman say as she stepped up next to him. He didn't look at the woman's face, though, and didn't answer. He just watched the way the bag the woman was holding swung beside her leg, then stopped. She coughed and the bag swung again, then stopped.

When the streetcar finally pulled up, Shelton waited for the woman, then stepped on behind her, dropped a nickel into the wire basket, and walked down the narrow aisle, holding on to the backs of the seats, one after the next, so he wouldn't fall when the streetcar lurched, which it did, before he sat down at the back.

Though he was tired and hungry and his whole body hurt, he had all the time in the world, didn't he? And when the streetcar had gone down that slick narrow street and swung around Lee Circle and headed up St. Charles, Shelton still sat in his seat and let the city shine in his eyes and didn't think of getting off — not even when the car passed the stop where he and Minou had stepped on that morning, not even when he thought of Isabel's kiss on his cheek, Olivia's welcoming smile, Elise's bare, red, stinging shoulder, her splayed naked body, her open mouth pronouncing his name, calling him.

He let the streetcar's swaying rock his body back and forth the way he'd seen it do to Genevieve when he was a child, when she'd let that rocking shake the stories loose from inside her. He had a story of his own to tell now, didn't he? But the story wasn't done. He heard Genevieve's voice say, *Where's your good fortune, poor Shelton?*

It's here, Shelton answered, looking out the window, watching the great free world shoot past and swirl around him. And now Shelton saw out the window, though it had turned wholly dark, the green stretch of Audubon Park. He saw the two stone lions guarding the entrance, lit up by a light the same way Jackson Square and the cathedral had been lit, the same way Genevieve's slumped, swollen body had been circled by the light of that single shaded lamp.

Here, he thought, and he reached up to pull the cord to ring the bell that told the driver to stop.

Shelton made his way to the door and stepped off. He crossed over to the park, walked up to the lions, put a hand on one, on its cold-stone back. He thought of Elise sitting here and of Olivia's warning that she ought to get off. He'd climb up there himself, he thought, but when he tried, he couldn't do it. It didn't matter, though, did it, for he could do what he liked. He wandered off, walking out of the lamplight and into the dark, down a path and then off from the path between one row of trees and then another. He was tired. He was hungry. But it didn't matter, did it?

Then Shelton stopped and knew just where he was, knew where he'd wound up — at the very spot he'd looked for with Olivia and Elise but hadn't found. Now he had found it, hadn't he?

Look: Here, towering over his head, was the oak tree where he'd fallen. Here, right here, was where his body had bounced from limb to limb, where his hands had clawed and scraped and scratched. Here, at his feet, was the dirt, were the oak roots and leaves. Here was where he'd struck the ground and lay wailing and wailing the way he'd wailed, he knew now, he'd figured out, on that doorstep on the day and at the very hour of his birth, where he'd been given up, abandoned, purchased, named by Mr. Edward. It was at this moment, wasn't it, standing beneath this tree, that Shelton first imagined the two dark hands raising him high, then setting him down, imagined the falling that would go on and on until that fall was from a tree and wouldn't stop even then and hadn't stopped until now.

He'd seen something before he fell. Well, what was it? It was something swinging way up high, fluttering there above the horizon, almost still but not, then sweeping down toward him with a message. Well, what was it he'd seen? What was it he'd heard? It was words of some sort, wasn't it? No, it wasn't words. Something else. Just a bird, wasn't it, just a black crow or red robin or dusty gray pigeon. Not a bird at all but a child's kite meant to look like a bird, the paper flapping in the wind as if it would speak, as if it had a message meant for him.

No, it wasn't a paper kite. It was himself he'd seen, his own body grown wings and fluttering there, the light like a warm blanket wrapped around him. From his place in the tree, from the spot to which he'd climbed, he'd looked out through the leaves and branches and seen himself. Just like he'd done with that portrait Minou had drawn, he'd looked out and seen himself, hadn't he, and he was trying to speak. His hands were raised in the air as if to say, *Watch. This is what happened to me. I'll show you.*

What happened? Shelton wanted to ask now. *Just tell me.* But he looked up at the tree and there was only darkness and one small slice of moon shimmering through the leaves, the light lifting the tree's limbs higher and higher, pushing Shelton down further and further until he felt how his feet stood there on the ground, as if they were buried in the dirt and oak leaves and roots, as if he'd just fallen and landed upright after all.

What'll I do now? Shelton thought, and as soon as he thought it, he knew. He shut his eyes, made the tree and limbs and leaves and moon all disappear. Then he took one step and another and, when he didn't fall, opened his eyes to see which direction he'd gone, then closed them and took another step and then another. This was Minou's trick, wasn't it, and not a trick at all. Just memory. Look and see and remember, and let memory guide you. So he walked and walked like that, opening his eyes, closing them, letting his body remember all it had done and seen and knew.

Here, right here, was the child's first step toward becoming what he'd wind up wanting to be. Eyes closed. Memory. Hands raised to speak all they know.

And soon, just like that, the child had stepped out from the trees to St. Charles Avenue. He waited for an automobile to pass, its headlights traveling across his body the way his own shape had traveled across the gold and silver items in the Royal Street windows; then he crossed and went down one street, turned into an alley, shut his eyes, opened them, shut them, walked.

And then here, before him, was the gate he'd swung open and

kicked closed that morning five years ago. Here was the patio garden of wisteria and oleander and persimmon. Here was the small house that had served once as slave quarters; here were the neatly appointed rooms of his unfortunate, privileged mother. He raised his hand to the door and knocked.

She's dead, Shelton heard in his head. *The poor woman.* But that was Genevieve's voice, not his own. He knocked again, and heard something, heard someone, shuffling inside, heard someone moving. It was covers thrown off a bed. It was feet on the floor. It was his mother, wasn't it, not dead but cured.

Then the door swung open. The light washed over Shelton so again he had to shut his eyes and open them, squint, and shut them again. And before he could see with any certainty, he heard a voice ringing in his ears the way he'd heard Minou's voice above him that morning, six mornings ago, when he'd run from the Milne Home: *There's a poor pitiful piece of work indeed.*

"What on earth are you wanting, young man?"

Shelton waited for the voice to take shape before him. It was a man, as old as Genevieve, even older maybe, his night clothes twisted on his body.

"Mr. Edward," Shelton said.

The man leaned in the doorway. "And what are you wanting with Mr. Edward?" The man reached over for something behind the door. Then the patio was lit up from a light shining above, and Shelton saw the man step toward him and shake his head. "Lord have mercy," he said, "what is it we have here?"

"I came to see Mr. Edward," Shelton said.

"This time of night?" the man said. "And looking as you do? You've got some nerve."

Shelton thought of Olivia's friends saying the same words in the shops on Magazine. "I do," Shelton said, and the man laughed.

"Yes, you do," he said. "Yes, you do." He looked at Shelton as if just by looking he'd find the explanation for why this child was standing there. When Shelton didn't speak, the man said, "Let's

186

just forget the pitch dark and go straight to why you're in search of Mr. Edward."

"He'll know why," Shelton said.

"Now, will he?" the man said. "You've got a prior acquaintance?"

Shelton nodded and looked straight into the man's eyes. "Who are you?" Shelton asked.

Now the man laughed. "It's mighty late for such chitchat, young man," he said. "You tell me who you are and I'll pass word along to Mr. Edward. I'll tell him you stopped by for a visit."

"I want to see him now," Shelton said. He looked at the man, looked up at his eyes. "Please," Shelton said.

"Maybe I don't even want to know what for?" the man said, and Shelton nodded.

"Well, he's not here, in any case," the man said. "He's gone abroad. He's away on business. It'll be another two months or more. You're welcome to call then."

"Please," Shelton said again, his body starting to tremble, his fingers curling into fists at his side.

"What else can I do for you?" the man said, raising his hands now as if to show how they were empty. "You should find your way home."

The man stepped back and placed a hand on the door. "Go on now," he said, and Shelton turned, felt the shaking grow worse, felt the ache in his legs and knees and hips, felt the fire burning there.

"Tell me your name," the man said. "I'll tell Mr. Edward."

"It's Shelton."

The man looked at him. He inched the door forward.

"Shelton Gerard Lafleur."

"Shelton Gerard Lafleur?" the man said. "That's quite a name. I'll tell him." Then he raised a hand and swung it back and forth as if he were swatting at a fly. "Go on now, Shelton Gerard Lafleur," he said. "Go on."

But Shelton stood still and didn't move. He saw the door close, heard the man shuffling inside, saw through the curtained window the light go out, heard the covers pulled back over the bed. "Go on, son," the man called. "Go on or I'll show you what for."

And Shelton turned now, opened the gate, let it swing shut behind him. He walked back down the alley, back to St. Charles Avenue. He went to the streetcar stop and waited. And when he'd waited and waited and the streetcar still hadn't come, he started walking. He headed back toward Minou's house, though he wasn't sure exactly where it was or how far and didn't even know if there'd be anyone there to greet him. He didn't know anything now, did he, beyond what he'd said to the man, and that was just his name.

Shelton Gerard Lafleur, he'd said, and again, as it had always been, even that was a question.

13 BLIND MAN'S BLUFF

So SHELTON DRAGGED his body along St. Charles Avenue, the question formed by his name still ringing in his ears. He walked past the park entrance and the stone lions, past one house after the next, the houses becoming smaller and smaller as the park disappeared behind him. Inside the houses, dogs barked and lights switched on as Shelton passed. "Who's there?" a man called out from the darkness, from the porch chair where he was sitting, but Shelton didn't answer. His feet scraped along the sidewalk like a rake through dry leaves, and Shelton saw the man stand, turn his head from side to side. "Edna?" the man said. "Honey, is that you?"

Shelton kept walking, though he tried to imagine who and where this Edna might be — the man's daughter, run off after some fight? The man's wife, passed away, the man waiting the way the boys at the Milne Home had waited for their mothers to come get them, the way he'd waited too?

Shelton turned off St. Charles Avenue when he thought he'd walked far enough, and he wandered from block to block until finally he found Foucher Street. He walked until he reached Minou's house, then he lifted himself up the porch step, so tired now that he felt he'd been carrying all day the cloth bag that as a young child he'd thrown over his shoulder and hauled back from Magazine Street to Mr. Edward's, that bag filled now not with a pound or two of flour and sugar but with a hundred pounds, a thousand, more.

On the porch of Minou's house, resting just beside the front door, were a blanket and pillow. Shelton was too tired and exhausted, though, to consider why they might be there, what Minou might be trying to tell him. So he reached for the door, and when he found it locked, he raised his hand and knocked.

It was a minute or two before Minou answered, and Shelton turned to look out at the street. He wouldn't have been surprised, would he, to find that the man on St. Charles Avenue, the one who'd called out, had followed him, certain he was trailing not Shelton but some ghost, the wife or daughter or mother who'd died and left him alone. And Shelton felt like a ghost himself now, his body so tired it seemed to slip away from him, disappear, leaving behind just the swirling thoughts in his head.

"Look here," Shelton finally heard from inside the house, and Minou swung open the door, standing square in the middle of the doorway just as that man had stood before him at Mr. Edward's.

"It's me," Shelton said, and his legs felt as though they might collapse beneath him.

"Dogs half the size of you get whipped for running off like that," Minou said. "Didn't I tell you to stay by my side?"

Shelton looked at Minou and saw the book tucked under his arm.

"I got lost," Shelton said.

"You didn't get lost until after you ran off," Minou said. He stepped back as if he meant to shut the door.

"Can I come in?" Shelton said.

"No, you can't," Minou answered. He pointed down to the

blanket and pillow. "But you're welcome to make yourself at home out here."

"But I'm tired," Shelton said.

"Then you'll be just fine," Minou said. "Try the chair."

"Please," Shelton said.

Minou took the book out from under his arm and shook it the way the preacher had done with his Bible in church. "Listen to me," Minou said. "I've taken on the job of looking after you. That's a promise I intend to keep. But I don't have the mind right now or the patience to listen to why it was you thought to run off when I said you should just stay put. They weren't coming to steal you, child. Who'd want to steal you back? What is it makes you think you're so valuable a property folks are going to fight over who gets the chance to look after you?"

Minou stopped and looked down at Shelton. "I'm the one looking after you. There's not another one on this earth who's made that promise. You understand that?"

Shelton nodded.

"But you've got to see, just like the girls, what's right and what's not," Minou said. "There's a right and wrong here, and the right is staying put, not running off. You understand?"

Shelton nodded again. He put his hands in his pockets and touched the coins there.

"Go ahead and ask, and you'll hear from the girls that they've spent a few porch nights of their own," Minou said. "Maybe they'll tell you it does some good to worry about what might be prowling around out here."

"What?" Shelton asked, turning again to look behind him, out at the dark street.

Minou laughed. "Dear Lord," he said, stepping out now and putting a hand on Shelton's shoulder. "It's nothing, child. It's nothing out here. That's what I mean. I've found a night spent sleeping on this porch leads to an appreciation of what's inside. Now get some sleep. Morning's not more than a few hours away."

Shelton stood there as Minou stepped back inside to shut the door.

"Wait," Shelton said.

"What is it?" Minou said. "I'm losing sleep."

Shelton pulled his hands out of his pockets, the coins gathered in his fists. "Here," he said, and he reached out to Minou.

Minou took the coins and looked at them. "I'll put them aside for you," he said.

"And this," Shelton said. He reached again into his pocket and pulled out the dollar bill. "A woman gave it to me."

"How'd she happen to do that?" Minou asked.

"I don't know. I think I scared her."

Minou laughed. "You did?"

"I think so," Shelton said.

"Well, I'll keep this for you as well. That's it?"

Shelton shook his head. "Something else," he said.

"Then maybe I ought to send you running off some more. Maybe we'd wind up rich. Maybe the whole world would want to shower coins on such a one as you."

"I took something," Shelton said. "A woman's pocketbook."

Minou stepped out onto the porch again. "What's this?"

"I took a woman's pocketbook," Shelton said. "I was running and she was there and I just grabbed it, I don't know why."

"Lord have mercy," Minou said, and he took Shelton by the arm and led him inside. He sat him down on the sofa, switched on the lamp, set his book on the table, and sat down next to Shelton.

"You're saying you stole a pocketbook off a woman?"

Shelton nodded.

"White or colored?" Minou asked.

"White," Shelton said.

Minou looked up, ran his hand over his head, then looked back at Shelton. "Where is it?" he said. "Where's the pocketbook?"

"I threw it down," Shelton said. "I was scared."

"That's worse than scared," Minou said. "That's out and out

dumb." He stood up and looked over at the hall and then at the front door, which he'd left open. He walked over and closed it, then sat down again next to Shelton. "You take anything from that pocketbook?"

"Some money," Shelton said. "What I gave you. Maybe it could be used for paying that man for burying Genevieve."

"Listen to me," Minou said now, taking hold of Shelton's arm. "I won't tell you what I'd do to my girls if they came home with such a story as that. I wouldn't care if it was true or not."

Shelton looked down at his lap, but Minou shook his arm. "Look at me," he said. "You even think of doing such a thing as that again and you'll be wandering the streets for good. I'll send you straight back to that asylum, that's what I'll do. You hear me?"

Shelton nodded.

"Now get some sleep," Minou said.

"Here?" Shelton asked.

"Right here," Minou said, and he turned off the lamp and walked away. Then Shelton heard him stop and walk back. He saw Minou's hand reaching toward him, then heard the coins clatter on the table.

As Minou walked off again, Shelton said, "I'm sorry."

"You better be," Minou said, and Shelton let him take a few steps before saying what he felt he needed to say before falling asleep.

"Minou," he said, and he heard Minou stop. "There's something else."

Shelton heard Minou sigh, one long loud breath. He could tell Minou that he'd stepped onto that patio, that he'd lain down and slept on that iron bench, that a white man and white woman had found him but let him go.

"I went home," Shelton said instead. "To my mama's house. To Mr. Edward's."

Shelton looked up into the darkness, trying to make out the features of Minou's face. "And?" Minou said, and Shelton heard, even in just that single word, what sounded like fear, like the voice of that woman who'd given him the dollar.

"He wasn't there," Shelton said. "Some man was."

"Who?"

"Like you," Shelton said, seeing the man standing in the doorway the way Minou had stood before him the morning he'd run from the Milne Home. "Like us, I mean," Shelton said. "A Negro."

"And what did this man tell you?" Minou asked.

"He said Mr. Edward was gone away on business. He said he'd be a while."

"And what did you tell this man?" Minou asked. He hadn't moved, but Shelton could see him now, could see the outline of his figure the way he'd seen it those mornings in the doorway.

"I told him my name," Shelton said.

"That's all?" Minou asked.

"Yes," Shelton said, and Minou didn't answer. Shelton, though, could see him shaking his head as he stepped away, out of the room and down the hall.

"Minou?" Shelton called out. He wanted to say he was sorry. He wanted to say he wouldn't steal again or run off or even go looking for Mr. Edward. But Minou was gone, and the child didn't know what to do except to get up and fetch the blanket and pillow from the porch.

When he opened the door and stepped out, Shelton was sure he heard a voice call out from the street. "That you?" the voice said, but it wasn't that man's voice, wasn't a man's voice at all but a woman's. Whose voice? It was Genevieve's, Shelton thought, calling to him from inside, from the dark room where she sat, her body bloated, slumped in the chair. No, it was like a woman's voice but not. It was a girl's voice.

"Joshua?" the voice said now, just a whisper, and Shelton heard something move, heard some weight on the clamshells near the house. "Joshua?" the voice whispered again. It must be Adrienne, Shelton thought, calling out through the window for Joshua

Warren, maybe calling out from her bed, still asleep. But that voice wasn't hers either, was it?

"Joshua," it said again, angry now, desperate, and Shelton recognized the voice. It belonged to Elise.

"Elise?" he said. "Elise, it's Shelton." But she didn't answer.

"Elise," he said again, louder. He waited, his hands shaking now as if she might appear before him, might say his name the way he'd imagined her saying it in the picture where his mind had placed her.

But she didn't answer, so he stepped back inside and shut the door. He'd imagined it, hadn't he? What would she be doing outside or standing at her window, calling Joshua Warren's name? He thought of the man calling for the woman named Edna. Had he imagined that too?

He lay down on the sofa now to sleep, hoping that for this one night at least, for what was left of it, his only dream would be of his own body, not of Elise's on that bed, her mouth calling out to him, not of Mr. Edward's lying here on this sofa, curled up like a baby. He wanted to sleep this one night without dreaming, peaceful and calm.

꙳ ꙳ ꙳

Once again, a few days passed on which Minou stepped out the door just before dawn and set off for work, leaving the child behind without a word passing between them. In the evening, when he returned home, he didn't mention what Shelton had told him about stealing the pocketbook or asking to see Mr. Edward. He didn't say when or if he'd again take Shelton with him to work.

Shelton spent those days as he'd spent the others, in the company of Olivia and Elise, though Isabel left instructions this time that they weren't to wander away from Foucher Street, instructions Shelton was sure had come from Minou: *Don't allow that child to stray too far, for I know how he is and there's no telling what he'd do.*

The first day, Adrienne received a visit from Joshua Warren. Shelton didn't tell Elise about hearing her call out that name the night before, certain now that he'd just imagined it. But Elise did tell him that Adrienne planned to marry this man a split second after he summoned the nerve to ask if she would. He was five years younger than Adrienne, Elise said, and he'd been married once already — to a woman who'd been unkind, who'd called him awful names and wouldn't sleep in the same bed, who'd decided to run up north with another man just for the promise of some fun. She'd left him a note saying that what she couldn't stand was the thought of him working on all his father's corpses, taking care of that foul business.

Joshua Warren, Elise told Shelton, hadn't set foot out his house for months on end after his wife left him, and he'd taken up with Adrienne only because she'd been kind enough to visit him, bringing plates of food and mindless gossip, acting sorry as could be about all that had happened to him but secretly glad for someone to pay her some attention.

"How do you know all that?" Shelton asked Elise. They were out behind the house, where Elise was washing clothes in a great tin bucket. She twisted the shirts and pants and dresses dry and then hung them one by one on the rope stretched from the house to a tree branch near the alley.

Elise laughed and looked up at Shelton. "I just do," she said. "I know a lot."

"Tell me how," Shelton said. "Tell me how it is you know so much. Is it just from snooping?"

"There's other ways beyond snooping," Elise said, twisting a wet dress in her hand. She shook it out, and Shelton saw that the dress was the green one Adrienne was wearing when he first saw her. "Maybe I'd say more," she said, "but you'd just go and tell it, the way you did with what I said about my daddy being put in chains."

"I didn't mean to," Shelton said.

"But you did," Elise said, turning her back as if she'd walk off.

"I'm sorry," Shelton said. "Anyway, he told me it wasn't true."

Elise turned back to him. "I know what's true and what's not," she said. "What's true is my daddy was smart, that's what. Along comes a man my daddy knows he can point his finger at and say how this man's the one, not him. Maybe my daddy didn't kill the one they said he did, but maybe this man didn't either. You see? But my daddy's smart enough to point his finger and say, 'Look how I've got a wife and family. Look how he don't.' He's smart enough to say, 'I've got me my own woman, a wife. What do I need to be killing for another one?'"

"But he said —" Shelton started, but Elise threw her hands up, and the wet shirt she was holding flapped in Shelton's face, covering his head. Though he couldn't see her, Shelton heard her laugh.

"It's Ichabod Crane," Elise said, and Shelton laughed too.

"Come to catch you," Shelton said, and he held the wet shirt over his head with one hand, reaching with the other for Elise. For just a moment he thought of Minou, imagined him reaching out like this to grab hold of some man the way he'd imagined Elise grabbing hold of Samuel Warren, and then, just like that, Shelton managed to forget it, hearing only Elise's laughter and his own, caring only about trying to catch her.

"Here I am," Elise said, and Shelton leaped forward and fell.

"Over here now," Elise said, behind him, and Shelton stood up, leaped again, his hand stretched out.

"Here," Elise called, off in the distance now, laughing. "Here," she said. "Try and get me." And Shelton followed her voice the way he'd followed Genevieve's voice through the dark house. But this time, beneath that wet shirt, he was smiling. He was laughing and laughing.

And when I'd grown, I came to paint that work: a green strip of lawn, clothes hanging on a line stretching the whole length of canvas, a child with a shirt thrown over his head, the child's arms reaching out the wrong way, reaching for the girl who stands behind him, who stands more like a woman than a child, her hip thrown out, a hand resting on that hip, her mouth smiling as if she knows she'll never be caught.

Blind Man's Bluff I called that painting, but even with such a name it was misunderstood. That's a work about fear, people said. That's a poor black child playing Klansman, white sheet on his head.

I could have said, I guess, that this was one moment when fear didn't have a place, when the child felt free of his fear, free of everything. So if there was anything at all behind that work, behind the child doing what he did, maybe it was just his coming to know through a children's game what Minou knew when he let his eyes shut tight — that there was something to be gained by not seeing, that there was a freedom in it beyond what he could have hoped to attain when his eyes were open, when he was forced to see how things really were.

Blind Man's Bluff. That was Minou's game, wasn't it? Eyes closed, hands reaching out, hoping and hoping through his lie to find not another but himself.

❧ ❧ ❧

Later that day, when Adrienne and Joshua Warren had gone for a walk and were sitting together for two hours on the front porch, Elise performed her usual trick and snooped on them, crouching behind the open front door, then running to the kitchen to tell Olivia and Shelton about what they'd said.

"It'd make you sick, hearing it," Elise said. "She's so funny and cute, he says, and she says, no, he is, and he says, no, her, and she says, no, him. Then they hold hands and kiss, and he wants to know if she's heard this new record by Count Basie or the one by Duke Ellington, and she says no but she'd like to, she wishes she could. Then they hold hands and kiss some more, and I swear I can see her waiting for him to ask her. Now that Maw-Maw's gone and doesn't need looking after, her answer's just quivering on her lips. 'Yes, yes, please.' Like that."

Elise pretends to swoon while Olivia and Shelton laugh, the three of them making a great din in the kitchen. "Yes, yes, please," Olivia says now, smiling and laughing and reaching over to take Shelton's hand.

"Yes, yes, please," Elise says, taking his other hand. The two girls pretend to fight over him, slapping at each other's faces, saying, "He's mine, he's mine," and Shelton laughs and laughs, even though he knows that there's some truth in this exchange, a truth that all his laughing can't chase out of his head. That truth's not with the girls, of course, it's with him. It's his own longing.

One or the other, I don't care, he thinks, and his body burns with rage and shame and want, with the wishing that he'd gone to sleep with as a child, the wishing that wasn't for this or that but was just the wish of *having.*

And with the second day comes the news that Adrienne has now been asked to marry Joshua Warren, not once but three times, and she's said "I don't know" and then "Maybe" and then, smiling, turning a happy circle in her dress, "Yes, I think I will."

"All in the blink of an eye or shorter, I bet," Elise says to her, and Adrienne shoots her a look that declares how not even taunting and teasing can steal this sweet joy from inside her. She holds out her hand to show them all the ring that Elise said was tucked away and always would be in Joshua Warren's dresser drawer.

"Here it is," Adrienne says. "Here it is." And she waves her hand around, Elise tells her, just like she is the royal queen of England and not some old maid.

"Don't I feel like a queen," Adrienne says.

And Isabel says, "You've got every right to, yes you do," and gives Elise a look that says she'd better quit.

So Elise marches off from the kitchen to her bedroom the way she marched off when the dishtowel stung her back.

"She just can't stand it that she didn't know," Olivia tells Shelton. "She wanted to be the one to tell us. That's just how she is."

Shelton wants to follow her to her room, knock on the door, sit beside her. Instead he just watches as Adrienne's ring sparkles and shines in the light, and when she walks over and lifts her hand near his eyes so he'll have a better look, he says, "That's the nicest ring I've ever seen," and she leans down and kisses him on his cheek.

"What a sweet thing for you to say, Shelton," she says, and when she straightens up, steps away, he looks for a moment into her eyes, at the tears there.

"What is it?" he asks, but Adrienne turns and throws her head back, happy and proud. "It's just sweet," she says. "That's all." But Shelton knows he is seeing something more and has seen it, hasn't he, since the first moment, when she paused before coming up to the porch to greet him the day he ran from the Milne Home. She is just like him, isn't she, just like Minou said — full of a fear she doesn't know what for.

Or maybe she does know, and he's the one who doesn't. So he tries to study her now, to watch how she moves and speaks and smiles, saying she doesn't know when the wedding will take place but wouldn't spring be nice, maybe outside somewhere, not in some stuffy church, flowers scattered here and there.

Shelton looks, tries to name what he sees, but can't. There is something of Genevieve in her manner, isn't there, some great tiredness in all her energy, some great sorrow in her smile. Is that it? Is that all?

When Minou comes home that evening and hears the news, he goes out and then returns with some wine to celebrate. "I am one happy man," he says, raising his glass. "One down," he says, "and only two to go." He waves his glass at Olivia and Elise. "Get busy, girls," he says, "because I'm preparing for my freedom. I'm dreaming of the day when you're both grown and married, yes I am. I can taste it. I can." And he finishes his glass of wine and pours another.

"Not too much," Isabel says when Minou lifts the bottle toward her glass.

"No such thing as too much with news like this," Minou says, and he raises his glass to Adrienne. "That boy mention the money we owe his fat-ass father?"

"Hush now, Minou," Isabel says, wrapping her arms around him.

"He didn't," Adrienne says, and Shelton can see how the question embarrasses her. "And he's not a boy, Minou," she says. "Don't be calling him that."

"Well," Minou says, "I just hope the man's father understands now how there's no point to it. It'd be like taking with one hand and giving with the other, wouldn't it? It'd be like stealing from your own wife's pocketbook."

And Shelton sees Minou's eyes turn toward him, letting him know that the mention of pocketbooks and stealing is no accident or coincidence, is meant in fact just for him.

"You go talk to Samuel Warren now," Isabel tells Minou, running her hand over his head.

"I'd rather talk to the devil," Minou says, pulling his head away. "I'd rather have a long drawn-out conversation with a white man than talk to that high-class nigger."

"Listen to me," Isabel says.

"I don't need to listen," Minou says.

"Well, you're going to listen," Isabel says, putting her hands on her hips and standing before Minou. "You go talk to Samuel Warren this very evening, right now. You tell Samuel Warren you're mighty proud his son is marrying my sister. You tell him that and shake his hand and let that be that. Let that be the beginning and end of this."

"And what if he asks for the money?" Minou says.

"He won't," Isabel says. "He's not going to let a funeral bill spoil this news, so don't you let it either. Now go on."

Adrienne walks over and kisses Minou's cheek. "Please," she says.

Minou turns to Shelton. "Like I said. Not just one queen in this house, Shelton. Four of them. Four." He holds up his fingers. "And a one-eyed Jack," he says, laughing now, taking the glass from Isabel's hand and drinking her wine. "Two of us," he says. "Two one-eyed Jacks."

He bows to Isabel. "Your wish —" he says.

"My wish," Isabel says, stopping him, "is for you to get yourself over to Samuel Warren's this minute."

"I'm going, I'm going," Minou says, and he turns again to Shelton. "You interested in accompanying me, Jack?" he says. "It'd make a pair of eyes between us."

"So you won't get lost, then," Isabel says. "You won't wind up somewhere else, will you?"

"We won't," Minou says, and Shelton follows him through the house.

"Now the fine time starts," Isabel calls out so Minou will hear. "The men's all gone. Now it's women's time."

Minou just laughs and shakes his head, and Shelton follows him down Foucher Street to Tchoupitoulas.

"Where do they live?" Shelton asks, picturing in his head Elise's story about punching Samuel Warren, picturing what he pictured before: Elise on top of him, hands at the man's throat, popping that woman's corset.

"Doesn't matter where he lives," Minou says to Shelton. "That's not where we're going."

"Where are we going?" Shelton asks.

"You'll see, child. You'll see."

They walk a few blocks down Tchoupitoulas until they reach Louisiana Avenue; then they turn and walk another block or two to where the street ends and the dark shape of a great levee looms before them.

"What's this?" Shelton asks, and Minou takes his hand and leads him up the slope, steeper than the side of Monkey Hill.

"Just wait a minute," Minou says, and when they reach the top Shelton sees where they are — at the Mississippi River. Down the bank, Shelton can see lights by the water and a line of square-shaped buildings. He raises his hand and points.

"That's the riverfront docks," Minou tells him. "That's where they unload all the boats."

Here, though, where Shelton and Minou stand, there are only rocks and a stretch of grass lining the river, and Shelton looks over at Minou.

Minou leans down and pulls a bottle from between two rocks. "Here we go," he says, and he takes the top off the bottle, raises it to his mouth, and swallows. Again he turns to Shelton. "Now, don't you go on about this," he says, and he takes a seat on one of the rocks. "There'll be plenty of chances to go see Samuel Warren. Tonight I just need some peace and quiet."

Shelton can't walk along the rocks and keep his balance, so he steps back to the grass and sits down there, the earth damp to the touch. While Minou sits with his eyes closed, his body swaying as if he is listening to music, Shelton looks out at the water and hears the sound it makes spilling over the rocks. He thinks of how he'd wanted, the day he ran from the Milne Home, to dip his body in the water of the lake. Now he imagines himself swimming out into the river, lying on his back and letting the water carry him farther and farther until he winds up, like a fish swimming home, in the Gulf of Mexico, which is ten times, his mother told him, the size of Lake Pontchartrain.

Then Shelton sees, imagines he sees from the water, that boy Emanuel Jackson sitting on the shore, looking over at him and laughing, laughing and shaking his head the way Minou just did when they walked out of the house.

"Minou," Shelton says, a whisper.

"What is it?" Minou asks, opening his eyes, and when Shelton doesn't answer, he says, "Go ahead. Tell me what's on your mind."

"There was a boy," Shelton says, "a boy at the Milne Home. You ever hear of Carville, Louisiana?"

"I haven't," Minou says, and he raises the bottle to his lips. "How come?"

"Well, this boy. He said that across the other side of Lake

Pontchartrain, they've got there a place named Carville. And that's where they keep lepers."

"Leopards, you mean?" Minou asks. "Like lions and tigers?"

"No," Shelton says. "Lepers. It's something that happens to their skin."

"Lepers," Minou says. "Leprosy. I understand now. But you see that boy again sometime, you're going to have to explain how he's mistaken."

"How come?" Shelton asks.

Minou sets the bottle down at his feet. "Because I know the place he means. I've seen it with my own two eyes, in fact, and it's nowhere near the Pontchartrain. It's down near Baton Rouge and right beside the river. My own father pointed it out to me that time I rode the boat with him. A world unto itself, that's what he told me. Ten or so big buildings, and there's a great wall around it, and those who go in don't ever come out. They won't let them." Minou leans toward Shelton. "I saw it myself," he says. "There's times I even imagined living behind those walls."

"How come?" Shelton asks again.

Minou shakes his head. "I can't remember now," he says. "Maybe it seemed safe. Maybe I figured the folks inside there didn't have to do so much as a moment's work. How is it you were thinking of that place?"

"I don't know," Shelton says. "I was just wondering if all he said was true."

"What all did he say?" Minou asks, standing up and looking out at the river.

"He said you could catch it by swimming in the same water they swam in."

Minou laughs. "Maybe you could if that water was a bucket," he says. "Beyond that, I don't think there's cause for worry. You're not worried about it, are you?"

"No," Shelton says. "I was just thinking about it, that's all."

"Good," Minou says, and he pretends to throw something out

into the water, or maybe he does throw something, because the child hears a splash.

Minou leans down and picks up a stick and begins scratching it against one of the rocks. "Now let me ask you something, Shelton, if you don't mind," he says. "The other evening, when you wound up at Mr. Edward's, what was it you were hoping for?"

"I don't know," Shelton says.

"Were you hoping he'd take you in? Is that it?"

"I don't know," Shelton says again, looking not at Minou but out at the water, trying to listen to its rippling and washing against the banks.

"I'm not angry, son," Minou says. "I'm just asking. There might come a time when you've got to ask such questions yourself, when you need to decide just what you want."

"I don't know what you mean," Shelton says.

Minou throws the stick out into the water. "I'm saying what if Edward Soniat comes back? You went by his house and spoke your name. He'll know now that you're around somewhere. What if he finds out where you are and knocks on my door? What is it I should tell this man?"

Shelton thinks about his dream of leading Mr. Edward through the rooms of Minou's house, watching him sleep on the front-room sofa.

"You gave that Negro man your name, Shelton," Minou says now, his voice rising as though he is angry. "You gave him your name, and if he's got half a mind, he'll give that name to Edward Soniat and he'll know."

"Know what?" Shelton asks.

Minou shakes his head and slaps his hand against his leg, a slap that echoes across the water. "Why'd you go there, son?" he says. "What was it you wanted? You've got to try to answer that. Not for me but for your own self."

"I don't know," Shelton says, and he feels his breath rush out of him, feels his legs twitching and his hands beginning to shake.

"Well, sometime you've got to know. You just do," Minou says.

Shelton looks down, looks away. "Mama," he says, and he hears Minou sigh, hears his shoes scraping against the rocks as he walks off and walks back.

"That girl wasn't your mama," Minou says. "That's something you've got to get straightened out in your head. She might have looked after you as best as she could. But you were purchased, Shelton. You were purchased. You understand?"

Shelton looks up at Minou, sees the anger on his face.

"Why are you mad?" Shelton says.

"There are times when you've got to see the truth," Minou says, "times when you can't keep telling yourself the same lies over and over again."

"Like that man being killed," Shelton says, and Minou kneels down, leans close to him.

"Who?" he says.

Shelton feels his body shaking, feels Minou's breath, the wine he's been drinking, blowing like a warm breeze against his face.

"Who do you mean?" Minou says again.

"Elise," Shelton says, and Minou grabs Shelton by the shoulders.

"That damn child," he says. "Don't you be thinking like her. I already told you. Don't you be listening and believing all that girl says."

"I don't," Shelton says. "She just —"

"Look here," Minou says, and he's shaking Shelton's shoulders now. "She's not the one who knows. She's just a child. You want to know something, you ask me, you hear. You want to know something, you step up to me."

Minou lets go of Shelton, then puts his hand on Shelton's head. "That's what you do," he says, his voice quiet now, just a whisper. "You come to me."

Shelton looks at him. "Tell me why I'm here, then," he says. "Tell me why you came to get me."

Minou stands up and turns away. Shelton hears him spit. "I can't do that," he says. "Lord knows you're sure to find out sooner or later. But I can't be the one to tell you."

"Then who?" Shelton says. "Why not?" And now he's crying, slamming his fists against his legs.

"Come on," Minou says. "Quit." He walks over to Shelton, helps him stand. "Quit now. You'll go hurting yourself again."

Minou holds Shelton's wrists and forces his hands down to his sides; then he lets go. "There," he says. "That's it. We've got to head back now. We've got to tell them how kind and understanding Samuel Warren turned out to be."

Minou holds Shelton's arm as they walk back up the levee. At the top, Minou turns again to look at the river. "You ready to try this again?" he asks.

"Try what?" Shelton says, thinking he means rolling down the side of the levee the way Shelton and Olivia and Elise rolled down Monkey Hill.

"Going to work with me," Minou says. "Maybe learning what I've got to teach you."

"Okay," Shelton says.

"You've got to, in any case," Minou says. "There's no other jobs stepping up and asking for you."

"Okay," Shelton says again.

"Tomorrow morning, then," Minou says, and Shelton stops walking.

"Listen to me," Minou says. "I understand this is nothing you want to do. I understand there's no joy in standing around and taking in money because there's white folks feeling sorry for you. You think I don't understand all that?"

"I don't know," Shelton says.

"Well, I do," Minou says. "I'll tell you this. I understand it a whole lot more than you. I know that people don't take home what I've drawn and feel they've acquired some great work. Maybe they look a few times and laugh. Maybe they pass it around to family and friends so they'll laugh too. But mostly what they do is feel good inside because they've given a dollar to a blind and hungry nigger. I understand all that."

"Why do you do it, then?" Shelton asks.

"Because I've got to," Minou says. "I've got a family to feed." He walks back to Shelton. "Some things are just hard," he says. "Look at us now. Think where we're supposed to be. I'm supposed to be shaking Samuel Warren's hand and slapping his back and telling him what a fine girl his son's got in Adrienne."

"How come you're not?" Shelton asks. "Why didn't we go there?"

"No reason," Minou says. "At least not one that makes any sense. I told you, didn't I, how my daddy was a superstitious one, believing all manner of this and that? Well, I'm not like that in most ways. Not at all, in fact. But there's something about what that man does, looking after those dead bodies. It makes me more like my daddy than I'd care to be. 'Don't take a step closer to death than you have to,' he used to say, 'or what you'll find is death's taken a step closer too.' I'd like to think that's just all superstition, but I see that man and I'm like you were the other day. I want to run in the other direction."

"That's what Elise said about Joshua Warren, about the wife who left him," Shelton says. "She said that's the reason why his wife ran off from him."

Minou laughs now. "There you go believing that girl again," he says. "Listen to me. There's a million reasons why a woman might leave a man. A million reasons." Minou looks up at the night sky as if, Shelton thinks, he means to count the stars there. "A million reasons, Shelton," he says, "and only one reason to stay. Doesn't sound like a fair deal, does it?"

Minou looks down at Shelton, and Shelton shakes his head.

"Well, it's not a fair deal," Minou says. "So you just try to hold on. That's what Joshua Warren will do with Adrienne if he's any kind of man. That's what any good man does. He just holds on."

"You too?" Shelton asks.

"With Isabel?" Minou says, and he laughs. "I've tried to. Sometimes I've been damn near close to not trying hard enough. I'll see when we get home, though, won't I? I'll see when I tell her where we have and haven't been. Maybe that will be one more reason for her to give up."

"You're going to tell her we didn't go there?" Shelton says.

"I've got to," Minou says. "Or else the not telling her would become a reason too. You see?"

Minou takes Shelton's arm, and they head down the levee. "No, it's not a fair deal," Minou says. "But let's wait and see."

When they get to the house, Minou stops on the porch and turns to Shelton. "There's one more thing I meant to tell you," he says. "I don't want you worrying about it now, though I suspect you will. I suspect I would too, if I was you. Adrienne has talked about this with us, with Isabel and me, and we've got to talk some more before it's settled. But I wanted you to know."

"What?" Shelton asks, seeing in his mind the way Adrienne's eyes filled with tears when she bent down to kiss him, the way she stepped toward him and then back, the way she lifted her hand to shake his hand but then dropped her arm to her side, the way she acted as if just speaking to him was so difficult and complicated she could hardly manage it.

And just thinking of all that, the child knows, doesn't he? He has the answer to the question that for years and years he didn't even know to ask. Now he does, though. And now he has the answer. It's Adrienne. She's his mother. But he waits for Minou to tell him.

"We've talked about once they're married and settled into their own home —"

Minou stops, and again Shelton says, "What?"

"We've talked about, considering how little room we've got and all, your going to live with them, with Joshua Warren and Adrienne, live in their home."

And the child surprises himself when he doesn't turn to run, when he doesn't cry out or let his hands curl into fists or let the shaking in his legs sweep him down to the ground, falling and falling.

"Fine," he says. And though he has to turn his head away and squeeze his eyes shut, he says it again. "Fine."

And it isn't just one thing now but two that he has learned this evening, the second being that Minou can lie to him, has lied to him again and again about finding out and telling him who is the one who gave him away, who left him on that doorstep. He has known all along, hasn't he?

So now, Shelton thinks, *I've lied too.* "Fine," he has said, as simple as that, and he has let his lie stand, let it be all Minou knows of the million and one thoughts swimming through his head, clawing at his heart the way his hands clawed when he fell, clawing for the grip of those branches, of just one branch, just one.

And Minou, as if some great gust of wind has stolen his breath, has swept him into silence, opens the screen door to the house and steps off to the side. He raises his arms to form a bridge across the doorway and lets Shelton, looking down, looking away, walk inside beneath them.

14 THE WRECKED, BLESSED
BODY OF SHELTON LAFLEUR

YES, THE CHILD had lied now. He'd said it would be fine if, come spring, once Adrienne married Joshua Warren, he was sent off to live with them. It wouldn't be fine, though. No, it wouldn't. No, it would not. It would be no finer than the child's quick fall from the sky, than his five years in the Milne Home. It would be no finer than enduring all the taunting and teasing only to learn, once he'd run from the home, that his mother, his white mother, had gone ahead and died.

That girl wasn't your mama, he heard in his head. That was Minou's voice, Minou's voice, speaking to him.

Yes, speaking to him still, though Minou had gone off to bed and Shelton had lain down on the front-room sofa, pulled the blanket over him, asked only for sleep.

And someone was listening — someone or something. Can't you see the sky split open? Can't you see the clouds tear apart the way they do after a sudden shower of rain? This is just a child's story, so maybe you've got to imagine turning the page and finding that split-open sky stretching out above the sleeping child.

And listen now. Does a child — any child, not just Shelton —

feel that each day dawns only once he has opened his eyes, that the day ends the very moment when those eyes shut, that the world is no larger than the reach of his hands, no older than the day when he took his place there, kicking and screaming?

Or can a child — and I do mean Shelton now — understand that the world carries on without him, that it's not his opening eyes that lift the sun on the horizon, not his feet that plant the ground beneath him? Does he understand that the sky can split open while he sleeps, that words are being spoken far beyond his hearing? Does he recognize that plans are forever being made?

If that's the case, then when Shelton lay down on that sofa, couldn't he have imagined, before he drifted off to sleep, all that had gone on beyond what he could see and hear? Wasn't that, after all, his life's story?

There's Mr. Edward plotting and scheming to acquire a child.

There's Genevieve doing the same to get the child back.

There's Minou planning to take Shelton away from the home.

There's Genevieve and Minou talking.

There's Minou and Isabel, Minou and Adrienne, Minou and Mr. Edward, Mr. Edward and Genevieve, Mr. Edward and Adrienne.

There's plans forever, forever being made.

Look now. There's that child lying down on the front-room sofa, asking only for sleep. He's reciting a list of names in his head, the names of those he cares for, who care for him or did: Minou, Mama, Mr. Edward, Genevieve, Olivia, Elise, Isabel, Adrienne.

But there's a question behind those names: Who is it, which one of them, has gone and twisted his life around so that no matter what he does or where he might be, his body always seems about to turn and go?

Minou lied and lied, refused to tell all he knew.

Mr. Edward didn't search for him, hunt him down, didn't find him and bring him home.

Genevieve had known where he was, had known all along, had watched and watched him like a waiting hawk. How come?

And Adrienne — she'd handed him over, hadn't she? Couldn't he feel how her hands had wrapped around his chest, how they'd held him up high, set him down on that doorstep?

Listen to the scraping of the child's feet on the pavement anytime he tries to get from here to there — isn't that like some wounded animal planting its bloodstained tracks in the snow, making a trail as jagged and curved as the hole in that tin-topped glass jar, a trail leading up to the very spot where finally those legs bend and buckle and collapse, a quiet thump when it's time just to lie down, to let the quickening breaths slow?

Which one of them, which one, the child wants to know, is responsible for his bent back and twisted limbs, for the shame he carries around every moment, the shame and fear and sorrow that his body holds out for all to see, gruesome and sickening, a strange and frightening display?

Which one of them believed or believes still that a child doesn't have reason to know the house he was born in, the woman whose body he'd slipped out of, the hands that first held him, the smiles or laughter or tears of whoever had witnessed the awful or magnificent wonder of his birth?

Oh, that's me, isn't it? That's nothing a child would think or say.

Well, forget what the child did or didn't ask. Isn't it still the case that the list of names he recited could perform like a mighty prayer, like a rising cloud of magic smoke? Isn't it possible that this evening could be the one where the sky split open and grace finally, finally turned its ear and thought to listen, thought to pay this one muttering child a visit?

Listen now. The child asked only for sleep. But what he got instead was another dream, one in which he's been set down atop some hill to look over the whole landscape. He looks from one direction to the next as if this is his final chance, as if he's being asked to see himself step down from that spot, set off without any cause or desire to look back.

There he is, there his body is, marching west into the sunset, north into the snow, east into the ocean, south down the river, the black scratch of a child he'd been before floating strong and steady now, slipping away like a leaping fish into the endless swirling blue of the Gulf of Mexico.

And grace doesn't think like miracles. No, grace has got its own trick. It's got other, truer business at hand. So in the child's dream his body isn't straightened and healed the way a miracle would choose to do. No, the child's body remains broken and twisted and wrecked. But here's what grace does, here's the trick grace performs: Every break, bend, and twist in the child's body serves now to wring the fear out from inside him, a steady stream pouring out the way all that water must have poured out from inside the body of Genevieve Simmons.

Now his limbs feel stronger, don't they, as if he'll stride down the hill in great, leaping steps, as if the awkward swing and scrape of his gait don't matter at all.

Well, they don't matter, do they, for the child can, if that's what he decides, just set aside his walking and fly instead, sweep this way and that, zigzag through the air, no longer a child at all but something else, some other kind of creature — a pigeon or dove or one of twilight's black-winged bats, looking down on the whole world, shooting up and up forever into the darkening sky, the world like a bright falling coin beneath him.

Look: There's the white Milne Home and Minou's shotgun house. There's Mr. Edward's great Garden District home and his mother's private quarters. There they all are, tumbling and turning, falling and falling while the child flies away.

Yes, what the child sees now, what he understands, is that at any moment he can just run again, run away for good this time, leave them all behind. That's what he'll do, won't he, when the time is right. He'll wait and wait, the way he waited at the Milne

Home, then he'll find his chance, find a moment when no one is set to look for him, when no one knows to look.

And in the meantime, he'll live with the knowledge of what is lying in wait, the world stretching out before him in whatever direction he'll choose to take.

And in the morning, when Minou steps into the front room holding his long wooden stick and his heavy wooden case, Shelton is already awake, already dressed. "Set to go, I see," Minou says into the darkness.

"Yes," Shelton answers, meaning more than Minou knows. *Set to go?* Shelton thinks. *Yes, I am. Yes, I am.*

So they walk to St. Charles Avenue, take the streetcar to Canal Street, step down Royal Street over to Jackson Square. The light's come up as Minou swings open his case, unfolds and assembles his easel, pulls out the yellowed paper and the charcoal square.

Shelton watches Minou now. He considers how Minou has gone through these same motions, this unpacking and assembling, this blind-man performance, every day for years and years. And Shelton wonders if there's a moment every now and then when Minou thinks to call out for a visit such as the one he received last night in his dream. Isn't there ever a time when Minou asks for the work of his hands to go beyond whoever stands before him, a work that calls out from this world to another, a work that shines like a light up to heaven, signaling the path grace might take if it had a mind to pay a visit, to bless the work of this one man's hands?

Isn't that what I've done with my own work? I've spent hours and hours trying to get right a flower's twist and curl, the straight spine of its stem, eyes filled with longing or sorrow or fear, a sloped shoulder, a store window, the patch of grass atop some hill, my own strange dark face time and time again — hasn't it all been one long, loud call to grace, asking it please to take the body of my work in its hands and somehow bless it?

The Wrecked, Blessed Body of Shelton Lafleur. I don't need to paint such a work, do I, for I've already painted it, and not just once but again and again, each and every time I lifted my hands.

Here's my question, then: Did Minou feel the same of his own work? Wasn't there something more to it than just the means of feeding his family, of fooling the whole world with his pretend blindness? Wasn't Minou waiting and waiting as well for that quick flash of light, for the single true note, for the one perfect work that is grace coming down, coming down, to touch him?

Look: At Jackson Square, not just on this day but during all the ones to follow, Shelton watches Minou, watches him the way he hadn't watched before. He's looking for the secret behind Minou's blindness — and finds it just like that, seeing how every few minutes Minou's eyes open, the smallest line but enough to see who or what stands before him, letting that sight become the picture he keeps in his head, the picture his hand then sets about drawing.

And Shelton listens to the stories Minou tells, the lies — they're all lies, aren't they? — that he makes up for his listeners' benefit, for the crowds that gather around not just to watch Minou draw but to hear him go on and on.

"Mexico?" Minou says to one man. "I know about Mexico, yes I do. Just a child, I was, but I've seen it for myself. Seen it, yes I have, for I wasn't always blind."

Shelton hears Minou's voice rise, as if he's delivering a speech, as if he's a preacher standing in the pulpit and those gathered around, though they're laughing and shaking their heads, are his devout congregation. "Yes, and there's Mexico in my blood," Minou says. "My own grandfather, my mother's father — he was a Mexican himself, skin dark as mine but red. He was a justice of the peace. Justice of the peace in a town called San Miguel de Mezquital and employed by the local priest. Now there's a crazy one for you, believing as he did that the Holy Spirit was fluttering inside his chest, just roosting on his ribs, feeding on his liver. Was my grandfather who painted the patron saint, hundreds of hundreds of times painted the same damn work, just so that priest could sell the paintings to the dirt-poor peasants for corn and bread, for wine and cheese, for their labor in building a brand-new church. This crazy priest, you see, the one with the Holy Spirit in his chest, was just hell-bent on having his own cathedral. Here you go."

And when the man walks away, Minou's picture in his hand, Shelton steps up and says, "That's not true, what you said."

"What's not true?" Minou answers, smiling and smiling and shaking his head, his voice still raised, his hands stretched out as if he's summoning the whole crowd nearer.

"About your grandfather," Shelton says.

"It's all true," Minou says. "You run along now. There's folks waiting to have a blind man draw them."

"It's not true," Shelton says again.

"Listen now," Minou says, and he waves Shelton over. "Let me tell you what my grandfather once told me. He was a Roman Catholic, though he wasn't much for believing such things. But he told me how once he left this world, I should look up to the sky for him every now and then. 'I'm going to spend my summers in heaven and my winters in hell,' he said. 'And the angels are going to fly me back and forth. So you better watch for me, child. Look up at the sky. Watch for me flying overhead.' That's what he said."

"I don't believe it," Shelton says.

"You hear me asking you to believe it?" Minou says. "You run along, then. There's folks here waiting for their picture."

And Shelton looks around now, sees the crowd gathered near, growing larger and larger. "But it's not true," Shelton says, pleading now, calling out as if he's the one who has lost Minou.

"It's all true," Minou says. "Sure it is. And I'll tell you what else. My grandfather lived to be one hundred years old, one hundred to the very day. Was only three years ago, in fact, that he passed.

It was his birthday, and what he did was just set off walking. He walked and walked until he found a mountain, and then he walked straight up the side of that mountain. Not very high, maybe, but high enough. Then he just threw himself off."

"Why?" Shelton asks.

And Minou stops and smiles. "I thought you said how this wasn't true."

"It's not," Shelton says.

"Then don't bother yourself doing what I do."

"What?" Shelton says.

"Come here," Minou says, and Shelton moves closer, lets Minou put his arm around his shoulder. "What I do is step outside every fall and spring and turn my head up to the sky. These eyes might be blind, but there's things they can see, and one of those things is the angels above. So I look for him, that's what I do."

"Have you seen him?" Shelton says, and he understands now, doesn't he? He sees how the crowd has gone silent, how they've stopped laughing and shaking their heads, how they're ready now to believe whatever Minou says.

"Not yet I haven't," Minou says, and his voice sounds as if soon it will give way to weeping. "No, sir. I haven't seen him yet. But with God's grace I will. With God's grace I one day will. I'll turn my head up, and wonder of wonders, there he'll be, two wings sprouting from out his back. That's just what my eyes will see."

And Shelton turns his head up toward the sky like Minou, and he hears what he now expects to hear, what this story has been about all along: the ring of coins on the pavement beneath their feet, a ringing that goes on until finally Minou lowers his head and says, "Thank you all. Thank you kindly. God bless you."

❧ ❧ ❧

It's at Minou's house, nights when Minou has gone off wherever he goes, that Shelton tries to find out the truth. He doesn't ask questions, can't make himself ask those questions of Adrienne,

218

but he watches her. He watches her cooking in the kitchen, watches her laugh outside on the porch with Joshua Warren, fireflies here and there like twinkling stars, Adrienne's laugh as bright as a candle flame, Joshua Warren nodding his head, waving his hands in the air, listening and listening to Adrienne.

Shelton watches her, looks at her face, trying to see something of his own face there. He sees it sometimes, he thinks, when she looks away, looks down to the floor, when she tries talking to him, tries to make conversation. *How are you doing with Minou at Jackson Square? Learning to draw, are you? No, and why not? Minou could teach you, should be teaching you, and would you care to go sometime with me and Joshua to the picture show or the park or just over to Magazine Street?*

And she puts her hand on his arm from time to time, asks if he'll give her a hand snapping beans, peeling potatoes, slicing apples, washing greens.

"Fine," he says. "Fine," almost as quiet now as he was at the Milne Home, watching, listening, waiting.

Yes, he's waiting for some word from her, for the one story that contains her secret message: *I'm your true mama, Shelton. Here I am.*

And with Isabel — the two of them alone, Minou gone off, Adrienne with Joshua Warren, the girls wandering along Magazine Street or sitting on friends' porches — Shelton asks about Minou, asks how she came to meet him, what she knows of his childhood. Did he have a grandfather from Mexico? Could his mother play piano just like Fats Waller? Could she grow a thousand tomatoes from a single vine? Did Minou once swim clear across the Mississippi? Were any of the stories he told more than lies?

And Isabel smiles, doesn't answer Shelton's questions but tells some story of her own — of how Minou asked to marry her by showing up one evening with a picture he'd drawn, a silly cartoon; of how Minou's father was big as a giant, strong as an ox, liked his drink just as much as Minou but was always gentle with his child, always gentle; of how Minou had once gone to college in hopes of becoming a true artist, but then his children were born and the hard times started and that was the way things seemed to go.

"Where is he?" Shelton asks one night. "Where is it he goes?"

"There's different places, I imagine," Isabel says.

"Like where?" Shelton asks.

"He likes his pleasures," Isabel says. "That's all I'll say. There are places. Maybe he just goes to drink. I could find him, I guess, if I wanted to."

And she turns to Shelton, looks at him. "You take the good with the bad when it comes to that man. There's more good than bad. That's something you ought to know."

Shelton looks at her, waits.

"You're happy here?" she says.

Shelton nods, looks away.

"Well, he'll look after you. That's enough. It's got to be."

❧ ❧ ❧

Then one day, late in the summer, at the end of a long day at Jackson Square, Minou tells Shelton he's got some business to attend to. "You stay here a while," Minou says. "I'll be back to get you."

"Where are you going?" Shelton asks, and Minou picks up his stick, taps it twice on the ground, then turns to Shelton. "I'll be back," Minou says. "Keep your eye on my things. Draw me a picture."

"I can't draw," Shelton says. "I've never drawn anything."

"You can see, can't you?" Minou says.

"Yes," Shelton says.

"Then you're already two steps ahead of me." Minou laughs. "Go on, then. I won't be long."

So Shelton watches Minou walk off, watches him head past the cathedral and then out of sight down Chartres Street. Shelton steps over to the easel and picks up one of the charcoal squares. He thinks of Minou closing his eyes, raising his hand to the paper. What is it that Minou, with no one standing before him, would draw?

Shelton closes his eyes and sees Olivia. That's who he'll draw, won't he — her bright smile, her gentle manner. Or Elise, though what he sees is her dress falling down to the floor, her body stretched out on the bed. There's Adrienne and Isabel; there's Genevieve slumped in her chair, his mother curled in her bed.

He can't draw any of that, can he? He doesn't know how to. Then he hears a shout, and he looks over toward the river. On Decatur Street, right in front of where the white people drink their coffee at iron tables, an old man is standing by a fruit and vegetable cart. His horse is lowering its head but refusing to drink from the bucket of water the man has placed in front of it. "Goddamn it, I'll just shoot you," the man shouts, and Shelton watches him struggle, watches him kick and curse.

Then Shelton lifts his hand and, just like that, begins to draw. What's the child doing? Who is it that's guiding his hand?

It's just chicken scratch, isn't it? No, it's something more. The child is trying to capture the setting sun washing across the stacks of fruit and vegetables, but not just that: the horse jerking its neck, the man straining against it, grabbing the horse's tangled mane, cursing.

Look how the cart's wood planks are weathered gray and knotted. Look how the muscles in the horse's legs are like the muscles of the man's arms. Look how the cart's spoked wheels are leaning, as if soon they'll break off, roll of their own accord down the street and away.

So Shelton draws and draws, continuing even when the man finally climbs back onto the cart, whips the reins up and down, clatters away. Shelton closes his eyes and thinks of Minou, tries to remember what he's just seen. He draws and draws and doesn't stop drawing until Minou comes up behind him and puts a hand on his shoulder.

"So you've seen something?" Minou says, and Shelton nods.

"Good," Minou says. "Good for you."

"You like it?" Shelton asks.

"It's fine," Minou says. "It's fine enough." He turns to Shelton. "You want to learn?" he asks. "That what you want to do?"

"Yes," Shelton says, and he looks again at the picture. That is what he wants, isn't it? "Yes," he says again.

"Then that's fine," Minou says, and he glances down. Shelton looks toward Minou's feet and sees the case there, a wooden case just like Minou's.

"You've got to carry that yourself," Minou says.

"I will."

"You got to learn now. That cost me some money."

"Okay."

Minou starts to pack the paper and charcoal in his own case. He folds the easel and puts it away.

"We're happy now, aren't we?"

"Yes," Shelton says.

"Yes, we are," Minou says. "And someday soon folks are going to be paying good money for you drawing them. Come on, now. Let's go on home."

But Minou stops. "You understand how the game is played?" he says, and Shelton looks at him, sees the frown on Minou's face.

"There's only one thing about as good as a blind artist," Minou says, and he raises his hand and places it on Shelton's shoulder.

"What?" Shelton says.

"A crippled one," Minou says. "That's the game. That's the sad truth of it. You understand?"

"I do," Shelton says, and he lifts his case, holds it up against his hip, and starts walking.

15   QUIET NOW

How to describe the child's happiness in Minou's presence as summer turned to fall with its quick burst of color, patches of red and orange among the city's never-changing green, a chill blowing in now across the wide Mississippi, north to south across Lake Pontchartrain, the wind carrying the news that soon, any day now, this cool dry weather would change to become winter?

The girls went back to school, spent their evenings bent over paper tablets and tooth-marked pencils and falling-apart books. Olivia nailed herself to her chair, while Elise darted here and there in search of distractions. Isabel and Adrienne told Minou that by all rights Shelton belonged in school right beside the girls, but Minou shook his head and said, "He's learning more than enough already."

"I am," Shelton said, smiling. "I swear I am."

And Minou turned, triumphant, to Isabel and Adrienne. "You see now? You hear the child? That's that."

"What's a child know, Minou?" Isabel said. "He's just a boy."

"No more," Minou said. "He's learning now from me."

"That's just what we fear," Adrienne told him.

"Well, you'll see," Minou said, and every morning he stepped into the front room to wake Shelton, to lead him over to Jackson Square.

And every morning Shelton set up his own easel right next to Minou's, drawing whatever Minou asked him to draw: the towering cathedral, the statue of Andrew Jackson, a pigeon perched atop the iron fence, the dark automobiles parked over on Decatur, the empty iron tables, it being too cold now for the white folks to sit outside and drink their coffee.

And from time to time now, along with all the other stories he told, Minou told Shelton's story too — how the child, this child right here, had fallen from a thirty-foot tree, how he'd been teased and taunted in the orphans' home, how a poor old blind man, Minou himself, had saved him, had stolen him away, had taken him home and given him a place to sleep. Now he was teaching the child, despite the child's being crippled and himself being blind, how to draw a good picture, how to make an honest living with the work of his hands.

"Winter's coming," Minou called out. "Want to know how cold we'll be? Frost on the windows inside and out. The poor crippled child's teeth chattering day and night. You think he's got a blanket? Well, he don't."

And Shelton stretched his hand out, took the coins that were offered, said, "Thank you. God bless you. You're kind, yes you are."

Minou wouldn't let Shelton draw people's portraits, though the child asked and asked. "Not yet," he said. "That's the last step. You're still trying. You're still making an effort. Once you learn to quit trying, when the drawing comes natural, that's when it's time to take on what's human. You don't want to be wrestling now with all that."

But at night, when everyone had gone to sleep except Minou,

who sat up in the kitchen with his book, Shelton would push the blanket off him, switch on the front-room light, and pull the paper and charcoal from his case. He drew his mother's face, her hair stretched out across a pillow. He drew a profile of Minou with his eyes closed, his head thrown back, his jaw clenched. He drew Olivia, tried to show the light in her dark eyes. He drew Elise, not just her face but her whole body, her whole shape.

And what was the child thinking drawing such a picture? He felt desperate in his longing, didn't he? He wanted to know the touch of that body, wanted to feel her hands on his own. His longing was so great that it was as if all his questions about his life had joined together, were towering over him now like a great marble statue or coiled inside him like a snake, frightening and dangerous, unnameable and endless, as large as the whole universe, as small and sharp as the point on the blade of a knife.

Where'd he come from? Why'd Minou come get him? Why wouldn't Minou or Adrienne or Isabel speak?

And one night, when even Minou had gone off to bed, Shelton stood up from the sofa and walked back through the house, stopping at the door to the girls' room and pushing it open until he could see the girls' beds. There was Olivia, a blanket pulled over her, even her head tucked underneath. And there was Elise, the blanket kicked away, the blanket lying on the floor by the foot of her bed, Elise in her nightdress, the nightdress twisted like a rope just above her knees, her arms thrown out wide as if she were dead.

Shelton walked over, took the blanket from the floor. He raised it to lay over her, but then Elise sat up.

"Shelton?" she said, sleepy, eyes half closed.

"I was just going to cover you," he whispered, his hands shaking, the blanket falling at his feet the way he'd imagined Elise's dress falling to her own.

"What else?" Elise said, laughing quietly now.

"That's all," Shelton said.

And Elise reached out, let the tips of her fingers touch his chest. "Go on to bed, little boy," she said.

"I'm not —" Shelton said, but now Olivia stirred.

"Here's Shelton," Elise said, and Olivia sat up.

"What?" she said, and Shelton turned to her. "What's wrong?" she said.

"He's just playing mama," Elise said. "Or he's walking in his sleep. Or something else. You still asleep, Shelton? Or maybe it's something else?"

"It's not," Shelton said. "I'm not asleep." And now both of the girls laughed.

"Quiet now," Shelton said. "I'll go."

"No," Olivia said, but he left the girls there, left them sitting up in their beds, left them laughing.

"Goodnight, Shelton," Elise called out, but he didn't answer. He walked back to the front room and pulled his own blanket over him, his hands still shaking.

What had he meant to do? What had he hoped for by stepping into the darkness of the girls' room? He'd just wanted to see her, see Elise. No, he'd wanted her to reach her arms out, call his name. And then?

He tossed and turned beneath the blanket. He tossed and turned until finally, in sweet relief, he fell asleep.

🍂 🍂 🍂

The colder it got outside, the fewer people strolled through Jackson Square, and Minou sometimes left Shelton now for hours at a time, walking off with his wooden stick stretched out in front of him, tapping the pavement. Minou wouldn't say where he was going, even when Shelton asked.

"You just look after things," he said. "Find yourself something to draw."

But Shelton wouldn't draw. It was too cold to draw. Instead, he'd walk a circle around Jackson Square, peer in through the shop windows, step inside St. Louis Cathedral, which was always empty except for a few old white women kneeling in the pews, their heads bowed, rosaries pinched between their fingers. He would look up at the dusty light passing through the cathedral's stained glass windows, and he'd imagine the voices of that white-robed choir of women. He could still hear them singing, couldn't he? He could still hear them singing that wordless hymn.

He walked along the cathedral's high walls and looked at the stone carvings beneath the windows: Jesus condemned by Pontius Pilate and taking up his cross, Jesus meeting his weeping mother and then a woman who wipes his brow, Jesus falling again and again until finally he's stripped and nailed and crucified, then taken down and placed in a wide tomb, with a great stone waiting to be rolled across the entrance.

That was a story, Shelton could see, just like the ones his mother had read, a story where you knew just what lay ahead: the stone rolling away, the tomb empty again, the miracle complete, the story done.

It was the stations of the cross, the first time the child had looked them over. Grown into a man, I'd go back to that same cathedral to look over those fourteen carvings again, deciding how to make my own paintings from them, how to tell that sad story with the work of my own hands.

Did the child know he'd make use of those carvings one day? He couldn't have known, of course, but what the child did do was step out of the cathedral, walk back to his easel, and try to draw his own picture: Christ fallen to the ground beneath the weight of his cross. That was Minou's face, not his own, he drew into that picture. That was Minou falling down to the ground the way he'd fallen, made himself fall, that first day at Jackson Square, when Shelton had run off.

And listen now: One day when Minou returned from his wandering, Shelton could see straight off that something had happened, something had made Minou frightened or angry. As soon as he stepped up, Minou started folding his easel, packing everything in his case, his feet practically stomping on the pavement.

"What?" Shelton asked.

"We're going home," Minou said. "We're going home right now. Hurry up with your things."

"What is it?" Shelton asked.

"Just hurry up now," Minou said.

And as they walked back to Canal Street to catch the streetcar, Shelton tried to imagine what had happened. Had Minou gotten into a fight? Had he been caught stealing something? Had he been with some woman, the same kind as the one who'd scratched those red marks on his face? Maybe he'd come across Samuel Warren, who still hadn't been paid for Genevieve's burial, whom Minou now refused to pay.

Shelton wanted to ask, wanted to tell Minou it would be all right, whatever it was, but he didn't know how to say that, didn't know what to say at all.

Then on the streetcar Minou turned to Shelton. "You're happy living in my house?" he said, his voice full of anger, his feet tapping on the streetcar's shifting floor, his eyes closed. "All's fine? You're certain all's fine?"

"Yes," Shelton said, and he felt his arms and legs shaking.

"Well, I've got to tell you something, then," Minou said. He put his hands up on the seat in front of them. "I had a chance meeting today. When I went off. I had a chance meeting." He turned to Shelton and opened his eyes. "It was Edward Soniat."

Shelton looked at Minou. He thought of his dream of Mr. Edward knocking on Minou's door, lying down to sleep on the front-room sofa. "Did he ask for me?" Shelton said.

"Yes, he did," Minou said. "He asked directly. It seems he's been gone most all this time since you spoke to that man. Gone abroad, he said, but ever since he's come back, he's been searching and searching for you. Wasn't searching now but conducting some business, but he took one look at me and knew. I don't know how, but he did."

"Knew what?" Shelton said.

"Knew you were living with me. Knew you weren't dead."

"What did he say?" Shelton asked, and Minou just looked at him, his eyes still open.

"Please," Shelton said.

"The long and short of it is he wants to see you." Minou looked away from Shelton now, looked up and out the streetcar window, over Shelton's head.

"When?" Shelton said. "When can I see him?"

"Listen now," Minou said. "I sat down with this man, Shelton. I sat down and let the man buy me a drink and we had ourselves a civil conversation. You don't know how hard such a thing can be, but that's just what we did."

"What did he say?" Shelton said.

"Look at me now," Minou said. "It matters less what that man said than what I said to him. I said you were happy living with my family, learning what little I could teach you. You weren't interested, I said, in returning to his home. That time has come and gone, I told him."

"I want to see him," Shelton said, and he thought of how he'd slipped to the floor that first day in Minou's front room and said the same thing of Genevieve Simmons: *I want to see her.*

Minou brushed his hands across his chest and then across his thighs, as if he were brushing away dust and dirt. "You'll see him," he finally said. "You will."

"When?" Shelton said, and when Minou didn't answer, he said "When?" again, his hands curling into fists the way they'd curled when he stood before Genevieve Simmons. Who was he angry at now? Minou, for all his lies and stories, for all he knew but wouldn't tell him? Mr. Edward, for not coming when he'd called out, when he'd fallen from the tree, for not being there when he'd stepped up to the door and knocked?

"In the morning," Minou said. "We'll go to his house. I told him we would. But listen now." He reached across Shelton to pull the cord above the window. "I don't know what this man is going to say to you. I don't know for sure, but I could make my guesses."

The streetcar stopped and Shelton followed Minou to the front and down the steps. They waited for the car to pull off, then they walked across the tracks and across St. Charles Avenue, Shelton trying to keep up, his case slapping against his hip and legs.

"Wait," Shelton called out, and Minou stopped and set down his case and sat down on top of it.

"What's he going to say?" Shelton asked.

Minou let his head fall back. He opened his eyes and looked up at the sky. "Most likely he's going to ask about you going to live with him." He turned to Shelton now. "Not because he wants or needs you there, you understand? Not because he's certain that's where you belong. Not because he's got any true strong feelings guiding him."

Shelton looked at Minou. "Why?"

"Because he owes it to you." Minou rolled a cigarette and lit it. "That's just what he said. He owes it to you. How's that?" Minou blew the smoke from his mouth and looked down at his feet. "Owes it to you because of taking you in the way he did. Because he took you out of your mother's arms."

And Shelton looked away now. "Why'd she do it?" he said.

"Your mother, you mean?" Minou said.

"Why'd she give me up like that?"

Shelton looked at Minou, saw him shaking his head.

"Adrienne," Shelton said.

Minou turned to look at Shelton. "Adrienne?" he said.

"I know," Shelton said, and he felt his hands curl into fists, felt his fists tighten.

"You know what?" Minou asked.

"Why she wants me living with her and Joshua Warren. I know why."

But Minou shook his head. "No, no, child," he said. "You're

mistaken." Then he smiled, a smile like Genevieve's had been, more sorrow than happiness. "Is that what you thought?" Minou said. "That she was the one?"

"I know," Shelton said, and he stepped away from Minou, turned as if again he would run.

"Listen now," Minou said. "Look at me."

Shelton turned. "What?" he said, and he felt his arms rise up before him, felt the fists of his hands.

"I'm sorry," Minou said. "I'm sorry, Shelton. You were looking to the wrong one. It's not Adrienne."

Shelton shook his head. It was time now, wasn't it? It was time to run. "Who is it, then?" he said. "Why won't you just tell me?"

"Listen now," Minou said. "It would have been a fine thing if you'd been right. Yes, it would. There'd be the chance of setting everything straight." He stood up and took hold of his case. "Let's go home," he said. "Let's go home and I'll tell you something along the way."

Shelton picked up his case and followed Minou. "What's true," Minou said, "is that Adrienne once had a child. I don't know how you guessed that. Maybe the girls told you, though I don't think they even know. But she did have a child. There was a boy she meant to marry on account of that child, a boy who meant to marry her. They were having this child together. But that child wasn't you, Shelton."

"Who was it?" Shelton said, and he thought of all the boys in the Milne Home, imagined that one of them, not him, belonged to Adrienne.

"It wasn't anyone," Minou said. "It was a child that died inside her. It came into the world already dead, but the one thing the child did was send that boy running off. He ran off in terror, like both him and Adrienne would be damned straight to hell if he stayed. They were young ones, Shelton. Both of them. My own girls weren't even born. I hadn't yet so much as come across Isabel. That's the child Adrienne had, Shelton. It wasn't you."

Shelton stopped and looked at Minou. "You swear that's true?" he said. "You swear it?"

"I do," Minou said.

"I just thought . . ." Shelton said, but Minou set down his case, reached out, and put his hands on Shelton's shoulders.

"I know," Minou said. "I see now what you thought. And I see how all of what I haven't said went and led you to think such a thing. But it's not true. Adrienne has asked to finish raising you. She's asked for you to live with her and Joshua Warren. And I guess it's true that the reason she wants to do such a thing has everything in the world to do with that child she lost. I should have told you that, I see."

And Shelton stepped back. "Tell me now," Shelton said, "why you came to get me. Why'd you come get me and not some other child?"

"Some other child?" Minou said, and he laughed. He took hold of Shelton's shoulders again. "Look at me now," he said. "You're seeing Edward Soniat tomorrow. If there's questions you mean to ask, you put them to him."

"Why don't you just tell me?" Shelton said, pulling away from Minou. "You're the one who knows. Isabel said you did. So why don't you just tell me?"

"You're going to see Edward Soniat tomorrow," Minou said. "It doesn't matter what I say now or what I don't. That's the time for you to decide who it is you belong to. If you were a baby, if you'd been raised with my family, maybe both your mind and my own would be made up. He's going to put that question to you, Shelton. And you're free to answer it however you like. You're more than free, in fact. You've *got* to."

Minou closed his eyes and waited, then he opened them again and looked at Shelton as if he were surprised to find the child still standing there before him. "You've got to," he said again, and he turned away, raising his hand to his face. He looked up at the sky as if the day had become night and he was searching for a star there that was falling, waiting for that star to draw a line of light across the sky and then, just like that, in a quick and silent burst of flame, disappear into the darkness.

Shelton thought of his dream of flying, the time he'd dreamed he'd walk down from that hill and disappear, the time he'd decided that one day, when no one was looking, he'd just run off.

"You've got to decide for yourself," Minou said now.

"Okay," Shelton said, and for the first time in his life, his body felt planted in the earth and not about to turn and go.

"Shelton?" Minou said, as if he were trying to read the thoughts in the child's head but couldn't.

Shelton looked up at Minou's face, saw how he turned away, saw the anger and shame and sorrow and fear, saw this man's million questions about the world. And the child understood at that moment the truth of Minou's doing what he did, making himself blind, turning himself into a clown, telling the million untrue stories he told. He saw the shame of it.

That face, turned away — that's the face the child put on the fallen Christ. That's the face I'd come to paint again and again through the years, trying still to understand, trying to see what the child saw a glimpse of at that moment.

And finally, when I thought I'd gotten it right, got as much into that work as my hands knew to do, I raised my hand again, scratching not just the red marks across the chin but a line of red across the brow, turning this man into the one, so the story goes, who endured all manner of pain and misunderstanding and torture, more than any before or after, who died the cruelest of deaths not knowing for sure if the heavens would, as he'd been promised, open up to take him in, not knowing for sure if his aim of giving his life for the sake of all others was truly what he'd done.

Minou would have laughed, wouldn't he, to see himself become the Holy Savior. He would have laughed and laughed but, I bet, understood.

233

A Final Prayer. That's a portrait of Minou. But that's my voice too, not just Minou's, crying out to heaven. That's both of us, our voices become one. That's a song, that's a call to grace, that's the both of us, together.

And the child, standing out on the street with Minou, understood all this at that very moment. He couldn't have named it, couldn't have uttered a word of what he knew. But he understood. He did. Just look.

Watch the child step toward Minou. Watch his hands reaching out. *It's me,* those hands say. *I'm the one now, the one who can offer some comfort.*

"I'm here," the child says, stepping forward, reaching out. "I'm here. I'm right here, Minou."

❦ ❦ ❦

So the child that evening found himself changed again, found that the earth had set itself spinning in a new direction, Minou clinging to this child now the way the child had once clung to him, Mr. Edward finding his way back just like the child had dreamed he would.

Couldn't I just leave Shelton there a while to consider the sweet pleasure of Minou's embrace, the comfort he could offer just by holding on to Minou, by telling Minou with the tight grip of his arms that he was right where he wanted to be? Now the end had come or the beginning had begun. Wasn't it enough for the child to learn, in the course of this one evening, that he'd been wrong about Adrienne, that he'd soon see Mr. Edward, that in just a few hours' time he'd step again into the house he'd run from for what should have been just one morning but turned out to be years and years?

Yes, that's how I'd like to leave the child, just for a while. But there was more waiting for Shelton that evening. And it's as if Shelton knew this already, for late that night, having seen everyone else off to bed, not a word spoken about Mr. Edward, Shelton leaves Minou standing in the light of the kitchen and makes his way through the house to the front-room sofa, strips off his clothes in the darkness, and lies down, pulling the quilt up over him and closing his eyes, wishing only for sleep, wishing for an end to all his questions.

Watch. The child sleeps. He sleeps, peaceful and calm, without a single dream to disturb him.

That's enough, isn't it? Just let the child sleep.

But then in the darkness he wakes to a touch on his foot, which has slipped beyond the reach of the quilt.

It's an angel, isn't it, come down to save him, to make his body whole, to tell him where he belongs, what he should do.

It's a hand there. A hand and then a voice, calling his name, whispering, "Shelton?"

How do I, a tired old man, try to remember this, try to explain a boy's wild imagining, the fierce push and pull of desire, the ache that makes its way like a burrowing animal through every single inch of the body, even one as twisted and wrecked as Shelton's?

The child feels the hand there, and it's as if some great wooden case, just like the one with his easel but bigger, ten times that size, has been suddenly set down at his feet, its top swung open, a voice from inside calling his name. The child wants to reach and reach into that case, though all his hands will touch is air, is more and more darkness. So he'll reach again, further and further, but it's still the same, only darkness and air, until finally there's a touch, a hand taking hold of his own, and he's found just what he wants, but by now the case has grown and grown and he is buried deep inside it, his own body, his every breath and ounce of blood and face and hands and limbs become now just a part of that endless darkness, a darkness that will never let him go because he'll never want it to let go.

Oh, that's just a dream, isn't it? The touch of that hand, the voice whispering his name. That's just a dream. That's Elise reaching out for him, calling his name. *It's me, Shelton. You want to see? You want to put your hands on me? You want to feel me touching you?*

"Shelton?"

Here she is now. She's going to touch him, isn't she? She's going to run her hands along his body, reach across his chest, along his twisted legs, moving her hands there until he has to call out, though he knows he can't, so calls out instead by kicking, by waving his arms, hands become fists, fingers stabbing at his palms tighter and tighter until she lets go of him, pushes herself away though he is reaching for her, reaching and reaching.

That's just what you wanted, isn't it? she'll say, and he'll nod, his eyes squeezed closed, his arms still reaching. He'll nod and say *More*, say *Again*, say *Please*.

The hand on his foot, the voice whispering his name.

He reaches out through the darkness, feels her arm, grabs hold of it, pulls her toward him, on top of him. "Please," he says. "Please."

But she's struggling now to get off him. "Let go," she says. "Let go, Shelton." And it's not Elise, is it? It's Olivia.

"I thought —" Shelton starts, but he can't say it. And maybe she already knows. Maybe she's seen the picture he drew, slipped it out from its hiding place beneath the sofa, seen how he looks at Elise, seen and understood his longing.

Now she sits down on the floor, her face just a few inches from his own though he still can't see it, can only feel her quick breath brushing against his chest and neck. Is it this girl he wants? He reaches his hand out into the darkness and touches the side of her head, and she doesn't pull away but lets her head lean down against his chest.

"Shelton," she says, and he hears in her voice not an echo of his longing but something else. "I've got to talk to you," she says. "I need your help."

"What?" Shelton says.

"Listen," she says, and he hears in her voice Minou's: *Listen now.*

236

"What?" he says again. "Just tell me."

"You can't tell anyone. You understand? Not a soul."

"Okay," Shelton says.

"Elise," Olivia says. "Listen. She's going to have a baby."

"Why?" Shelton says, and he hears Olivia laugh quietly, then hears her laughter turn to tears.

"I don't mean why," Shelton says. "I mean who."

Then Shelton knows, realizes he knows already. He hears that voice again calling out into the darkness, the voice he heard when he stood on the porch and listened. "Joshua Warren," Shelton says.

"You knew," Olivia says. "How'd you know?"

"I just did," Shelton says. He imagines it now, imagines Elise lying down with this man, calling out this man's name, not his own. Shelton pushes himself up on the sofa. "Adrienne," he says.

"I know," Olivia says, and Shelton can see her now, her face streaked with tears, the tears lined with light as if they're pulling the light over from some distant place.

"Why?" Shelton says.

And Olivia runs a hand over her face. "I don't know why," she says. "I'll tell you what Elise said. She said, 'He wanted me,' as if it was as simple as that. She said he just found the time and place to put his hands on her and say her name. She said it was like he was saying something holy, like he'd been waiting to speak her name his whole life."

"That's all?" Shelton says, and he feels the shame of his own thoughts, how he has imagined the same thing — Elise speaking his name, calling to him.

"No," Olivia says. "That's not all. Remember that money Daddy owed for Maw-Maw's funeral? Daddy never paid it. Joshua told her he'd see that things got settled."

Shelton thinks of the story Elise told — how she'd punched Samuel Warren, how she'd felt what he wore, the woman's corset. Was that just a lie? Just like her father's lies, just like Minou's?

Olivia pushes herself up and sits down on the edge of the sofa next to Shelton. "She was just trying to help, she said. That was it, she figured, that one time, and then he'd go on and marry Adrienne. But he kept coming to her, Shelton. He kept coming."

"She called from your room," Shelton says, and he realizes now what Olivia hasn't said — that she knew all along, that she knew what Elise was doing. "You knew," Shelton says.

Olivia cries and cries now, and Shelton reaches for her, pulls her body against his own. "My sister," Olivia says, and she leans her head against his shoulder.

"What?" Shelton says. "What can I do?"

Olivia lifts her head, looks at Shelton. "Tell Daddy," she says, and she puts her hand on Shelton's arm. "Please," she says. "I've thought and thought on this. Tell Daddy it was you."

And Shelton feels his arms and legs tighten like four taut ropes.

"Please," Olivia says, crying, sobbing. She pushes herself off him and stands by the sofa. "Please," she says again. "There's nothing else to do."

And before Shelton can answer, she turns and walks off.

"Olivia," Shelton says, and he sees her stop, sees her body turn in the darkness. "Olivia," he says again, pleading now, desperate.

"Please," she says again, and she turns away. "If you don't . . ." she says, shaking her head.

"I can't," he says. "I can't do it." But Olivia is gone. She hasn't heard him. "I can't," he says, louder now, but Olivia doesn't come back, she still doesn't hear him.

So he lies down on the sofa and pulls the quilt over him, over not just his body but his face as well.

Quiet, he tells himself. *Quiet now.*

He makes his eyes close. He smells the musty cloth of the blanket, feels it pressing against his face, feels it lift and fall with his every breath.

Quiet Now. There's a child asleep on a sofa. There's a child whose eyes are closed, a child who is peaceful and sleeping. There's light at the edge of that work, coming in through some unseen window, a light that sorts itself out among the woven strands of the child's blanket, that touches the child's face, slips into the lines beneath his cheeks and at his chin and at the corners of his eyes, a light that shows how at any moment now that child's face will change, will look more like a grown man's than a boy's.

But it's as if the sofa is opening up beneath the child, opening up as if it is opening to the dark and empty center of the earth, and once again, though now in the pitch-black darkness, faster and faster, more quickly than he could have ever imagined, the child's body is tumbling down through the air and darkness, twisting and turning now, changing and changing as it falls.

16 HOME

IN THE MORNING, it was Minou who woke him. Holding his wooden case and stick, Minou watched Shelton dress in the darkness, then led him out the door, across the porch, and down the steps. They walked with the first light of dawn from Foucher Street to St. Charles Avenue, then got on the streetcar, heading not for the French Quarter but in the other direction, toward Audubon Park, toward Mr. Edward's.

Shelton could hardly bring himself to speak. He couldn't do it, could he? He couldn't tell Minou what Olivia had said to tell him. He'd just tell him the truth instead, that's what, but then he looked down at his hands and thought of how he'd longed for the touch of Elise's body, how he'd longed for her hands to touch his own. That was part of the truth too, wasn't it? It wasn't the truth without those thoughts of touching, of being touched.

"You know where to get off?" Minou asked, and Shelton nodded, looking out the window as if what he was searching for were the right stop and not which words to speak and how. There, just ahead, was the entrance to Audubon Park. There were the stone lions. Somewhere near was the tree where he'd fallen, the tree he'd found again months ago now and, closing his eyes, used to make his way back to Mr. Edward's, to pronounce his name, to ask that man in the doorway his questions.

"Here," Shelton said, and Minou reached over him to pull the cord on the car's side. The streetcar screeched and stopped.

They got off and walked away from the park and down the alley in silence. Minou swung the case in his hand, paused from time to time to let Shelton catch up. Shelton listened to the echo of their steps in the alley. He looked up at the windows of the houses, all of them dark. It was too early, wasn't it, for people to be up.

"This is it," he said when they reached the gate behind Mr. Edward's.

Minou looked at the house, nodded. He turned to Shelton. "That's some kind of home, isn't it now?" he said. "That's a white man's home for certain."

"Back here," Shelton said, pointing to the rooms behind the patio. "This is where we lived. It's where that man was."

Minou looked for a moment before speaking. "You go around to the front this time," he said. "Go and knock on the front door."

Shelton looked at Minou. "I will," he said. "You're coming too?"

"I'm not," Minou said.

"Please," Shelton said. "I want you to."

"I've got to get on to work," Minou said. "I'm late already. Go on."

Shelton swung open the gate and stepped through it. "Can't you just wait for me?" Shelton said.

Minou set the case down and stepped up to the gate. He reached into his pocket and handed Shelton a nickel. "That's carfare," he said.

"No," Shelton said now, and he felt his body shaking, felt the nickel resting in the center of his palm, just like one of Mr. Edward's worthless — weren't they worthless? — foreign coins.

"You know the way back," Minou said. "It'll be fine."

"No," Shelton said again. "No."

"I told him you'd be here," Minou said. "I gave the man my word. He gave me his. He wants to talk to you, that's all. This isn't the place for me. He's going to tell you all you want to hear. You'll be fine."

"I won't," Shelton said. "I'm not fine."

Minou swung the gate open and stepped up to Shelton.

"What's wrong?" he said. "This is just what you wanted."

He took hold of Shelton and held him; then he turned and walked back through the gate. He picked up his case and headed off down the alley. For a moment Shelton watched him, watched the way Minou let his shoulders slump and his feet drag along beneath him. Shelton heard the stick knocking against the ground, echoing through the alley, and though there was no one looking, no one to see him, Minou had already, Shelton knew, let his eyes swing closed. He'd already become the blind man of Jackson Square, already left his own life for the one he'd made up.

And if I could call to the child through this story, make my hands rise up and reach back through time, I would do just that. I would take my hands, these hands, and place them on the child's shoulders. I'd lean my mouth close to the child's ear. I'd say, *Let him go, child. Let him go.*

Years later, years ago, I did what I could. I painted this moment, made a work of it just as if I were recording the truth of what happened, of what I'd let Minou do. There he is, slump-shouldered and turned away, dragging himself through that quiet alley, his figure bent by my curving brushstroke, his shoulders and legs straining as if inside that case is some great weight, are all his years of pretended blindness, his earning nickels and dimes and quarters for making a clown of himself, a dark nigger trickster.

No. Something more. The one who disappears inside his work, inside that wooden case, inside the very sweep of his raised arm, inside that small charcoal square — there he is. There's that Negro artist, you know the one. What's his name? What is it?

And where's he going now? Where's he going?

Home.

Look at him now. Look. The alley where he walks has become just a narrow path between two rows of tall houses, squeezed one against the other, leaning into the alley, over the man's head, as if at any moment those two rows might touch, their separate roofs become one. There's a light in every window and each one a warning to let things be, to let this man keep walking, let him get where he's going.

And here and there, there are faces in the windows. There are elbows propped on the windowsills, hands dangling down like weary, drooping vines. No one cares about this man's coming and going. They don't pay it any mind.

But in one window, ahead in the distance, there's a woman who leans out above the street, her arms stretched wide, her face shining in what's left of the moonlight, her mouth open. She's calling the man's name, isn't she? She's calling and calling. Is that some devil, some wild, laughing woman who doesn't care who it is, who just wants to give herself over, give up whatever's hers to give? No, that's Isabel, that's Minou's own wife, and she's calling Minou home.

That work's a lie, isn't it?

No, it's something else. It's me, it's my hands raised to the canvas. It's the sad-ass crippled artist Shelton Gerard Lafleur hoping to use his one gift, though he knows both that hope and that gift are useless. He wants to change the world, change his memory of it. No, he wants to change just this one morning's unfolding circumstance, that's all.

And now if I could I'd just grab that child. I'd shake his shoulders and shout. I'd wrestle him down to the ground, steal the life from inside him — I'd do whatever it took to keep him from saying Minou's name, from causing this man to turn and ask, "What is it now, Shelton? What?"

But the child has called out, and Minou has turned, has let his eyes swing open. And now the child has got to say something, hasn't he? He's got to find the words to speak.

"Can you come here? Please?" Shelton says. He's willing to forget his million questions for Mr. Edward. He's willing to walk away too, never to know who set him down on that doorstep, never to speak another word to Mr. Edward, never to hear how his mother grieved at the loss of him.

"Please?" Shelton says again. "Just come here." And Minou must hear something in the child's voice, something that says this isn't anymore just a child's shyness and fear. It's something more, something worse. So he sets his case down, lets the stick rest against it. He walks back to the gate, opens it, approaches Shelton.

"What is it?" he says. "What are you thinking?"

That's the right question, isn't it? What is the child thinking this moment, backing away from Minou now as if he's been threatened, looking this way and that, seeing for just a moment a dark shape in the upstairs window? It's Mr. Edward, isn't it, waiting for the child to knock on his door, to announce his presence, to say he's returned, to let himself be swept up in the long embrace that has waited all these years.

Shelton turns back to Minou, watches him approach. He thinks of the first time he saw him, the first words Minou spoke. *There's a poor pitiful piece of work.* That's what he was, wasn't he, terrified and shaking. Now he's something else, something more. He's got to speak.

And surely there's a steady stream of thoughts in Minou's head, just as there is in the child's. *He's afraid,* Minou is thinking. *He fears he won't come back, won't want to. He fears the man will hurt him or steal him or do him some harm or tell him something about the girl who raised him or the mother who birthed him, tell him something about Genevieve Simmons and her devilish trickery and lies, her terrible deception that took a living and breathing child and just as well buried him, left him abandoned in that home for orphans. He's afraid of everything, everything, except that which he ought to be fearing — the mention of my name on that man's lips, my own name.*

244

"Tell me," Minou says, and Shelton backs and backs away. "Tell me now."

"Elise," Shelton says, and now he's standing in the center of the patio garden, surrounded by wisteria and oleander and persimmon, the wisteria's limbs twisted and knotted like his own. He remembers kneeling in that French Quarter garden when he ran from those white-robed women and the crowd of boys, remembers the dirt on his shoes and hands, the footsteps approaching, the sound of one voice and then another.

"Elise?" Minou says. "What?"

Shelton's body shakes, his hands curl into fists at his sides. He could do what he'd done with Genevieve, couldn't he — raise his hands to his own face, leave it bruised and bloody and swollen. Minou would sweep him up into his arms, wouldn't he? He'd say, *Quiet, quiet. No, you didn't, child.*

And all would be fine, all would be fine.

"She's going to have a child," Shelton says, and he looks at Minou, makes himself look, keeps his head from turning away.

"No," Minou says, and Shelton watches how his body straightens, how it grows and grows, to twice the size it was a moment ago. Minou's hands, gigantic, take hold of his arms.

"It was me," Shelton says, and Minou's grip tightens. Shelton braces himself, plants his feet. "The child is mine."

Then Shelton feels his body rise, two hands on him now, and for a moment he isn't falling but flying. Here is grace, isn't it, come to pay another visit. Here is grace come down again just to save him, to sweep him up through the air. He'll look down on Minou, say how he's sorry, say he'll see him again sometime. He's flying through the air like in that story Minou told, like the grandfather Minou said he looked for in the sky.

Then his back and shoulders and head strike the ground, crash against brick, and he feels the cold air enter an opening in his head, hears a long loud scream — not his own voice. Minou's.

He's bleeding, isn't he? It's just blood. He's fine.

Then Minou is standing over him, kicking at his legs, kicking at his chest. "My child!" he says, spitting, screaming. "My flesh-and-blood child!"

He leans over, grabs Shelton, makes him stand. He slaps Shelton's face, slaps it again. He stares into Shelton's eyes. "I took you in," he says. "I took you in, no-good rotten-ass cripple child."

I was trying to comfort her, Shelton thinks, but then he knows that's not the truth, not the whole story.

He'll just tell Minou, won't he, tell him everything, explain how it's not his child but should be. *Look,* he'll say, and he'll raise his hands before him, show them to Minou. *Look,* he'll say. *Here's all my longing.*

But now Shelton is flying again, flying back and back, tumbling, falling, and before his body hits the ground, before his head and shoulders strike the bloodstained brick, he hears a voice calling him, calling his name, calling out to Minou.

And he is lying on the ground, his arms and legs burning. That's his own voice now, isn't it, screaming and shouting. "Stop!" his voice says, and he finds that his body has turned on its side.

There's Mr. Edward become an old man, black hair turned gray, running and running. There's Minou grabbing hold of him, the two men struggling, hands thrashing and reaching and grabbing, and the two of them falling, Mr. Edward screaming, "Stop it now. Stop," and Minou cursing and cursing, "Goddamn you. Goddamn your dead white daughter. Goddamn your nigger child."

Shelton tries to move, tries to stand but can't. He watches Mr. Edward and Minou struggle, Minou's face in the ground now, pressed against the brick, Mr. Edward's knees on Minou's back, his hands on Minou's throat.

"My child?" Mr. Edward says. "My child?" And Shelton hears Minou choking, sees his legs kick and kick. "Stop it now," Mr. Edward says, "or I'll kill you. I swear I will."

246

Now Shelton stands up, manages somehow to stand. He reaches for Mr. Edward, summons every ounce of his strength, then pushes him over. Now Shelton is on top of Mr. Edward, hands at the man's throat. It's Mr. Edward, not Minou, who's choking now, who's kicking and kicking. It's Minou calling to Shelton from the ground. "Quit now! Quit!" he calls, calling and calling.

What is it the child has taken into his hands — a man's throat, yes, a man's very life, but much more, much worse: all his years of hope and longing, his million and one questions, the two black-robed nuns and this man's dying daughter, his own twisted limbs, the tree where he fell, the branches tearing at his fingers. He hears the women's singing voices, hears the boys' taunts and teasing, hears the strange and silent child crying out now, screaming.

"Quit!" Minou calls, but he's already gone, isn't he?

And the child doesn't quit, does he? He feels his hands tighten, strong as Minou's. He feels his hands around the man's throat, sees the black-robed nuns, hears them laughing. *Dark as you are, child?* they say. *Dark as you are.*

And Mr. Edward is coughing now. Minou's hands are grabbing Shelton's shoulders, pulling at him.

Now Shelton's hands are gripped around nothing but air. Mr. Edward, still coughing, pushes himself to his feet, stands.

"I'm sorry," Shelton says, crying now. But he's not sorry, is he?

"Set him down," Mr. Edward says to Minou, waving his arms. He leans forward, bends over, coughing.

"I'll do no such thing," Minou says, his arms locked around Shelton's waist.

Mr. Edward stands up straight. "Put him down, I said."

"I won't," Minou says.

Mr. Edward turns now. "Stevens!" he calls out. "Stevens!"

"Hush up now," Minou says.

"Stevens!" Mr. Edward says. "Where the hell are you?"

The man opens the door and steps out. It's the same man

whom Shelton spoke to, the same man he told his name. He looks at Minou, then at Mr. Edward.

"Go get the police. Get anyone," Mr. Edward says.

"Yes, Mr. Soniat," the man says, and as he walks toward the house, Shelton sees his eyes meet Minou's.

"Go on, nigger," Minou says, and the man looks at Shelton, then back at Mr. Edward.

"That's right. Go on," Mr. Edward says. Then he turns to Minou. "Set him down now. Set him down and you can go."

"Set him down?" Minou says, and he turns and walks toward the gate. "That's just what I'll do."

He puts Shelton down, puts his hands on Shelton's arms, looks at him. "You just —" he starts, but he stops and stares at Shelton, who sees Minou's eyes open wide, staring at him.

Minou shakes his head now. "No, no," he says. "You've not told me the truth, child," he says, and he laughs, a wild laugh, frightening. "Tell me now," he says. "Tell me quick."

"Elise," Shelton says, shaking. He looks at Minou, looks into his eyes, says, "Joshua Warren."

"Joshua Warren?" Minou says. "He's the one?"

And Shelton tries to speak but can't. He looks at Minou and nods.

"Well, that's simple enough," Minou says, and he laughs again. "That's simple enough." And he lets go of Shelton and turns to Mr. Edward. "Here he is," Minou says. "Just send him home when you're done."

Minou walks toward the gate and Shelton calls after him. Minou turns. "It's fine," he says. "I've just got some business to attend to."

Shelton calls again, but Minou opens the gate and steps into the alley.

Shelton tries to follow him, but now there's a hand on him, two hands, Mr. Edward's. "Shelton," Mr. Edward says, arms wrapped around him now. "Let him go," Mr. Edward says.

Shelton holds on, speaks into Mr. Edward's chest. "I tried to kill you," Shelton says, and he feels Mr. Edward moving, looks up to see Mr. Edward shaking his head. "I meant to," Shelton says. "I did."

Then he pushes himself away, twists out of Mr. Edward's arms. "That's what he'll do," Shelton says. "That's what he'll do with Joshua Warren."

Shelton runs now, runs again, though this time it's different. It's all different now, he knows.

He does know, doesn't he?

He stops, turns around, hears again Mr. Edward's voice. *My child?* Mr. Edward had said to Minou. *My child?* he'd said, his voice mocking, accusing, final and complete.

So Shelton stops at the gate, turns back to Mr. Edward, looks at him. "He's my father," Shelton says — not a question this time, not a question at all.

Mr. Edward looks at him, nods.

"Why?" Shelton says, a final question, complete.

Why'd he give me up?

Why'd you take me?

Why wouldn't anyone, anyone, just tell me?

Mr. Edward raises his hands toward Shelton. "He wanted to save you —" he says, and he looks down, looks away. "We both did. He wanted me to make up some story. I said I would."

Now Shelton doesn't need to ask, for he can see it all, see Minou lying down with some woman, wild with laughter, with drinking, blind. He can see Minou's shame and fear when he learns how this woman is carrying a child, his own wife and two children safe at home, and now he's got to choose, hasn't he, but he won't choose, won't leave this child in the filth of the house where it will be born, and he learns from Genevieve, who knows all, of what Mr. Edward wants for his daughter. A child, and here's a child, and all that's required is a story, a story to tell to Isabel, to his two little daughters, a story he can just make up in the blink of an eye. *I found him in some alley. I took him from some whore. I won him in a card game. I got paid a handsome price.* So it's Minou who takes the infant child from the bloody bed, carries it to that Garden District doorstep, makes his deal with the man, makes a deal that neither of them, no one, will ever speak the truth of this, then sets the child down.

Yes, Shelton feels still the grip of Minou's hands wrapped around that infant, feels those hands, gigantic, wrapped around his ribs now, thumbs touching, and he hears Minou speaking to Mr. Edward, hears him say, desperate, pleading, *You look after him. Look after my son now.*

And he's gone, gone forever, but still there's Genevieve Simmons, who knows everything, who has never once in her life been blind. She'll look after him too, teach him all she knows, watch him like a hawk, patient and waiting and plotting for the one day when she'll take him home in her arms.

"He wanted a home for you," Mr. Edward is saying. "I wanted—" but Shelton is already a million miles away, already gone. Then he turns back to Mr. Edward. He could ask now, couldn't he, where his name came from. He could ask anything at all — who that woman was, where she might be now, how Mr. Edward and Minou might have managed to speak such words as must have passed between them. He could ask, and surely Mr. Edward, his promise useless now, would tell him, would go on and on about how the deal was struck, the words traded between them, the secrets they swore to keep, how it was all managed, this transaction, this purchase.

But it's all gone, isn't it? It's all gone, even the child — for look who's standing there before Mr. Edward now: not some wailing infant, not a child at all, but Shelton Lafleur, Shelton Gerard Lafleur, not a single question swirling inside him now but how to get where he needs to be going, how to try to save Minou.

So the child starts to run, but it's different now, for he's not running away this time. Mr. Edward is calling his name, calling and calling, but it doesn't matter now. Shelton runs down the alley, runs out to St. Charles Avenue, looks up and down the wide street, calls out for Minou. He's already gone, though. He's nowhere in sight, and Shelton waits and waits for the streetcar to come, and it's only when it pulls up that Shelton realizes he's lost the coin Minou gave him.

The door swings open and Shelton looks at the conductor. "I don't have any money," Shelton says. "I lost it."

The driver looks at Shelton, shakes his head, and reaches his arm out to shut the door. "You got to pay," the conductor says, and Shelton turns away. He hears the door close, sees the car jerk forward, watches it move ahead, swaying from side to side.

"That's fine," he says, and he starts to run again. He won't make it, he knows, he won't make it there in time. But he runs and runs and keeps on running, stopping just to catch his breath, to quiet for a minute the screaming ache in his legs. Then he starts to run again.

When he has finally turned off St. Charles and found Foucher Street, Shelton sees up ahead, as if it's been summoned on his behalf, a miracle: a car parked in front of Minou's home, the engine running. Shelton knows who the car must belong to, who it is that must have gone inside.

And when Shelton steps into the house, he sees him: There's Mr. Edward, standing in the front room with Adrienne. "There he is now," Mr. Edward says. "Shelton." He's calm and smiling, as if nothing has happened. He's pretending that everything is fine.

"Minou," Shelton says, and he sees how his saying that name, just the way he's said it, has changed the look on Adrienne's face.

"What?" Adrienne says. "What is it?"

Shelton looks at her. "Where are the girls?" he asks. "Where's Elise?"

Adrienne raises a hand to her mouth, takes it away. "They're both in school," she says. "Why? Where's Minou? What's happened?"

"He's fine," Shelton says. "He's fine." Then he turns to Mr. Edward. "We've got to go now," he says. "Let's just go."

"What is it?" Adrienne says, and Shelton looks at her, wishing now he'd been right in thinking that here was his mother. "What is it, child?" she says, and Shelton tries to make himself smile, tries and tries and then manages it.

"Oh, it's nothing," he says. "Minou just left me with Mr. Edward. He got angry at something I said and got on the streetcar without me. I was just scared, that's all."

Adrienne looks at him, then sighs. "Well, I thought," she says, "something had happened."

"No," Shelton says, shaking his head. "I was just scared about being left with Mr. Edward, that's all." He turns to Edward Soniat. "But now I'm fine. We've got to get going, don't we?"

"We do," Mr. Edward says, and he puts his hand on Shelton's back, steers him to the door.

Shelton turns to Adrienne. "I'll see you later," he says. "I'll just see you later, okay?"

Shelton turns to step through the door but then realizes he doesn't know where Joshua Warren lives. He's never been there, never seen his house. "Adrienne," he says, "where's Joshua live? Mr. Edward's got something to talk about with his father. A friend of his passed away last night. A Negro man."

Adrienne looks at Shelton. "Where's that man taking you?" she asks. "Tell me, child."

"He just wants to know where does Mr. Warren live," Shelton says, and he turns to Mr. Edward, who has already stepped onto the porch. He smiles and waves at Adrienne.

"General Pershing," she says. "A block this side of Magazine. You sure that's why?" she says. "You sure there's not something going on?"

"There's not," Shelton says. "I swear."

Then he heads out the door, and Mr. Edward is waiting in the car. "General Pershing Street," Shelton tells him. "It crosses Magazine."

"I know," Mr. Edward says.

And only now does Shelton feel his body start shaking. "We have to go," he says.

They drive over to Magazine Street, Mr. Edward leaning forward to watch the street signs. When he finds the street and Shelton feels the car turn, they see the crowd gathered in front of the house a block ahead. Mr. Edward slows the car down, and Shelton sees first a group of women holding each other, weeping, and then, past them, a circle of men. As they pull up before the house, Shelton looks at the men and sees it, sees the body lying on the ground inside the circle, at their feet.

It's not Minou. It's not. It's Joshua Warren.

"Keep going," Shelton says. "They'll know." So Mr. Edward makes the car shoot forward. Shelton sees the men turn their heads, looking for who's come and gone, who'd want to drive by like that. A white man and a black child? What is it they're up to? And when they've gone two blocks, Mr. Edward turns onto another street, pulls the car to a stop.

"It's done now," he says, and he shakes his head, lets his head fall, his eyes close. "I'm sorry, Shelton. Let's just pray they don't catch him."

Pray, Shelton thinks, and he closes his eyes. He sees the white-robed choir of women, their hands raised to the sky, swaying like tree branches. He sees the faces he saw in St. Louis Cathedral, the faces he looked at one by one, looking for someone to save him. And he hears them all singing now, hears them singing that wordless hymn, voices raised now, raised high and loud, reaching up to heaven, asking please please please, won't the sky tear itself open, won't grace come down, won't it come down now.

Here he is. Here's Minou. Here's his son, the child named Shelton. Here they both are now.

17 THE FINAL FLOWERING OF SHELTON LAFLEUR

I SAID BEFORE how this is just a child's story, and even sitting in that car, his head bowed, Shelton knew that the child he'd been was now gone, had run off with Minou, and neither one, though he called and called out, was there to be found.

They looked and looked, of course. Shelton led Mr. Edward over to the river, to the rocks where he and Minou had gone the night they were supposed to go see Samuel Warren. They went to the park on Tchoupitoulas Street. They went up and down Magazine Street and then drove over to the French Quarter, parked the car and walked to Jackson Square. Shelton hoped and prayed that here would be Minou's final trick, that he'd be standing before his easel, before the yellowed paper, charcoal square in his hand, his arm raised, the smile on his face saying, *Well, isn't that a shame about Joshua Warren, but look, all this time I've been right here.*

The sky began to darken, and Mr. Edward drove Shelton back to Foucher Street. Mr. Edward led him inside, back to Minou's family. They knew everything now, had heard Elise's story, had quieted Adrienne's fit of screaming, of pulling at her hair and striking out at anyone who came near, and together now, and each for her own reasons, they all cried.

And Shelton, in the center of them all, couldn't stop himself from imagining Minou over Joshua Warren's body, choking him, Minou's hands around Joshua Warren's throat until Minou saw the man's head fall to the side, the straining muscles in his neck stretching now, stretching tighter and tighter.

My child! My child! Minou is shouting, until he sees what he's done and peels his fingers off, sees the purple crescents his fingers have left behind. Then he lets out a scream, a terrible wailing, that Shelton knows he'll hear forever, that I still hear now.

And Shelton imagined Minou running off, running to the river, washing his hands clean, washing his whole body until the rushing water takes him, sweeps his body away.

He imagined Minou catching a ride on some north-traveling train, telling himself that soon he'd find the place named Harlem, where he could open his eyes, do as he pleased.

No, he imagined Minou setting off from the city, wooden case still in his hands. He saw Minou following the crooked line of the Mississippi River, then stepping up to that lepers' home, asking please won't he be welcomed inside. And the doors, the great gates, swing open, take him in.

And that image, that idea of Minou winding up at the lepers' home — that one would stay with Shelton too, would appear again and again to him as though it had to be true, and there would come a time when I'd go there, when I'd make the drive along the river to Baton Rouge just to be certain I was wrong, that this wasn't where he'd gone.

They'd let me in, let me ask my questions, let me show them a picture I'd drawn. "Minou Parrain," I'd say, standing among them as if I were one of their own. "Minou Parrain," I'd say, "though he might have used some other name."

And though I didn't say it, couldn't bring myself to say it, I thought of how that name he used might have been — would have been, wouldn't it? — the very same as my own.

Lafleur, that dark flower rising up out of nowhere, suddenly gone. Look, there's my own face. There's Minou's. *The Final Flowering of Shelton Lafleur,* painted with fierce, angry strokes, lines running up and down the dark throat, red and white cut into the dark eyes, cut throughout the dark face. Whose face? My own? Minou's?

He's not gone, is he? All these years, and all Minou has done is grow inside me. I look at my two hands and see the works they've made, see the way they've reached out for grace, felt it touch them. That's Minou's touch, isn't it?

Yes, this is just a child's story, and that child's come and gone. He's grown into a man, an old man, and in his lifetime has done all of what Minou, had he gotten the chance, would have asked him to do. I tried to look after Minou's family, be a good son to Isabel, a brother to Olivia and Elise.

And maybe there's no way of a lie becoming the truth, but I was, as much as anyone, father to the child that Elise would give birth to, that Olivia would look after for years and years, until it was grown, Elise being unable to look after it, unable, I suppose, for all her shame.

And one by one we all watched the years pass, even that child, that little girl who is now a woman with children of her own, the child who's now the woman who wept at each one's passing — Isabel's, Adrienne's, Elise's — but not like she wept when Olivia, dear Olivia, passed on.

I don't need to say how or why I stayed near Olivia, how she remained the one clear and true song of my life, even when she found a man to marry, a man she loved, a man who was kind to her, accepted the presence of her sister's child, accepted the presence of her father's son.

It's Olivia's being gone now, more than anything else, that has let me tell the child's story, let me make it known, the story of this strange and silent child who one day, for no reason at all, fell from the sky, the earth rising up to meet him, to hold him and carry him forward through the years.

There hasn't been a time that I stopped, that any of us stopped, looking for Minou. Any minute now, we prayed, let him just turn the corner. Let him step through the door, call out our names or his own.

Each work I painted, when I raised my hand to sign my name, there it was, there was my question: Shelton Gerard Lafleur? And I'd lower my hand, wait for Minou's answer, wait for him to come back and tell all he knew.

Mr. Edward, good man that he was, gave me money. He wanted to see me every now and again, see that I was being looked after, cared for, and loved. I was, I told him, and didn't ask all the questions the child had longed to ask. What use were they now, just so many clattering coins?

Mr. Edward, though, became the one who showed my work to all who'd care to look, telling everyone my story, the little of it he knew and understood. But it's been Minou who has stayed with me. Old man that I am, my hands still feel guided by his own. And I've come to believe, though it has taken some time, at least one of the stories he told me.

Yes, late in the evening from time to time I drag my old body outside. I look up to the sky filled with darkness. I look up, look for the form of Minou flying by.

Someday before I die, he'll swoop down, won't he? He'll come to pay me a visit, come to take my hands again into his own and bless them.

That's him now, isn't it?

Watch. That's him now.

Look. Just look. I'll show you.

There he is.

Listen now. Listen.

Here I am.

257

I would like to thank the Lyndhurst
Foundation for its generous support
while I worked on this book.

J. G. B.